CW00926567

SECRET WATERS

SECRET WATERS

A guide to the quiet and unspoilt rivers, lakes and canals of Britain and Ireland

John Watney

Frontispiece:

Brundon Mill on river Stour near Sudbury, Suffolk

First published in Great Britain 1988 by
Webb & Bower (Publishers) Limited
9 Colleton Crescent, Exeter, Devon EX2 4BY
in association with Michael Joseph Limited
27 Wright's Lane, London W8 5TZ

Designed by Vic Giolitto

Production by Nick Facer/Rob Kendrew

British Library Cataloguing in Publication Data

Watney, John, *1919–*
Secret waters: a guide to unspoilt rivers
and canals of Britain and Ireland.
1. Inland navigation—Great Britain
2. Boats and boating—Great Britain
3. Great Britain—Description and travel
—Guide books
I. Title
914.1'04858 DA650

ISBN 0-86350-144-3

Typeset in Great Britain by August Filmsetting, Haydock, St Helens

Colour reproduction by J Film Process, Bangkok, Thailand

Printed and bound in Spain by Graficromo, Cordoba

Contents

Foreword

After many years of sailing round the coasts of the British Isles I came to realise that the most interesting part of any cruise was making a new landfall and 'discovering' places and people. As most harbours and anchorages are associated with a river or sea loch I often extended my discovery by going further inland by water in the boat's tender. But cruising stop-overs are usually very short so I would often return another time by car taking with me an inflatable boat to make my own mini-cruises further and further inland. Eventually my interest in tidal and, therefore, navigable waters led me to explore further than heads of navigation, into the tideless reaches of rivers – even to their very sources. I have never found a waterway entirely dull, and most are full of interest, character and history; after all at one time they were the main lines of communication and, until the coming of steam, the most prolific source of power.

This book is a reminiscence of many years of ditch crawling in a variety of small boats on tidal reaches, driving and walking where no boat could go or was not allowed, and scrambling about over sometimes rough terrain in the wilder parts of the country in search of water sources. I hope it will encourage more people to take an interest in our liquid landscapes and get away from roads and car parks to contemplate placid pools, clamber round roaring waterfalls and seek out fine viewpoints overlooking great river valleys. And on the way discover a little more of our social and industrial history, so much of which was dependent upon water for transport, power and irrigation.

River Tamar

OS 1:50,000 Sheet 201, 190

The Tamar is one of the finest sheltered-water cruising grounds in the British Isles, yet it is one of the least crowded. With its tributaries and creeks, or lakes as they are called, it offers some 100 miles of navigable water amidst outstanding and much changing scenery, with enough shoreside sites worth visiting to keep an inquiring family busy for a week or more. The river itself is the boundary between Devon and Cornwall, and from Plymouth Sound it is navigable for twenty-three miles inland. For at least three hours either side of high water the lower reaches are expansive with ample room for fleets of yachts to race and manoeuvre at will. But higher up the mud flats start showing much earlier, spreading out from both shores until, at low water, only narrow channels are left trickling through reed-fringed mudscapes. Therefore, once out of Plymouth Sound visits ashore need to be carefully planned; those who know our east coast rivers will be familiar with the situation. On the Tamar it is the planning ahead which adds interest to the act of driving a boat, and the scenery and unspoilt rural simplicity ashore more than compensate for the need for muddy wellies. Sailing boats do make their way to the limits of navigation, but these waters are more easily discovered under power when one can keep ahead of the flood and the ebb or, with a little speed, even catch them up after a stop. With an iron sail there is no need to inadvertently tack into a mud bank on the ebb. The fast shallow-draught, trailable boat is ideal for those who want to see everything in a short time, while the inflatable dinghy equipped with oars as well as outboard can penetrate deep into parts normally visited only by the birds. OS sheet 201 is essential for navigating the countryside of the Tamar valley and it is also far more useful for interpreting the landscape, and deciding where to go ashore, than any chart. Self-sufficient types seeking to escape the urban environment would do well to launch into the upper reaches, while those who cannot forget supermarkets, souvenir shops and jukebox pubs will want to be based in Plymouth.

Coming in from the sea is no problem because Plymouth Sound is very easy of entry either side of the breakwater in all conditions, although in heavy weather the western channel is recommended. The first sheltered anchorage for crews needing to get their breaths back after a hairy passage is immediately to the north of and behind the breakwater. Pleasanter – but only in settled weather – is Bovisand Bay, *490 505*, on the east shore opposite the end of the breakwater, or Jennycliff Bay, *490 520*. Both are picturesque rocky coves but with nothing ashore. Alternatively, for the more gregarious, a first stop could be the anchorage in Cawsand Bay, *435 504*, if the wind is in the west – otherwise the swell can be sick making. The steep streets of Kingsand and Cawsand, twin villages with precariously perched cottages, make this an interesting and pretty stop-over out of season; during the holidays it is too small for the crowds that descend upon it. There is a slipway reached through tortuous narrow streets, and trail boat owners might consider staying at the Boatel on the sea front and using that as a base for any excursions up the Tamar.

If you want all amenities, Plymouth has two marinas: Sutton Harbour alongside the Barbican, and the Mayflower Marina at the entrance to Stonehouse Pool. The latter is perhaps better described as being on the Devonport shore just through the narrows, *456 536*, between Cremyll and Stonehouse. A less salubrious, but convenient, resting place is Millbay Dock where you can dry out alongside or lock in and stay afloat. The entrance is due north of Drake's Island and is dominated by a conspicuous silo rising above all other buildings. Round the corner from Cremyll, which is where the foot ferry starts for its five-minute run to Plymouth, there is an anchorage at the entrance to Millbrook Lake in the area opposite an obelisk on high ground. The ferry brings the shops of Plymouth within walking distance of your boat, and there is the Edgcumbe Arms Hotel for local refreshments in the ambience of low beams and stone-flagged floors, or for sitting outside watching the boats passing through the narrows. A few minutes' walk uphill takes you to Mount Edgcumbe Country Park with its deer, panoramic views over the Sound and restored sixteenth century house which is open to the public.

Cawsand, a pretty stop-over out of season; during the holidays it is too small for the crowds which descend upon it

Millbrook Lake, which is only a mile long, is navigable to its end for less than an hour either side of high water. Its main attraction is Foss Point, *432523*, on the north shore where a variety of multihulls have long made their homes round the old quay of a former brickyard. St John at the head of the next lake up river is well worth a visit, but it needs to be a brief visit near the top of the tide or a long one sitting on the mud. High hedges half hide old cottages with very English gardens, and for added quaintness the village is approached from one direction through a ford. The countryside about is bright with fruit blossom in season. Going on upstream the Tamar becomes the Hamoaze past the Devonport dockyards on the east bank and Torpoint opposite, both of which can be passed without comment. Then comes St Germans, or the Lynher, river as it is variously called winding six miles westward to St Germans Quay, *364 571*, which is actually on the bank of a tributary, the river Tiddy. Well inland and set among trees, it is the home port for a lot of boats both on its grassy hard and in drying berths. If forced to sit out the two hours around low water, the time can be well spent walking the half-mile uphill to the church of St Germanus built on the remains of the original Saxon cathedral of Cornwall. The present church is the most complete example of a Norman building in the county. The Tiddy is navigable by tender for a further two miles to Tideford, as also is the Lynher after it turns north before St Germans. Altogether there are six little lakes to explore off St Germans river, and at the entrance a mooring off Jupiter Point is convenient for a run ashore to Antony House above the south bank. This National Trust property is the finest Queen Anne house in Cornwall; it has been altered very little in the 250 years

The river Tamar is not navigable beyond the weir at Gunnislake in Cornwall

The great cliff of Bishop's Rock rising sheer over a hairpin bend of the Tamar.

The nascent river Tamar below Lower Tamar Lake

The river Dart owes much of its beauty to the woods which line its banks

The footpath beside Devonport Leat provides an easy walk across large stretches of Dartmoor avoiding the hazards of bog, rock and river

The Blackbrook river, a tributary of the Dart, is crossed by this clapper bridge near Princetown on Dartmoor

since it was built and still contains much original furniture.

Back in the Hamoaze and going north the Royal Albert tubular railway and Tamar road bridges dominate the scene. Do not just pass under the tubular railway bridge in your hurry to get into the quieter upper reaches. Throttle back and circle around below its two great spans and consider how it took ten years to build and was one of the wonders of the Victorian Age, designed by Isambard Kingdom Brunel and opened by Prince Albert in 1859. The two central spans complete with their suspended permanent ways were prefabricated and floated down-river on barges, to be lifted into position by hydraulic jacks. Brunel directed the whole operation with flags and numbered boards from a platform atop each span after ordering that the delicate manoeuvres be carried out in complete silence from the thousands watching from the banks. The spans fitted perfectly into place with less than an eighth of an inch clearance. The modern single-span suspension road bridge is as aesthetically pleasing as Brunel's is powerfully impressive. There is a convenient launching site right under the suspension bridge reached by taking the left hand road off the roundabout just before the bridge, and the first left again where a steep street leads down to the riverside and a wide public slipway which is ideal for a trailed boat.

Once upstream of the bridges the river reverts to its proper name of Tamar and the real adventure can begin. Up until here the tides in the main river will have been of small consequence with plenty of deep water in every direction at all states. From now on attention must be paid to the channels which wind through great banks of drying mud. Although the river opens out to its greatest width at its confluence with the river Tavy, it is possible at that point at low water to scrub your bottom while standing ankle deep in water on the edge of the fairway half a mile from the shore! The Tavy, which comes from the middle of Dartmoor and gives Tavistock its name, should be entered on a rising tide when the passage between the mud banks can be followed without difficulty. The limit of navigation is just over three miles up at Lopwell Dam, *424 650*, where there is a convenient quay and neatly landscaped car park-cum-picnic area. But you can soon get away from that; a half-hour walk up a steep road through the woods to Milton Combe, *489 660*, will give you the thirst to appreciate the excellent real ales and history of the pub called The Who'd Have Thought It. By then your boat will be safely aground back at the quay, so you might as well go on walking uphill a further mile to Buckland abbey, *c* 1278, which is now a naval and folk museum containing many nautical relics including Drake's Drum (which I had always thought to be a poet's invention!). A quick drink with less effort can be had at Bere Ferrers, *460 685*, on the north shore, half way to the Dam. The quay is by the church which sits beside the water with its slate and granite gravestones almost falling into the river. It contains some of the best stained glass in Devon and a most beautiful Norman font.

Continuing up the Tamar the village of Cargreen on the Cornish side has little to offer of aesthetic or historical interest, but there is the Spaniards Inn, *436 626*, whose landlord has laid moorings in twelve feet of water so that his nautical customers may remain upright at all times. Tables set beside the river wall make it an ideal spot in sunny weather. There is a curiosity a mile south of the pub in Landulph church, *432 615*, which can only be reached by road. It is the memorial tablet to Theodoro Palaeolus who died in the parish in 1636 and is believed to be the last known descendant of the Byzantine emperors. A little beyond Cargreen on the Devon side are Weir Quay and Hole's Hole, two adjacent clusters of cottages on the waterfront. Weir Quay is made up of several quays which originally served the local farms and lime kilns. Kilns, or the remains of them, and quays in every state of repair and disrepair can be spotted at close intervals along both banks of the Tamar and its several tributaries. Few of the country lanes inshore existed a hundred years ago; they were no more than tracks used by horses. Bulk transport and such commuting as there was all took place on the water. Lime was brought to the kilns by sailing barges which returned downstream to the towns with farm produce. Other quays served ships of up to 300 tons which collected copper, manganese and arsenic from the nearby mines. The now ivy-clad engine house chimneys of those mines can be seen everywhere on the slopes of the Tamar valley.

The surprising sight of Hole's Hole is a pair of houseboats, bows to the wooded shore. The bigger, said to be the hulk of an old clipper ship, is owned by a TV scriptwriter, and the smaller and prettier by the local salmon netters who use it as a night shelter. Weir Quay is a good place to wait for a tide, being at the end of the wide estuarial part of the river and at the start of the narrowing reaches through deep valleys where only a blind Philistine would want to travel fast. From here on every arrival and departure from a place of interest has to be by agreement with the tide if too much time is not to be lost waiting for mud to cover. Above Hole's Hole a bend takes the river in an almost complete loop so that you start heading north west, then due south before coming out facing north east. The Devon shore is flat and swampy while the slopes on the Cornish side are covered with woods which hide from view Pentillie Castle, *410 645*, built in 1689 and recently so restored as to look quite modern. But its whereabouts can be noted by its quay and quaint boathouse with leaded windows and decorative red and black bricks.

Granite, fruit and vegetables were once shipped out from Halton Quay, *414 655*, just up river from Pentillie Castle, but it is now neglected and overgrown with weeds. A row of Georgian cottages make the spot a tiny hamlet, and a building looking just like a whitewashed brick signal box arouses curiosity. In fact it is a chapel, and closer scrutiny reveals a cross on the wall facing the river and a small bell on one corner. It is said to mark the place where St Interact, son of an Irish king, and St Dominica, his sister, landed in the seventh century. The ubiquitous lime kiln completes the scene. Between Halton and Cotehele Quay, *424 681*, which comes two miles further on, the woods give way to open views of the Cornish valley slopes which are a coloured patchwork of market gardens. Whether serious traveller or frivolous tripper on the river, you should stop by at Cotehele. The eighteenth and nineteenth century quayside buildings have been sensitively restored, and in one a small museum gives a very digestible lesson, in pictures and models, on the Tamar as a commercial river serving the mining and agricultural industries of the two previous centuries.

A fully restored and commissioned Tamar sailing barge, the *Shamrock*, lies in its small basin waiting for charter parties as it would have waited for cargos two generations ago. She was built in Plymouth and made her maiden voyage in 1899 to Fowey carrying a deck cargo of sailing dinghies for a regatta. Then for twenty years she worked up and down the Tamar under sail before an auxiliary engine was installed, after which she spent forty-three years at sea carrying road stone from Dartmouth to Falmouth. Acquired by the National Trust in 1974, she was restored at Cotehele Quay with the help of the National Maritime Museum. There is a good slipway off the quay, and the National Trust provides some boat storage space. Above the quay, a good puff uphill, is the mediaeval Cotehele House, 1485, which is still furnished with much original material. Its large gardens on several levels overlook the river, and within the grounds there are a mediaeval dovecote, a working manorial water mill and a large cider press. This National Trust property could well occupy the four hours during which the quay dries out. A visit during spring tides could leave you stranded there for a very long lunch hour, but there is a restaurant by the house and a café on the quay.

A flood tide would then take you a mile round the bend to

The harbour office at Cotehele Quay, restored by the National Trust to its dusty late-Victorian state

Calstock which clings to the hillside along the river in the shadow of a great twelve-arched railway viaduct built in 1906 of concrete blocks in an area of abundant granite. It was once a mining and shipbuilding town which virtually died when the mining ended, and the railway killed the river trade and, therefore, the yards. It is now a tiny dormitory linked to Plymouth by a single track railway service through exquisite scenery. The restaurant at The Boot, which is a short walk up from the quay at the east end of the village, has had a wide following for a great many years, and the bar and snug are conducive to making your number with the locals. There is no need to have your own boat to cruise the Tamar; there is a pleasure steamer which sails from Phoenix Wharf in Plymouth to Calstock and back with an hour ashore in the village. Sailing times vary as the steamer has to be at Calstock over the top of the tide. An alternative, if the tides serve, which allows you as much time as you want to walk along the river from Calstock to Cotehele would be to take a morning train from Plymouth and catch the evening steamer back. British Rail issue combined tickets for rail and river journeys.

Most people do not consider going on further than Calstock, but they miss the most exciting bit of the whole navigable river – three great loops below steep cliffs and three miles to the river port of Morwellham, *424681*, said with the emphasis on the 'ham'. It is a bit like driving through a wooded gorge and wondering if you will ever get out of it as gouts of mud thicken your wake to send frissons of apprehension through the crew. But if you take it slowly with the rising tide and wait patiently for more water when you stray from the deep ditch – channel would be too grand a word – you will get there with no more harm done than a prop polished by the soft mud. It can, of course, be more easily taken on the plane, but that might be considered anti social. Morwellham itself is one of those places which must please even the most blasé voyager. It is a magnificent slice of industrial history being daily re-enacted by people in the appropriate costumes and using contemporary tools and artifacts. The port was built to ship copper from the mines up in the hills which was brought there by the Tavistock Canal, cut in 1802, to a point high up above the river. From canal barges it was taken down to the quays on an inclined railway. Parts of the Devon Great Consol mine have been opened up and can be visited by a narrow gauge railway.

The silted up harbour at Morwellham, a magnificent slice of industrial history, where a family could easily spend the whole day

The *Shamrock*, a fully restored Tamar sailing barge, in its small basin at Cotehele Quay waiting for charter parties

There is everything there – a working forge, a restaurant, arsenic furnace, lime kiln and a nature walk, and all is well explained. A family could easily spend a day at Morwellham, but to go by boat means taking a very quick look and turning back before getting stuck in the mud unless the trip is planned so as to arrive on an early morning flood and to leave again that evening.

The river is still navigable for an hour or so of each tide a little further on to the now derelict lock of the Manure Canal, *435 709*, at Gunnislake, which must be the shortest and oddest canal in the country. It ran less than a mile alongside the Tamar from below the weir at Gunnislake to the New Bridge – the first one over the river until the Tamar road bridge was built in 1962 joining Plymouth to Saltash. As its name implies, it was used by fifty ton barges which brought manure and human effluent from Dock Dung in Plymouth to Gunnislake for spreading on farmland and gardens. They also brought coal and lime for the kilns and bones for the bone mill. Just a big village now, it was a busy place in the last century. The lock into the canal is part rotted away and overgrown, but most of its component parts can be recognised beneath a thick coat of moss and lichen. The canal today is a series of still ponds richly carpeted in summer with brilliant green duckweed. I tried to visit the owner of the old lock keeper's cottage which stands on an island between river and canal, but was repulsed by a savage sounding dog. The owner, I was told by a water keeper, was an 'ennit' who did not welcome visitors. Ennit is the Cornish for ant and the local name for incomers and tourists. In Devon we are called 'grockles'.

The river is not crossed again until, after several miles of great meanders, it comes to Horsebridge, *400 749*, which was the first bridge over the Tamar when it was built by monks in 1437; in those times monks carried out all the civil engineering in the country. They were usually funded by people who had made a bob or two and were worried about the manner in which they had done it, so used some of it to buy indulgences. The road that it carries is now a very minor one, but it used to be the main route into Cornwall. On the Devon side of the bridge the monks built a small nunnery; when Henry VIII dissolved the monasteries the land was given to the Russells – the Dukes of Bedford – and it became an inn originally called, inevitably, The Packhorse. It is now The Royal, a name granted by Charles I when he stayed there. His seal is on the doorstep to this day. Kings in those times were always pleading poverty, and a landlord who rendered a service to the monarch was more likely to be told he could call his pub 'royal' than receive any payment. The Royal is definitely worth the drive through winding lanes for its food and its beer – both home-made. Terry Wood, the landlord, brews his own beer, or at least his son does. 'You have to have a brewer; you can't run a pub and brew yourself', he told me. 'Fortunately my son is very competent. We have a single barrel plant so we can only brew one barrel at a time, but with three fermenting vessels we can brew three times a week. A barrel is thirty-five gallons, so we can serve 840 pints a week'. Even so he can run out. Of the six real ales he offers, two were 'off', finished, when I last called in. It would be unwise, if not criminal, to go beer tasting at The Royal and then try and drive, for his brews are strong drink with gravity up to 1060, which is almost a barley wine, against the average keg beer which runs out at 1032 to 1034 – about half the strength. The interior is all low ceilings, wood beams, three-foot-thick stone walls and open fires; or you can sit on the lawn and look at the river. From the outside it could be mistaken for a rectory with its arched seventeenth century windows in a Gothic pattern of small panes giving the place an ecclesiastical air.

The place with an ecclesiastical character of quite another sort is Bishop's Rock, *368 780*, in the woods at Carthamartha. This is a ledge of rock almost lost from view when the rhododendrons are in bloom jutting out over the edge of a great cliff rising sheer over a hairpin bend in the river. It is said that the Bishop of Exeter preached from it to a congregation in the meadows 100 feet below him. This giddy perch overlooks the Tavistock Woodlands now owned by the Earl of Bradford; looking one way the river is seen flowing down from Greystone Bridge and in the other direction it snakes away to be lost below the canopy of mature trees. A visit to the foot of the cliffs is equally satisfying. The river is shallow here and you can walk in it and through a copse on a small island. On one side the cliff rises vertically all covered with tenacious trees, on the other is a meadow hardly sloping at all. This peaceful spot can be reached across grazing fields from a farm road, *373 794*, off the A384 leading to a house called Woodtown.

The Tamar rises near Woolley Barrows, *271 167*, barely four miles from the north Cornwall and Devon cliffs below Morwenstow so that it very nearly makes Cornwall an island. For most of the nineteenth century it really was an island, albeit artificially made so by the building of the Bude Canal which was fed from the river Tamar. The canal opened for traffic in 1823 and all but a few miles of it closed in 1891, but most of its route and the remains of many of the engineering works along its course can be found with the help of OS 1:25,000 maps. Bude on the north Cornish coast is still a registered port with a massive sea lock which could take vessels up to 300 tons. One branch of the canal ended at Blagdonmoor Wharf, *362 059*, just north east of Holsworthy, and the other at Crossgate Wharf outside Launceston. The total length was about forty-six miles, and barges worked from Bude to Helebridge, a distance of only two miles. From there on the canal narrowed and was used by tub boats ten feet long and five and a half feet beam which carried about five tons each and were pulled by horses in strings of six. The main cargo was sea sand but coal, limestone and building material were also carried. The summit was on the Holsworthy line where it reached 433 feet. There are two locks on the stretch from Bude to Helebridge and six inclined planes for lifting and lowering the tub boats. The first is at Marhamchurch to which there is a three and a half-mile walk along the towpath from Bude. The tub boats were fitted with iron wheels, and at the top and bottom of each incline they were hooked onto a chain, driven by a water wheel, and lowered or hauled up from one level to the other.

The exception was the great Hobbacott incline, *245 047*, which was worked by buckets in the well system. The buckets held fifteen tons of water and the chains were prone to snap, so a steam engine was kept in reserve to do the hauling. Hobbacott is probably the most impressive site to visit. If motoring park in the layby, *244 051*, at Habbacott Down on the Red Post-Stratton road. A footpath to Thurlibeer Farm, in the grounds of which are some old canal buildings and a hole in the ground which was one of the bucket wells, leads to the top of the incline. It is a steep walk down and steeper walk up the 320-yard long incline which rises 225 feet. At the bottom there is at first nothing to see other than a clearing in the trees, but careful searching soon reveals some dressed stones, thoroughly overgrown, which are the remains of two miniature basins into which the incline rails dipped and also into which the tub boats were floated to be attached to the chain. These basins still have a little water in them so remain wet and muddy. The canal sides have fallen in and become overgrown so that it is no more than a ditch, but it does become a bit more like a canal back towards Marhamchurch and there is quite a believable section at the top of the incline. Near Red Post where the canal passes under the B3254 the canal bifurcates, one arm going to Holsworthy while the other follows closely alongside the Tamar down to Druxton. On the way are vestiges of Merrifield Incline Plane, *271 015*, Tamerton Wharf, *318 974*, Tamerton Incline Plane, *318 966*, and Bridgetown Aqueduct, *342 891*. Off the Holsworthy branch can be found the soggy ditch which was once the short feeder canal from Lower Tamar Lake, a reservoir through which the river flows. Beside the weir is a tunnel which took water to the feeder, and a year or two ago the South West Water Authority used the Youth Opportunity Scheme to start clearing the feeder canal and in 1987 there were a few hundred yards of water in it. When that feeder and the Bude Canal were last full of water then Cornwall was an island.

River Dart

OS 1:50,000 Sheet 202 and Outdoor Leisure 1:25,000 Sheet 28

The Dart is every yachtsman's dream of what a sailing river should be – no bar, no shallows and beautiful scenery. It is in fact a ria, or drowned valley, routed out by glacier and flooded when the ice melted. It is the thick woodlands on its steep slopes, in places up to 500 feet high, that give it much of its beauty. But it is largely a man-made beauty, the trees having nearly all been planted by late Victorian and Edwardian landlords; early nineteenth century prints show the hillsides to be largely bare. There were exceptions like Long Wood on the east shore above Higher Noss Point, Gallant's Bower above the castle on the west side of the river entrance and Sharpham Woods up near Totnes; all survivors of even more ancient oak woods which were cut down over the centuries. Their bark was used for tanning, the branches went for charcoal, and the trunks and some of the heavier limbs for building ships. That the trees were re-planted is only right because the river could not be the Dart without them for the name Dart is the old Celtic word for oak.

The river is both tidal and navigable for eleven miles up to Totnes with a deep channel as far as Dittisham, after which the depth varies, but on spring tides 1,000-ton, timber-carrying ships, 240 feet long and drawing twelve and a half feet, have no difficulty getting up to Baltic Wharf in the town. The river is most certainly best seen from the water because the roads on either side keep well inland and only at a very few places do they afford a view of the valley, let alone the river itself. It is an experience which anybody can enjoy because there are plenty of pleasure boats plying between Dartmouth and Totnes, but of course they do not reach those tucked away parts up little creeks which your own boat can get to – and where it can be stuck in the mud if you do not watch tide and time. Bayards Cove at the southern end of Dartmouth town is the most preserved part of the original waterfront; it was used to represent the port of Liverpool in the BBC series *The Onedin Line*. The *Mayflower* put in there after being battered by a storm on her way down the English Channel before going back to Plymouth for repairs. The oldest part of the town is along Higher Street which in Elizabethan times ran along the riverside ten feet above the high water mark. It is now well inland. Here and there are examples of the once close-packed, half-timbered houses with overhanging upper floors of the Tudor era. Everybody goes to look at The Cherub, a beautifully restored wool merchant's house dated 1380 which, unbelievably, was allowed to become utterly derelict until 1958 when a Mr Creswell began restoring it and opened it in 1972 as a free house and restaurant. It is named after a type of boat once built locally for carrying wool. The cellar holds a fine selection of English wines to go with their locally caught fish – bass from the Skerries Banks, Dart cockles, Dover soles from Dartmouth, salmon from the river and crab.

Thomas Newcomen was born in Dartmouth in 1663 and his Memorial Engine – the first ever commercially used steam engine which he built in 1712 – is housed in a glass building in the public gardens. His invention came sixty years before James Watts' improved design, by which time at least 200 Newcomen engines were at work pumping water out of mines. The one on display was working as a canal pumping engine up to 1913 and could be made to work again today. The town rises in terraces, and from the highest point is overlooked by the red brick Britannia Royal Naval College. Everybody associates Dartmouth with the College, but it may not be generally realised that the building was only completed in 1905 and prior to that it was housed in a couple of warship hulks moored in the river.

Upstream from Dartmouth the river twists and turns with never a straight reach so that each successive scene comes into view on its own, which makes for surprise-surprise all the way. Dittisham on the left bank is the first. Its main street – it would be no more than an alley in a town – rises steeply from the beach beside the Ferryboat Inn, *866 548*; the foot ferry crosses to Greenway Point where Agatha Christie lived. If driving into Dittisham leave the car in the park on the outskirts of the village. The temptation to drive down to the water should be resisted; if the

Tuckenhay on Bow Creek off the river Dart was once a centre of industrial activity with a gas works, corn mills, cider stores and a paper mill

tide is out you may get bogged down turning on the narrow foreshore. If it is in you will have a very tedious job backing a long way up with hardly any width to spare. You should walk down; it is a most pretty street between the stone and thatched cottages with only a narrow strip of river visible at its end across which sailing boats hurry in and out of sight. Dittisham is famous for its damsons called Ploughmen, possibly because the trees originally came from Germany where they are called *pflaumen*. The village church has a unique wine glass pulpit with carved and painted saints encircling it.

When leaving Dittisham go out on the road to Cornworthy, even if it means going back on your tracks, because along that road there is probably the best panoramic view of the Dart. It is from near the crown of the hill, *845 555*, out of East Cornworthy and it looks across a reach of the river and into the creek below

Stepping stones across the head of Bow Creek above Tuckenhay

Stoke Gabriel whose houses sit on a hill above a large mill pool. Like almost all nice villages it has been suffocated by dormitory sprawl, but its core is still intact, centred around Church House Inn which bears the date 1111 on one of its beams. It has an enormous inglenook in which a whole pig was roasted as recently as New Year's Eve 1982, and maybe others since then too. A back oven big enough to take a man was used to bake all the village bread, and the inn itself is thought to have been built to house and feed the stonemasons while they were building the church. The Exeter Registers of 1300 refer to the dilapidations of the old church at Stoke Gabriel, but the present one is largely a fifteenth century rebuild. The church register records the baptism of John Davis who sailed to the Arctic in a ten-ton pinnace in 1587 and discovered the Falkland Islands in 1592. The churchyard is partly covered by the outspread branches of a great yew estimated to be over 1,000 years old.

Across the river from Stoke Gabriel, Bow Creek flows through virgin countryside with not a building in sight and the only sign of life a flock of sheep moving as a solid block under command of a sheepdog. This long finger of water invites the unwary to explore it all the way up to the hamlet of Tuckenhay where a most convenient stone quay and the Maltsters Arms, a typical white-painted pub, conspire to tempt one to stay too long only to find that there is only enough water left outside to keep a shelduck afloat. Tuckenhay has many curiosities for so small a place – you can walk from one end to the other in three minutes. Sleepy now, it was once a compact centre of industrial activity with corn mills, cider stores on the quay and a paper mill which, until a few years back, was producing the highest quality hand-made paper. The village was lit by gaslight as early as 1806, the same year that it was introduced to London. The shell of the gasworks – gas hut would be a more accurate description – is still there beside the quay at which coasters unloaded coal and took away paper and cider. The quay is now the car park for the Maltsters Arms which, I regret, has been well and truly 'done up' inside with a smart restaurant to pull in the carriage trade. It also brings a lot more cars to clog the narrow local lanes. No wonder one old gentleman in the village prefers to go to Totnes in his motor boat to do his weekly shopping.

Back in the main river there is a winding channel between the mature trees of Sharpham Wood, rising 200 feet from the water, and Ham Copse, then a straight bit and you are in Totnes lying against a concrete ledge below the bridge. If stopping alongside there for long beware of the high tide which covers the ledge and can leave your boat like an old maid, on the shelf. When navigating those bends at high water springs watch out for the masts of a big coaster showing above the trees round the bend in front of you or coming up behind you; it will be a timber boat and you will need to get out of the channel to let her pass. By road one sees nothing of the river after Tuckenhay until crossing the bridge in Totnes. The head of the tidal salt water is the weir, *801 612*, two miles upstream of the bridge and can only be reached in a dinghy. From there on it is all rich peaty water pouring out of the great sponge of Dartmoor. The highest possible point from which any navigation can be attempted, and then only by canoe, is Buckfastleigh, from where down to the weir the river winds swiftly over rocks and boulders, which call for some skill to negotiate. Every October a hair-raising raft race is run for charity along that reach to the weir, which is shot at high water.

By far the best way to look at this part of the river is to take a return ticket on the Dart Valley Railway from Totnes to Buckfastleigh, making sure to get a seat on the left side facing the engine. The line runs within a few yards of the water for the seven miles. Dartington Hall, *799 627*, stands amid water meadows embraced by a great sweep of the river between the weir and Staverton. It is a mediaeval courtyard house on a site occupied since Saxon times. A tilt yard for jousting and bear baiting has raised grass terraces for spectators who now watch *son et lumière* spectaculars. The house is surrounded by a garden, open to the public, with 400-year-old Spanish chestnuts and masses of azaleas, rhododendrons, hydrangeas and camellias. Next-door is the school of the same name but of somewhat different fame. The Dart makes one last tame appearance as it flows through the grounds of Buckfast Abbey, *741 674*, a monumental building of yellow stone built by Benedictine monks between 1880 and 1938.

For the next few miles the river can be followed much of its way on foot as it comes foaming down through the glens of Holne Woods, Holne Chase and Southpark Wood, much of the way through National Trust property and the River Dart Country Park. The road from Ashburton to Tavistock switchbacks up and down meeting the river first at Holne Bridge and then at New Bridge, after which it climbs up onto the high ground by Sharp Tor, *686 729*, and then down to Dartmeet where the East Dart comes down from the north to meet the mainstream West Dart – or is it the other way round? No matter; there is a big clapper bridge across the tail end of the East Dart with its centre stone missing, and that has justified a huge car park, cafeteria and shop.

Buckfast Abbey, a monumental edifice of yellow stone on the banks of the river Dart, was built by Benedictine monks between 1880 and 1938

The Dart Valley Railway is the only way to follow the river from Totnes to Buckfastleigh as it runs within a few yards of the water for seven miles

Dartmoor ponies graze beside Cherry Brook, a tributary of the West Dart

Few of the thousands who stop there see Dartmeet, that is the meeting of the two rivers, which is some little distance downstream south of the road. To get a view of the actual meeting point, *627 731*, cross over the bridge and walk a few yards up the road to the start of a footpath beside a stone cottage. Immediately after passing through a gate the path bifurcates, the left one going down to stepping stones over the West Dart. On the other side the real Dartmeet can be seen. Continuing along that footpath a very steep climb will take you to Combstone Tor, *670 718*, for magnificent views north over Dartmeet, up the East Dart valley and east along the forested Dart Gorge leading to Holne Woods. While down by the start of the West Dart you may come across some woebegone and very hungry looking teenagers peering at you from bivouacs made from mosses and rocks or fallen branches. They will be Royal Marine recruits from the Commando Training Centre at Lympstone on the Exe on their three-day survival course on the Moor.

The best known site along the East Dart is Postbridge with its clapper bridge, *648 789*, the most famous one of them all, which attracts crowds of tourists all through the summer. From there until its source some seven miles to the north the East Dart flows across bleak open moorland most of which is a military range Danger Area. It is up on that wilderness that the Teign, which flows east to Teignmouth, the Tavy which flows west to the Tamar, the West Dart as well as the East Dart all have their sources within a mile or two of each other. The West Dart above Dartmeet keeps well away from the road although it can be seen in the distance most of the time, until it turns north towards Two Bridges from where it can be followed on foot to its source, subject to the red flags not flying on the ranges. There is a car park outside the Two Bridges Hotel and in the disused quarry on the other side of the road at the start of a track along the east bank of the river. The first time I took that walk I met with two surprises. The first, two miles along the track, was Wistman's Wood, a famous but then unknown to me plantation of twisted dwarf oaks literally growing out of great granite boulders and thickly covered with mosses and lichens. Altogether twenty-six mosses, twenty-one liverworts and some seventy lichens have been identified. The average height of the trees is a little over twelve feet, but their branches hang low so that it takes some hunting and agility to find a way to walk upright through the wood. If you have the energy it is rather fun scrambling over rocks and under branches to find ever more grotesque shapes. The wood is in the care of the Nature Conservancy Council and access is not restricted, except to one or two experimental plots which are fenced off.

After leaving the wood that first time and feeling rather exhausted I went over the West Dart, no more than a jump across that near to its source, and walked up a slope towards what looked like a level contour path. I was puzzled to find that it was a narrow footpath beside a neatly dug stone-lined leat which curved away to the south, back the way I wanted to go. I had come across the Devonport Leat which carried the water supply from the West Dart just above Wistman's Wood to Devonport. The digging of the leat was started in 1793 and was not fully completed until January 1802 at a cost of £23,400. It is basically an irrigation ditch or micro canal at the most ten feet wide and three feet deep which winds across Dartmoor following one contour line for as long as possible before dropping down a few feet to another. It remained in use as far as Dousland until 1951 when it was terminated above Burrator Reservoir, and from where it now cascades out of a pipe, *551 683*, down a cliff to run under the road and into the reservoir. Dartmoor can be a dangerous place for the ill-prepared and in bad weather, which can come suddenly, it is all too easy to get lost. But the path beside the Devonport Leat is always a safe and easy way of walking across a large section of the moor avoiding the obstacles of bog, rock and river. To complete the whole length as it is today would be a walk of about twenty miles, but by careful study of the OS 1:25,000 map it is possible to trace its course as a very thin blue line to find the points at which it is accessible from roads.

Devonport Leat tumbles off Raddick Hill and over the aqueduct above the river Meavy on its way to Burrator Reservoir

Two most interesting walks, each occupying about two hours, would be first from Two Bridges up to Wistman's Wood and back beside the leat to Beardown Farm, *604 754*, and so back onto the road just west of where you started. The other is from Cross Gate, *562 695*, up a lane from the north side of Burrator Lake, through the woods of Norsworthy and Stanlake Plantations, out onto the open moor, past a group of old stone settlements to the aqueduct, *573 714*, over the river Meavy to climb up beside a cascade down the side of Raddick Hill. Either return the same way or cross-country to Crazy Well Pool, *582 704*, and then west along the footpath below it back to Cross Gate. When it ran its complete course into Devonport, was a large chunk of Devon surrounded by the waters of the Dart and Devonport Leat an island? Not quite, because the water eventually ended up in pipes and storage tanks and did not flow freely to the sea.

Exeter Ship Canal

OS 1:50,000 Sheet 192

Exeter has a guildhall which is claimed to be the oldest municipal building in Britain, having been on its present site since 1160. The cathedral has no heaven-seeking spire, but is flanked by two massive Norman towers and its west façade is decorated with the largest surviving fourteenth century stone sculpture in the country, while inside the thirteenth century Gothic vaulting is the longest in the world. Houses in the cathedral square go back to Elizabeth I, there is a section of Roman wall still standing, and the present High Street was an ancient Celtic ridgeway. All that one would expect of a cathedral city. It also offers the visitor two unusual walks. One, most suited to a wet day, is its system of underground aqueducts built in the thirteenth century to carry water from local springs. It is entered down steps from the pavement in Princesshay. The other one, which could fill in a whole day and be worth it, is a ten mile return walk along the towpaths of the Exeter Ship Canal which runs parallel to the river Exe.

The start of this walk is bound to be delayed by a visit to the Martime Museum housed in a number of warehouses by the quay and by the canal basin, which in themselves are recognised as being among the best examples of industrial architecture. Those by the quay are particularly impressive, built of red and white limestone about 1835 and five storeys high set back against a cliff topped by a terrace of Georgian houses. The museum has more than eighty craft on display – coracles, a sampan, several Arab dhows, a Tagus lighter, a steam tug and a reed boat from Lake Titicaca in the Andes is a random sample. Among those afloat in the canal is Brunel's steam dredger built in 1844 which is the oldest working steam craft in the world; she is regularly put into steam. Her engine room has to be entered almost on all fours, and is occupied by one cylinder with a few pipes and a crankshaft to a

Exeter has all that one would expect of a cathedral city including this Elizabethan building, Moll's Coffee House, which stands opposite the cathedral

huge flywheel, half of which protrudes up through the deck, a contraption which looks too crude to have ever worked.

Boats may be hired to row round the boats-afloat part of the museum and through the canal basin, which is filled with a collection of privately owned boats, old and new, as interesting in their way as those in the museum. By south coast standards berths are very cheap, although going up and down the canal is expensive, so they are mostly long-stay while being worked on by their owners.

These impressive five-storey warehouses on the quay at Exeter were built of red and white limestone in about 1835 and now form part of the Maritime Museum

John Bridger, who owns the chandlery, called it: 'A bit of a graveyard; a lot of boats come up here to die'. Looking out of his office window we watched an elderly bearded gentleman working on a very old wooden craft with a clapped out van for a workshop. 'He works on her year after year and never gets much further with it; he is part of the scenery. We have more than a few of them, enthusiastic diehards all going to go round the world, but I don't think they really want to go. All they want to do is work on their boats – that is their joy in life'. John Bridger's shop is stocked with the latest in electronic equipment, expensive, high powered, outboard engines and designer sailing clothes, and his customers come from far and wide – from everywhere except the basin itself. 'Its all do-it-yourself here. They make their own chain plates and get bottle screws off scrapped telegraph poles'.

If making a day of it I would suggest starting without a proper breakfast and, after spending some time at the museum, walk the one and a half miles to Double Locks Hotel, *932 900*, where they serve breakfast until 12.30 – a big fry-up and a pint of beer of your choice for £2.50. The Breakfast Club, whose members are mostly local business executives, meet on the second Thursday morning of every month to talk business over a pint and breakfast. The hotel stands beside Double Locks, so called because it can take two ships side by side, and is thought to have been built by the Dutch in 1710. There is no record of this, but it is made of Dutch metric bricks of that period which were used as ballast in ships which came over to Exeter for timber and wool. It was originally the lock keeper's house before it became a pub, but lock keepers were in the habit of selling food and drink to bargees and ships' crews before the days of licensing. A pub is only as good as its landlord, and Double Locks has a charismatic one in Jamie Stuart. It was his own favourite pub as a youngster, and when it came on the market he was sailing a big charter boat off the coast of Turkey. He bought it over the telephone, and in four years he had earned a recommendation in all the good food and beer guides, and justifiably so. He is a landlord who identifies with his customers, a young version of the traditional Mine Host. His pub is immensely popular with students at Exeter University, is patronised by gourmets who study the menus chalked up on blackboards, and has a reputation for its folk music and jazz sessions.

From here it is a further three and a half miles to Turf Lock, *964 861*, where the canal flows into the tidal reach of the river Exe. And there, as you might expect, is the Turf Hotel, at the end of the outer embankment with the canal on one side and the river on the other. It is a watering hole which can only be reached on foot or by boat. Apart from walking down the towpath, you can get to it by a footpath up the west bank of the Exe from Powderham Castle, *968 837*, which can be a bit muddy, but it makes a very pleasant walk of about a mile, especially at low water when you should see avocets. During the summer local watermen run tripper boats at lunchtime and in the evening from Exmouth and Starcross to the Turf Hotel, which is also used by the fishermen who go up there for a drink at the end of a day's work.

The local fishing in the estuary and immediately out at sea is for bass, which is so much sought after that in early spring and summer it sells for up to £4.50 a pound when wild salmon is fetching only £3.50. The bass season starts between April and May, depending on the weather. The female fish lay their eggs in mid-channel somewhere off Cherbourg when the surface tem-

The Canal Basin in Exeter with its collection of privately owned boats, mostly long-stay and being worked on by their owners

perature reaches about 9°C, which would not be before the end of March. From there they then make their way to the mouth of the Exe. The peak period is mid-June to October. No licence is required, but salmon and sea trout caught by accident are supposed to be thrown back. The locals mostly use sand eels as bait which are actually baby herring but, because they are long and thin and live around the sandbanks, are called sand eels. These are caught by trawling a very lightweight net at about one and a half knots along the sand-bars at half tide. They are put in keep tanks off Exmouth Dock and individual fishermen pull up alongside to buy them by the bucketful. The method of fishing for bass is with rod and line drifting as close to the sandbanks as possible without running aground. Most locals fish for the sport and the pot, while a few fish commercially. There is a strict legal limit of fifteen inches, but of course twelve inches is a better size for a restaurant dinner plate. Steve Rush, a keen amateur bass fisherman, told me that in his opinion the best way to cook them is by baking for ten minutes per pound plus another ten minutes at 180-200°C in a tinfoil envelope with butter, lemon juice, a few herbs, salt and pepper. 'Gut and scale it first but leave the head on because the best parts of bass, and salmon too or any game fish, are the cheeks below the eyes. Small ones or less than three pounds can be barbequed, but if any bigger you will burn the outside before the inside is properly cooked. Score the skin on both sides and throw green fennel or rosemary on the coals while grilling it to infuse the flesh with a beautiful flavour'.

The Exeter Ship Canal would never have been built and we would not be able to enjoy that walk if it had not been for Isabel, Countess of Devon, who had a weir built across the river above Topsham to block navigation up to the port of Exeter, so diverting seaborne trade to her own town, Topsham. The City Fathers, after an exhaustive legal battle which came to naught, had a canal dug to by-pass Countess Weir, *942 897*, as it is now called. It was sixteen feet wide and three feet deep so could only be used by lighters, but when it opened in 1566 it was the first lock canal to be built in Britain since Roman times. In 1698 work started on enlarging it to fifty feet width and ten feet depth, as it is today. It then ended at a lock, *962 880*, opposite Topsham which is now derelict, but in 1825 it was extended a further one and a half miles to Turf Lock where ships could enter deeper water. Commercial traffic on the canal started to dwindle at the end of the last century when it became too shallow for the deeper draught cargo ships. Only one big ship uses it now, the sludge boat from the sewage works which was designed specially for the depth of the canal and to go under the M5 bridge which gives a clearance of only thirty-five feet. It is followed up and down by a man on a bicycle who opens the locks and the swing bridge which carries the Exeter by-pass over the canal. Because of the high cost of these openings private boats usually get together to form a convoy to reduce the expense, which still averages out at about £12 one way. It also takes from two to two and a half hours for the passage, waiting at the swing bridge, at the locks and for slow boats to catch up with the faster ones. It is quicker to walk if you do not stop too long at the pubs.

Wiltshire and Hampshire Avon

OS 1:50,000 Sheets 173/184/195

And were those great stones in ancient times rafted down the Avon river from below the Marlborough Downs, then hauled out at Amesbury and up the curving slope of the Avenue to form the great sarsen circle of Stonehenge?

We will never know, but it is an interesting theory that adds a touch of historical mystery to the Wiltshire and Hampshire Avon which has its beginnings in several streams below the Downs and flows into the sea at Christchurch. On the way it passes through Salisbury where it is joined by three other rivers of comparable size, and from there on does have a verifiable history. The idea that it was the highway by which stones were brought to Stonehenge was mooted in 1961 by a Canadian geologist, Patrick Hill of Carleton University, Ottawa. His thinking runs contrary to the accepted belief that the sarsen stones were brought overland on tree trunk rollers from the Downs with up to 800 men and women hauling each stone and perhaps 200 more clearing the way and shifting the rollers. It has been calculated that several thousand people must have been thus occupied for at least seven years. More likely, they only worked on stone hauling in winter when their primitive farming was at a standstill, so it could have taken several years longer. The upper reaches of the Avon today are no more than a series of streams at best two feet deep, but Hill theorises that in those days the Avon might have been deeper, or was dammed south of Amesbury to increase its depth. Alternatively, he suggests that the climate was more extreme with long, frozen winters, when the stones could have been slid over the gently sloping ice of the river. He reckons that twenty-five men could pull a fifty-ton, laden sledge over ice.

If the sarsens did not come down the Avon then perhaps the smaller four and five ton blue stones from the Prescelly Mountains above Milford Haven came up river after being floated along the Bristol Channel, the Bristol Avon and the river Frome, then overland to the river Wylye which flows into the Wiltshire Avon at Salisbury. In search of support for the romantic notion that the now gentle Avon was once a great transportation system for the Henge builders, I asked for an opinion from the leading authority on Stonehenge, Professor R J C Atkinson. Sadly he threw cold water on the idea, telling me: 'Two things make it impossible. First the weight of the sarsens which, for the uprights, varies between twenty-five and fifty tons. This would require a raft far larger and deeper than could be accommodated on the Avon even in its present state. In 2,000 BC the climate was much drier than it is today, and the volume of water must consequently have been less. Also it is almost certain that at the time much of the Avon was split up into narrow braided channels which would make the use of a raft quite impossible. Like most rivers, its present course is largely the result of artificial canalisation. I'm afraid therefore that what would otherwise be an attractive idea must be abandoned'.

Even so, I like to think that the river did have some important connection with Stonehenge, otherwise why does the Avenue (now only visible from the air, but marked on the OS map, *123 423–141 418*) – which must have been the main approach road to the circle whether for goods, traffic or ceremonial – follow a gentle contour slope in a long sweep towards the Avon just south of West Amesbury House? On the OS map the Avenue is shown as stopping just short of the river which, at that point, meanders in two great loops; but it will doubtless have changed its course by a few hundred yards in 4,000 years. Trying to trace, or rather decide upon, the true source of the Avon is a thankless task geographically because at Scales Bridge, *134 559*, just north of Upavon, it splits into two rivers, both called Avon, which both divide again before finally breaking down into numerous brooks, streams and ditches. There are no footpaths along these little streams so they can only be traced where they run under roads, and in the villages through which they pass. Pewsey, on the eastern arm of the upper Avon, lies in the centre of the green vale of the same name. Although it has the usual spread of council houses and loud shop fronts, the centre is still remarkable for its Wiltshire thatched cottages and Georgian houses. The cottages

The Double Locks Hotel on the Exeter Ship Canal, built of Dutch ballast bricks, is popular with students and businessmen from Exeter

St Peter's Tower on the foreshore at Lympstone was built as a memorial to his wife by a local man

Topsham, on the tidal reach of the river Exe, once rivalled Exeter as a major port

Was the Wiltshire Avon used to raft the sarsen stones from the Marlborough Downs to the building site of Stonehenge?

Britford, with its ninth century church and seventeenth century rectory, lies alongside the old navigation which brought barges from the sea to Salisbury

The garden of Waterside Mill at Downton is an island formed by the mill's tail race and the Avon

are traditionally built of porous chalk stone with overhanging thatch to keep rain off, and damp-proof foundations of sarsen, a hard sandstone found in the form of large boulders and blocks lying about the surface of chalk downs and particularly prolific in Wiltshire. Because sarsen requires no quarrying and can be split to size in situ, it was logical to use it to construct Stonehenge and it has remained a local building material up to recent times. Downstream from Pewsey are the three Manningfords – Abbas, Bohune and Bruce, with its complete pre-Conquest church. The Avon has now swollen from a lively stream, just capable of taking a canoe after heavy rain, to a small river as it enters Upavon before cleaving its way through the heart of Salisbury Plain.

The Avon is a chalk stream with trout fishing along its whole length and salmon below Fordingbridge. It is all private water and even the harmless canoeist is hard put to find short stretches which are not strictly reserved for fishing and patrolled by water bailiffs. Permission to paddle through the many estates is difficult to come by, and most unlikely in spring and summer. The only pleasure boating that I have found is on a very boring stretch through the outskirts of Salisbury and in Christchurch harbour which, of course, is tidal. But all things are possible, they say, and for a bet in June 1947 the whole seventy mile length of the Avon from Pewsey to the sea was navigated by a rowing boat.

Upavon lies in a deep cleft overlooked on either side by ancient earthworks. On the high downs to the west is sixty acre Casterley Camp, *118 361*, which can be visited when there is no red flag flying to indicate firing on nearby Larkhill Artillery Range. From the rough road leading up to the camp there is a fine view to the north across the west Avon valley to Mill Hill, White House Hill and Golden Ball Hill on the Marlborough Downs. To the east you look down into Upavon with the Early English tower of its flint- and stone-banded St Mary's Church rising above the few remaining thatched roofs in the heart of the village. From here on downstream to Amesbury the high ground on both sides of the river is given over almost totally to the military with their camps, ranges and tank training grounds. This 'occupation' of Salisbury Plain started in 1897 following a War Office Committee recommendation that more extensive open land was needed for troop manoeuvres and the War Office started purchasing large areas of farmland, a process which was accelerated by the Boer War. But down in the valley one sees almost nothing of the military as one passes through a string of riverside villages with more big churches – almost one for every mile – than could ever have been filled. Some are well worth a visit, but they all stand as monuments, not to a once greater population, but to personal wealth in a most fertile valley during the centuries when the rich built churches because they truly feared God and wanted to ensure a ticket to heaven, while demonstrating their importance in the community.

Bernard Coombs, now in his eighties, is the landlord of the Red Lion at East Chisenbury, a pub which probably looks today as it did in the 1930s

As with the east and west headstreams north of Upavon, there are virtually no footpaths which keep company with the river and it has to be followed along the roads down either side. The A345 runs almost straight so that it only touches the river where that bends towards it, but there are some moderately high-level views across the water meadows and the pattern of the meanders can be seen. The minor road down the east side lies lower, is much more intimate, and passes through a dozen riverside villages between Upavon and Bulford. The first village on the minor road is East Chisenbury, which has a small priory in private grounds and a row of perfectly coiffured thatched cottages. From a public footpath on the opposite bank you can admire the pretty gardens and manicured lawns sloping down to the water's edge – lovely weekend retreats in which no locals will ever again live. A village so desirable that a few years back the tiny roadside chapel – a brick box – was sold for £58,000. But one place remains as it always was – the Red Lion, a long, low, dark, rough-floored cosy barn of a place with barrels up on trestles and beer decanted from a jug. Time has stood still in the Red Lion which, I suspect, looks today as it did in the 1930s. The most up-to-date decorations are wartime photographs of Will Fyfe, Freddie Mills and Jack Dempsey, one-time mates of the owner, Bernard Coombs, now into his eighties. One of his customers is Baroness Vickers ('she slips in for a drink occasionally') who lives next door and of whom he is very proud. 'Imagine a woman of her age going to the Falklands in a Hercules, and the only woman on it'.

The OS map shows as many footpaths and tracks down to the river as there are roads with bridges, but all the fords are now lost, overgrown or fenced off. 'They should be open as they are public rights of way', says Bernard Coombs. 'Some of the older people in the village remember when carts used to bring corn off the downs along the track beside the pub here, straight across the river and over the hills to Devizes. They used to put horses in at the fords to dredge the river of weeds and break up any mud banks which would then be washed away; it used to do the horses good too. Each farmer would do his own stretch of river, not during the fishing of course. Now nothing is done to keep it tidy'.

Untidiness is not the only problem with the Avon, and so many other rivers these days. Water extraction has reduced the flow of water and caused areas of silting, and the proliferation of fish farms is bringing damaging effluent into the water despite settlement tanks and filters which do not always do their job properly. An angler to whom I fell talking just below Upavon said: 'It's asking the wild fish to swim in sewage. They fined a fish farmer £1,000 recently for putting too much effluent into the river; that sorted him out a bit'. Worse pollution comes from the ordinary farms. He told me of a farmer who built a slurry pit too near the river, which was illegal; one day the bank collapsed and some 30,000 gallons of slurry were released into the water. The local water board got their equipment to the nearest army tank crossing and pumped millions of cubic feet of oxygen into the river in time to save the fish. When slurry gets into a river it produces a chemical effect which removes all oxygen from the water so fish are literally asphyxiated.

The river leaves the roadside after East Chisenbury to return to it a mile downstream at Littlecott, which is joined by a bridge to the village of Enford on the west bank. Littlecott Mill, *143 518*, is both a good example of a water mill complex and of how beautifully they can be renovated as homes and their grounds landscaped into water gardens. The large brick mill house with decorative bands of chalk stone has not been used for its original purpose since before the First World War when it was a centre for the repair and maintenance of the local steam-driven farm machinery. The cottage beside the house was the forge. After steam machinery was phased out during the 1920s the mill continued to look after first paraffin (TVO) and then diesel driven farm equipment. It lay derelict after the last world war until 1974 when the present owner moved in. The river below the weir, the curving mill race, an overflow leat and the tail race make a pattern of blue water when there is a cloudless sky, dividing emerald green lawns into islands joined by little footbridges. Small trees and shrubs give it the character of a miniature park. All this is best seen by going up the metalled track which forks to the left just north of the mill. The undershot water wheel is inside the building so the mill race disappears under the house.

In 1676 the patronage of All Saints Church in Enford was sold to Christ Hospital, now the famous Blue Coat School. Since then every vicar has been an old boy of the school. In the early nineteenth century the display of parish loyalty to the crown was much in vogue, and Enford was no exception as is shown by the large five foot by five and a half foot, carved and painted coat-of-arms of William IV which dominates the nave. The pulpit has a mediaeval hour-glass stand, and in the Lady Chapel there is a funeral bier purchased by public subscription as recently as the beginning of this century. The earliest method of telling the time was by using scratch stones, and some of these can be seen about six feet above the ground on the east wall of the south aisle. A clock was installed in 1728, but it had no face and told the time by striking the hours. The face was added in 1846. It is by close looks at minor items in churches that one can get glimpses of the way of life in small communities in the past.

At the next meeting of road and river, about another mile downstream, is a tiny mill at Coombe, *148 505*. It has none of the landscaped elegance of Littlecott, being no more than a white painted cottage. But to look across the rich, vivid green algae-covered mill pond to the gable end, against which is set a wooden water wheel, is to experience a time warp back into the last century, especially when the family cow walks into the picture to graze. All is as it ever was except that the wheel no longer turns. Inside the mill room are the last vestiges of machinery.

Until the later half of the nineteenth century every village and farming community along a river had its mill for grinding corn and milling flour, many of them going back to mediaeval days. Their numbers grew during the industrial revolution with the increase in the consumption of flour in the growing towns. There were also fulling mills where woollen cloth was pounded in water to thicken it out; and water wheels drove hammers and bellows for forging iron, provided power for saw mills, joinery works and even for grinding gunpowder. The Avon had its share of water mills, probably one almost every mile, to complement its villages. It is not, nor probably ever was, a fast flowing river, but the old corn mills would not have required a great deal of power – just a great, big wheel and a sluggish, old flow to keep it slowly turning. Two grindstones would be low-geared from the wheel, and they would grind exceeding slow. What was needed was plenty of torque and not much horsepower. This constant flow was achieved most of the time by the judicious use of weirs and mill ponds with controlling gates or sluices. In times of spate, water was stored and released as needed to supplement the natural flow in more normal or dry periods. This control over the water became more and more impossible during the last years of the nineteenth century as land drainage affected the water tables and local towns extracted huge quantities for domestic and industrial consumption. A few mills were still working after the First World War, but by the end of the 1930s all but a handful were either derelict or converted to more prosaic use. The structures have been saved but the character of the mills as the pivot of local economic life – the place to which all paths led so that people could bring their corn for grinding and take away flour for their bread – cannot be revived.

There is a big, gaunt mill at Netheravon on the west bank which is variously described as Haxton Mill or Old Mill, *147 491*. It stands on the site of an earlier corn mill (probably several over the centuries, since there is mention of mills at Netheravon in Domesday Book), which had two water wheels and ground for

Bunces Brewery at Haxton beside the river Avon brews traditional cask-conditioned bitter with water pumped up from a deep layer of green sand

the military from 1898 to 1911. The present building was erected in 1914 as an electricity generating station, a speculative venture to provide electricity to the newly built Royal Flying Corps' Netheravon airfield across the river. It produced 110 volts DC, and the upper floor was massively built to take the weight of many tons of storage batteries. These enabled electricity to be accumulated during the hours when there was little or no demand from the airfield and to even out the load on the generators as the flow of river water fluctuated. The mill stream flowed under the floor to power a vertical shaft turbine which drove the generator. It seems that the electricity maker got his sums wrong for there was rarely enough water flow to maintain the voltage and there was considerable voltage loss in the two mile cables to the airfield. DC current, unlike AC, does not travel well! By 1929 everybody was turning to AC supplies, and the mill power station was forced to close down.

Between the wars the empty mill was used for a number of purposes including silent film shows, boxing and local 'hops'. But the collective memory of the older inhabitants is of a cold and draughty place which was never popular. In recent times it was empty and vandalised until it was discovered by Mr Bunce, a civil servant who was contemplating early retirement to do his 'own thing'. The mill is now Bunces Brewery. It is not that he had ever considered being a brewer, a trade for which he had no qualifications other than '. . . having messed about with home brewing in the kitchen'. It was the size and shape of the mill which planted the idea in his head. 'The twenty foot high generating room looked just right for a small brewery, and the battery floor above would make a very large flat with high level views of the river'. He now has a weekly capacity of ten barrels of thirty-six gallons each of traditional cask-conditioned bitter beer with the reasonably high specific gravity of 1043. He uses about 500 gallons of water a week which is pumped up from a deep layer of green sand. It certainly makes a most palatable bitter, a veritable real ale. There is a small bell-push by the door marked 'off licence'. From there, from Tuesdays to Saturdays, Mr Bunce will serve you with take-home containers of four to thirty-six pints at well below pub prices.

The Bunces' hobby is canoeing and ironically, although they live beside the river, their canoes have never been on it and the paddles are used for stirring the mash. 'The river is tightly controlled by the fishing interests, in particular the powerful Services Dry Fly Fishing Association which manages eight miles between Fifield and Bulford. Although theoretically canoeable with quite a bit of portage from Upavon to the sea, it is called the Forbidden Avon to distinguish it from other Avons like the Stratford one which is full of boats. In five years we have seen only two canoes come down the river, and those were both in winter when there was no fishing'.

Going on south we come to Durrington of which Pevsner remarked: 'Much suburban military housing'. And so it is still today. One of the few nice, old houses is Pinckney's Farm House, a reminder that this army dormitory town was once an agricultural village. The house dates back to 1765 and was built by the Pinckney family, then the local squires, who came over from Picardy with the Conqueror in 1066. Their ancestral village was Picquiny where, by coincidence, thousands of troops from Wiltshire were billeted during the First World War. The present owner is Dr Richard Joseph Basil Heritage Jones, the senior partner is a three-handed practice which covers the Avon valley between Amesbury and Pewsey, a thin sixteen mile strip enclosed on either side by military camps. 'When I joined the practice in 1958 there were accounts going back to the turn of the century, all written in Latin. We made up our own mixtures from scratch with pestle and mortar, scales and measuring jars'. Asked what brought him to the valley, he replied: 'The fishing – fifty yards from the surgery'. His enthusiasm for fishing the Avon has waned somewhat in recent years. 'What used to be absolutely fantastic natural fishing twenty-five years ago is now very much diminished. It is virtually put and take; the river is stocked every year and by the winter they are all taken. It is the advancement of time that has spoilt it. Now people have running water, instead of closets in the garden they have flush toilets, they have washing and bathing facilities so they use a lot of water. The water is abstracted from aquifers deep in the chalk so cutting off the supply of water to the river. Nature intended the rain from heaven to soak into the chalk like a sponge all the year and then be released through the aquifers or subterranean springs to run into the river and provide clean fresh water for the fish. Every year there are more and more applications from farmers to abstract millions of gallons which is all lost, or at least when it comes back it is poisonous, full of nitrates. Then there are the fish farms. It is intensive farming with intensive fish defaecation into the river. You can cope with pollution if you have a good flow of water, but with pollution and abstraction the oxygen drops and the fish do not thrive, and natural regeneration no longer takes place. So the keepers catch trout in late December when they are ready to spawn, get the ova out of the hen fish and milt from the male; they strip them and fertilise the eggs. The fish are bred and raised in stew ponds which are fed from fresh water springs, not from the river. In the Middle Ages stew ponds were where the monks raised fish; the word stew means brother. When they have grown to about three-quarters of a pound the keepers put them in the river. They only live for a short span until they are caught'. Like all anglers he is mighty jealous of his rights and protective of the sport. He says: 'Canoeists have no right over the water, much to their dismay. They think they can paddle down a river like they walk down a road. But it's not the same because the ground under the water belongs to the person who owns the shore and the riparian rights. If you take a boat over the water over his ground you are trespassing'.

If Durrington is at all known outside army circles it is for Durrington Walls, *152437*, and Woodhenge, *151434*. The former is a thirty acre site surrounded by a now much reduced circular earthwork with a ditch discernible on the inner side which makes it seem unlikely that it was a defensive structure. The main road cuts right through the circle, and while it all means much to the expert there is little to entertain the rest of us. Woodhenge was unknown until it was discovered by Squadron Leader Insall, VC, on 12 December 1925 when, flying at about 2,000 feet over Stonehenge, he noticed a circle of white chalk marks nearby. The pattern looked remarkably like that of Stonehenge, which he could see at the same time. So he flew over again when the sun was low in the sky and saw a distinct depression inside the outer ring and a slight mound in the centre. He waited until the following year when the crops were fully grown and he was able to photograph a number of rings set close together. Excavation began in August 1926 revealing six concentric circles of oval holes which had once held wooden posts thought to have supported a roof 140 feet across. In a position which relates to that of the so-called Altar Stone of Stonehenge was found the skeleton of a child with its skull cleft, and elsewhere the skeleton of an adult. Today stubby little concrete pillars indicate the position of the original uprights, but they provide no sense of awe and it is impossible to imagine what the original edifice looked like. It is there, it is very old, older than Stonehenge, but not at all impressive.

The busy A303 holiday route to the West Country crosses over the Avon on the outskirts of Amesbury, which the river almost encloses in a great meander. Amesbury remains unmentioned in most guide books of the area, but is nonetheless the oldest and most historically important place in the valley of the upper Avon. Its name is a modern form of Ambrosebury, or Ambrose's Town – Ambrose being Ambrosius Aurelianus, a noble Roman who remained in Britain after the withdrawal of the legions of the fifth century, becoming a great general and commander of the Christian Britons against the pagan Saxons who were endangering the legacy of the Romano-British civilisation. There are as many legends attached to his name as to that of Arthur, his contemporary. Strong among them is the belief that he was born and lies buried in Amesbury; but the Cornish and the Welsh have also claimed him as one of theirs, and in Hampshire they say that he came from Winchester.

These days few citizens of Amesbury will have heard of Ambrosius, but they may very well know that it was in their town that Guinevere took the veil on the death of King Arthur and became abbess of the nunnery she founded there. It may be pure fiction that it was from Amesbury that her former lover, Sir Lancelot du Lac, carried her corpse to Glastonbury for burial beside Arthur, but there certainly was a nunnery in Amesbury in the sixth century. Soon afterwards the town fell to the Saxons who destroyed everything. A new convent was built by Ethelfrida in 980 to expiate her sin of murdering her son-in-law, and a new town grew up around it. In 1177 the morals of the nuns had so deteriorated that they were dispersed to other convents, their abbess was expelled from the order and left to her own devices. But the convent was given a new lease of life when a prioress and twenty-four nuns were imported from Anjou in France; it was to

The river Nadder, near its junction with the Avon, curves round Salisbury cathedral and through the Queen Elizabeth Gardens

become one of the greatest female houses in the country – actually it was a mixed community of men and women, but totally ruled by women. Many females of the royal line became nuns there, and it prospered until Henry VIII's dissolution. The present abbey, *151 418*, is a stately porticoed mansion built in 1830 following closely the design of a previous building by Inigo Jones. As the Avon curves away from Amesbury there is a stretch downstream of the weir which is a favourite and permitted bathing place for the local children, after which it is again severely protected by angling organisations.

From Amesbury to Salisbury the valley opens out with more arable land than water meadows. Still the river wanders about between two roads, touching first one then the other. At Lake there is a picture-postcard mill cottage, *135 391*, now a weekend home, where the mill stream still turns a horizontal wheel to drive a generator supplying electricity to heat the greenhouse of Lake House. The old Edwardian switchboard inside the generator house has ivory labels below two switches marked 'Lake Village' and 'Lake House'; the village is now on the mains. The river has been diverted below the mill to provide Lake House with an intriguing water garden laid out with exotic plants, trees and shrubs which is very occasionally opened to the public. The house, of flint and stone chequerwork, looks very much like an Elizabethan mansion, but in fact is a re-build after a fire at the turn of the century. A curiosity at the entrance gate is a pair of large ammonites set into the well either side. Heale House, *127 364*, perhaps the loveliest of all the manor houses in the Avon valley, two bends down the river, also has a water garden which is open to the public with the added attraction of a genuine Japanese gazebo, imported complete in 1890, which spans one of the artificial 'canals'.

On weekdays you may have the riverside lawn outside the Bridge Inn at Upper Woodford almost to yourself to admire the swans which grace the scene. This is a part of the river where a heron can sometimes be watched spearing fish and there are plenty of ducks, moorhens and coots darting in and out of the reeded banks. The kingfisher is a rather rarer sight. Old Sarum, along with Stonehenge and Salisbury, is one of the big tourist attractions along the Avon, but from the river it looks no more than a low hill topped with trees; nothing can be seen of the hill fort with its Neolithic, Roman and Norman remains nor those of the original cathedral lower down. From the top of the ramparts you get only glimpses of water where there are gaps in the trees.

As the Avon enters the northern suburbs of Salisbury it loses its personality for a while to become a straightened up, walled in and culverted waterway, until it is let free again where it is joined by the river Nadder coming from the west to curve round the cathedral precincts before turning south again on its way to the sea. Before reaching the Avon the Nadder is fed at Wilton – of carpet fame – by the Wylye coming from near Stourhead and through Warminster. While still in Salisbury the Avon is also joined by the Bourne which has its source in the Vale of Pewsey, not far from the nascent east Avon. All three are chalk rivers, and the Avon has become nobler for their waters by the time it leaves the city. But it is a stolen nobility for, in fact, in prehistoric times, the Nadder was the main river flowing on eastwards into the then great Solent river, and the Avon was only its tributary. When the water level fell the eastern end became what is now the Hampshire Test, and the Nadder, Wylye and Avon, blocked on their way east, had to find a southerly course to the sea at Christchurch.

Looking at it now, it is inconceivable that Salisbury was, for a very short period, an inland port, but there are records that barges navigated the Avon from Christchurch to Salisbury in the 1680s, taking on average two days for the journey. On William Naish's map of Salisbury, published in 1751, ten navigation cuts are shown down this twenty-eight mile stretch. Some of these are still shown on the current OS maps, and the best-preserved one which can be reached on foot starts just to the west of the big roundabout by Harnham Bridge, *145 292*, on the A354 out of the city, and goes past Bridge Farm, *156 284*, and Manor Farm, *158 277*, where a dilapidated lock can be seen, the only one on the navigation still recognisable. The cut meets the river again in the grounds of Longford Castle, *173 267*. Traces of navigational cuts can also be found at Downton, Fordingbridge, Ibsley, Ringwood, Avon, Sopley and Winkton. At Fordingbridge there is a place named Horseport which may be connected with barge horses, and in current literature issued by the town's Chamber of Commerce the introduction starts: 'One time smuggling centre, Fordingbridge . . .', which suggests a connection with the sea. There is a written statement of 1737 in which a farmer affirms that he remembers the navigation being started forty-five years before, and that in places windlasses were used to haul the barges. The navigation had certainly been abandoned by 1730, and there was a petition to parliament in 1772 to have the river cleared of obstructions caused by the navigation which had proved too inconvenient and was wholly discontinued.

In 1705 Thomas Newcomen had patented the first steam pumping engine and the Industrial Revolution was underway.

But transport was still mediaeval, with goods being moved by horse and cart over rutted roads, and the first unreliable railway line was not to open until 1825. Meanwhile there was a boom in canal building, and in the second half of the eighteenth century many fortunes were to be lost and won. One that was lost was the £90,000 invested in a canal between Southampton and Salisbury incorporating nine miles of the existing Andover Canal. Work started in 1795 was still in progress in 1799 when John Rennie made a survey of the job and gave it a most unfavourable report. It got as far as Alderbury and there it stopped; goods had to be carried the last few miles to Salisbury by road. Traffic slowed to a halt in 1808 when the Salisbury Southampton Navigation Co collapsed. The OS map does not show the line of the old canal, but bits can still be discovered along its route such as a farm bridge over a dry trench at East Grimstead, *270 225*, and the remains of one of fifteen locks near the bridge at West Dean.

The old cattle bridge at Britford across a section of the navigation alongside the river Avon which once brought ships from the sea to Salisbury

A far more satisfying exploration is to Britford off the A338 Salisbury-Bournemouth road. Take the lane to Bridge Farm and stand on the bridge to look up a straight length of a cut towards the 402-foot spire of Salisbury Cathedral, then continue to St Peter's Church at the end of the lane. It dates from about AD 800 and the south door is original Saxon. Inside it seems heavy with the weight of centuries; one might almost expect to intrude on a Latin mass attended by Saxon farmers. On the lectern is a Breaches Bible of 1582 bound in with a 1640 prayer book. Beside the church a seventeenth century rectory wreathed in roses stands looking at itself in the still water of the cut. To live there undisturbed at the end of a lane, a deserted waterway on their doorstep, water meadows beyond and Salisbury's spire always watching over them, must be a taste of heaven on earth – a thought with which the lady of the house was in absolute agreement.

At Charlton All Saints, ex-Marine commando Mike Trowbridge is Water Keeper to Lord Radnor of Longford Castle, *172 267*, and responsible for the river from Britford to Downton, a reach of five miles, and the river Ebble from Homington to Longford Park where it meets the Avon. In these lower reaches the Avon is as much a salmon as a trout river, or was. In 1986 the estate stopped selling salmon rods on Mike's five miles because they could not guarantee a catch. There used to be catches of eighty to ninety salmon a year, but in recent times there have been as few as four. He puts the blame on the fish farms because of the effluent they cause, and also on the water authority for taking so much water out of the river that the salmon are trapped in shallows and cannot get up to their spawning grounds.

From the keeper's cottage, a public footpath crosses the meadows, a section of the old navigation and the river proper to Standlynch Mill *c* 1690, *182 235*, a large, warm brick building encircled by trees. Empty but not crumbling when I was there, it was just longing to be renovated. Maybe something will have been started by the time this is read. Standlynch is the centre of Mike's operations; it is here that he has his fish ponds and eel traps. The working of the traps is very simple. A trench dredged in the bottom of the mill race leads the ground-moving eels towards a series of hatches which can be opened so that they are swept by the force of water onto a sloping grid, where they are left stranded high and dry to be raked off by the eel fishermen.

Rob and Jan Buckett live in Waterside Mill in Downton, their garden an island formed by the river and the tail race. In its later working years the mill was used by the CEGB as a power station, but had been taken over by pigeons for twenty years before the Bucketts bought it; everyone in the village thought they were mad. However, they have done a wonderful conversion, and at the top of the building among the original roof trusses have devised two little flatlets for bed and breakfast guests. Not the usual hushed breakfast in a small room crowded with large

Christchurch, at the confluence of the rivers Avon and Stour, is a yachting centre with a yacht club and three boatyards, but is not an easy harbour for big boats to enter

families round small tables; each flatlet has a kitchenette where Jan cooks the breakfast of your choice while you enjoy your morning paper. Most civilized. Downton has a ring and bailey which must have been most attractive when it was laid out as a garden complete with temple and pond. Sadly it has been vandalised and now serves as a wall of death for the local bikers.

Leaving Downton one passes out of Wiltshire into Hampshire for the last wanderings of the Avon. At Breamore a big mill stands by the road bridge, *163 175*, which, although no longer working, is lived in and has been left looking its good, old self. On the other side of the river Castle Hill, *170 165*, provides the best of all views of the Avon. It is the only viewpoint marked on the map for the whole of its seventy mile length. Fryern Court, *143 163*, just north of Fordingbridge was the home of Augustus John, and in the grounds of the house there is a 1930s building, reminiscent of the superstructure of a cruise liner, which was his studio. The burghers of Fordingbridge were ambivalent about the fame which he brought to the town, many of them feeling that the stories of his promiscuity precluded him from a public monument. Eventually a sculpture, a fierce cartoon in bronze which had been wished upon them, was found a site half-obscured by bushes in a corner of the recreation ground.

Sopley's old mill, *156 967*, complete in structure but gutted of its machinery, is now leased to a cosmetic company. Its arrangement of hatches and eel traps is worth a close inspection. Now that the mill no longer works the mill race is diverted to provide a cascade of white water into a charming pond, the home of a family of swans. From a footbridge upstream you can look down on the mill, hatches, traps and pond; a rustic river scene almost certainly looking now as it did a hundred years ago, if not as it did in 1086 when it was valued at ten shillings and provided 875 eels a year for the lord of the manor. On a bluff above the river is the parish church of St Michael and All Angels which, when the trees are not in full leaf, gives a long view down the river towards the priory at Christchurch. It is built largely of ironstone rubble, a clumsy and intractable material, which almost certainly came from Hengistbury Head. One of the church windows is dedicated to Mary Anne, a girl of nineteen who drowned while bathing in the run at Mudeford. It is a reminder that we are virtually at the end of the Avon's journey as a river for it is very soon to meet with the Dorset Stour to form Christchurch Harbour, a great tidal lagoon of quiet water but tortuous channels, which empties into the sea through the run.

In its last few hundred yards the Avon splits into two arms through Christchurch old town which are lined with moored yachts and cruisers. Some of them are big, but this is not a harbour for big visitors in fact they are actively discouraged by the Harbour Master. It would be all too easy for one to go aground on a falling tide and block the channel until the next springs. But small sailing cruisers, dinghies and sailboards have a lot of fun on the great expanse of shallow water. The entrance is very difficult through the narrow run where the maximum rate of stream is reputed to reach nine knots on equinoxial springs, and that is after negotiating the ever-shifting bar outside. Christchurch is a boating resort with a yacht club and three boatyards, but it has a much older history having been a real harbour in mediaeval times when coastal rivers were the transport routes inland. It has been protected by Hengistbury Head ever since an Iron Age fort was built on it. The Head is actually named after Hengist who landed there on his second invasion. The priory, which dominates the yachts moored along the town quays, presents a catalogue of church architecture – a bit of Norman, Early English, Decorated windows and a Perpendicular stone rood screen. Wandering inside and out will occupy a pleasant hour. The two arms of the Avon are navigable through the town because they are tidal, and I have been a mile or so up river in an inflatable – there are now too many obstructions for anything heavier although the tidal reach goes inland another five miles and tidal water is, with very few exceptions, always a public right of way. There is a boatyard and moorings at the mouth of the Dorset Stour, and it would be delightful if one could navigate upstream into Hardy country, even to the elegantly landscaped Stourhead, but a low bridge in the town puts a stop to such a notion.

Newtown River

OS 1:25,000 Sheets SZ 28/38/SZ 48

Tall-masted ships lay along the quayside at the end of which steam rose all day from the salt works, and further up river men were tending the widely famed oyster beds. The town sloped up from the water; there was High Street, Broad Street, Gold Street and Silver Street, names that might be found in any important town. The population numbered some sixty families and the borough land was divided into seventy-three plots, most of them held singly at a rent of one shilling per annum. The arable land around the town was divided into strips, known as land-shares or furlongs, one being allocated to each household. The mayor and twenty-five burgesses made up the corporation of this thriving English seaport, the time was the fourteenth century, and the name of the town was Francheville. You will not find this name on the map any more although it was the capital of the Isle of Wight until the French, who were always attacking it, finally sacked the place burning all the homes in 1377. It was partially rebuilt, but the capital was moved to a place of greater safety at the head of the tidal reaches of the Medina river and was called New Port.

In place of Francheville there is today just the small village of Newtown which sits atop a slight rise above the low lying flats of the Newtown river estuary. There are only ten houses, but it has a large church and a fine town hall, *424 906*, looking grand enough for a bustling market town. Of the mediaeval houses there is no trace for they were made of wood and thatch, but one can still walk through the streets of the old town, which are now grass lanes bordered by small, hedged fields marking the site of the original borough plots. Ships of 500 tons once sailed into the river and unloaded alongside quays, but it has long since silted up. The last commercial craft to use the river were flat-bottomed barges which sailed up to Shalfleet Quay with cargoes of shingle and coal, returning with potatoes. A few continued under motor until just after the last war when this traffic ceased altogether. Silting has continued, so these days visiting yachts wanting to stay over a tide are limited to anchorages just inside the entrance unless they are prepared to sit in the mud for several hours.

I had sailed up and down the Solent for many years without ever putting in to Newtown river, and knew nothing of this backwater of history until a friend who keeps his boat at Lymington on the mainland shore offered me the prospect of 'a very peaceful weekend full of pleasant discoveries'. And so it was.

We crossed the Solent on board his forty-two foot power cruiser *Echo Pilot* which is used as a floating test bed for his firm's sonar depth sounders – and what better boat on which to enter Newtown river where the depth of water, or in most parts the lack of it, is of paramount importance? If you sail there on a weekend in the season when high water comes in the middle of the day you will be one of a crowd; at other times it will be less crowded but you will be restricted in your movements around the creeks to early morning and evening and need to take to the tender to explore any distance from the deep channels or reach the one and only hostelry where the food is quite memorable. The entrance is three and a half miles east of Yarmouth and is marked by two posts, the outer with a Y top mark and the inner with a disc; from there on in the channel is marked by perches. Keep to the channel and pay attention to the shingle spits and mud banks which abound at all times other than at the top of the tide. Short cuts are not advised unless you draw nothing.

We moored in the river level with Newtown Quay, *419 912*, which is on the port hand after passing the wide mouth of Clamerkin Lake, also on the port hand and a popular anchorage surrounded by the saltings of Newtown Nature Reserve. The quay is plain to see by its black, wooden boathouse which stands proud above the flat terrain. As a quay it is rudimentary and only suitable for very small boats and tenders, being little more than a low, rough, stone embankment which dries out. It is difficult to imagine that this crude landing place was once a part of the island's most important port. From the quay a 100-yard long, one plank wide, wooden bridge spans a mud creek and some of the old salt workings to take you dryshod to the grassy footpath leading sixty feet up the hill to Newtown itself. A notice tells you that it

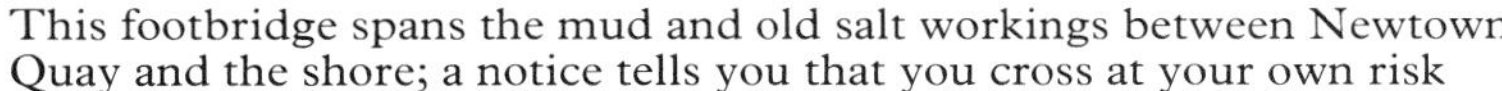
This footbridge spans the mud and old salt workings between Newtown Quay and the shore; a notice tells you that you cross at your own risk

The old town hall at Newtown is owned by the National Trust and contains records of the corporation from 1636

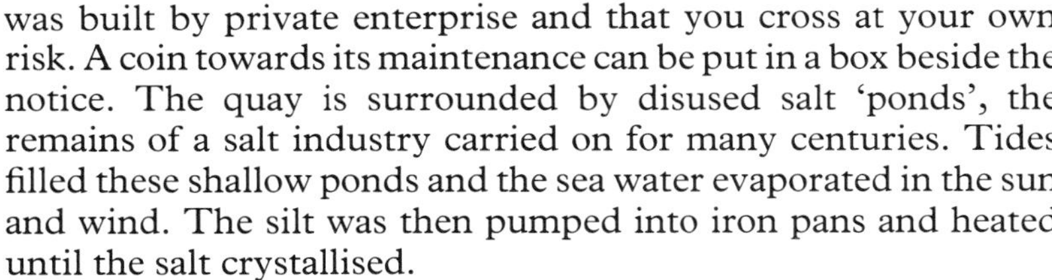
was built by private enterprise and that you cross at your own risk. A coin towards its maintenance can be put in a box beside the notice. The quay is surrounded by disused salt 'ponds', the remains of a salt industry carried on for many centuries. Tides filled these shallow ponds and the sea water evaporated in the sun and wind. The silt was then pumped into iron pans and heated until the salt crystallised.

All the river and creeks to the high water mark are owned by the National Trust who have left well alone so that nature reigns with the hand of man firmly slapped down. *The* sight in Newtown is the Old Town Hall, isolated on a green and looking incongruously grand for so tiny a village. It was built in 1699, and indicates the political importance of Newtown at that time, even though it was by then no more than a hamlet. It had become a parliamentary borough in 1585 when Queen Elizabeth I summoned more members to her parliament; from then until it was declared a rotten borough in 1832 and disenfranchised under the first Reform Act, it elected two members of parliament. This despite the fact that a map of 1636 shows only twelve inhabited buildings. In their 1832 report a government commission stated that: 'not only does no burgess reside within the borough, but . . . it is not probable that there is an inhabitant capable of exercising any municipal function'. Among the most eminent of Newtown MPs were John Churchill, who became the first Duke of Marlborough, and George Canning who became Foreign Secretary and Prime Minister.

When the corporation was dissolved the town hall, being redundant, became in turn a school, a private house and then a ruin. It was restored in 1933 by an anonymous group of benefactors who signed themselves 'Ferguson's Gang' and handed it over to the National Trust with an acre of land. Subsequently, a number of local residents formed themselves into the Newtown Trust and, little by little, bought up all the land of the former borough, gradually reassembled the plots of the ancient town and gave them to the National Trust. The town hall is brick built with stone dressings, the windows have round heads and stone keystones, and the interior is richly panelled. On the north façade Gothic fenestration and a columned Tuscan portico are late eighteenth century additions. It is now open to the public. Largely furnished in Jacobean style, it contains many ancient charters and documents together with the records of the corporation from 1636. There is a council chamber, robing room, mayor's parlour and a lobby.

The Noah's Ark nearby is thought to be the oldest house in

Lower Hamstead Quay, opposite Newtown, is a rickety wooden walkway across the mud to the edge of the deep channel

the village. It was once a public house, and the sign which still hangs over the door is reproduced from the old borough seal depicting a boat looking not unlike the ark, hence the name. Newtown now has no pub, no shop, no garage, not even a bed and breakfast sign, but it does have a telephone kiosk. Most of the present church dates from 1835, although the square tower goes back to about 1070 and has walls over five feet thick. It was a place of refuge for the population when the French invaders arrived in the nearby creeks. Elsewhere around the church there are remnants of previous buildings from Norman times to the end of the eighteenth century.

After visiting Newtown I took a tender cruise by inflatable round the fourteen miles of creeks, going first over to the other side of the river, a third of a mile at high water, to Lower Hamstead Quay, *415 913*, which is a rickety, wooden walkway reaching out across mud to the edge of the channel. At the landward end a notice invites crews to drop fifty pence per boat through a slot in a capped length of scaffold pipe set upright in concrete. How does the owner of the land, Colonel Kindersley, recover the coins? I have watched him do it, but will not reveal for no longer are all boating people as honest as they should be. Not that he has much to lose. In the height of summer with his landing in constant use his pipe yielded only one fifty pence coin and several coppers. Until a few years ago there was a boatyard by the quay run by a Mr Marshall, and he must have been a hardy character. He worked in the open in all weathers as he had no building, only a wooden toolbox the size of an outside privy laid on its side, which is still there. But he could cope with hauling out and repairs to hull and sterngear. In another wooden box an old Bedford truck engine hides its rusting shame; its drive shaft runs to a winch now well camouflaged with long grass and weeds, and nearby are the remains of a slip.

Lower Hamstead Quay is a popular port of call for yacht tenders because a couple of hundred yards up a lane Lower Hamstead Farm, *414 911*, has a shop which sells milk, whisky, gin, bread and a limited assortment of canned and packaged food. Whether you get an answer to the door bell seems to depend on the demands of the farm, except during the holidays when your ring is likely to be answered by one or other of the children in charge of the shop. From the farm the coastal footpath wanders through woods a mile or so alongside the creek called Western Haven to a road which runs into Shalfleet. It is possible to take a fairly large boat at high water to the top of the Haven, to where the coastal path crosses it over a stone bridge, *403 896*. Looking somewhat like a miniature reach of the Amazon when the foliage is at its summer thickest, this is a lovely away-from-the-world little trip to make. But the National Trust intend to keep it looking that way and anchoring is frowned upon; it might even be forbidden if there were anybody about to forbid.

The more popular trip is up the river and into the central creek, Shalfleet Lake, with, at its entrance, a sizeable stone quay and Bob Woodford's boatyard, *414 904*. Anybody old enough to have been boating before marinas were invented will find themselves on a nostalgic trip when they step ashore here. The yard has no water, no electricity, no telephone, no VHF and certainly no hoist. A prehistoric tractor does the hauling out at from £1.20 per foot. Bob provides mud berths and hard standing, repairs and fitting out at somewhere near 1960 prices! If the cross-Solent ferries were not so expensive, I am sure that many more yachtsmen would use his services. As it is he gets winter refugees from Quayhaven, Lymington, Beaulieu and Cowes. You will recognise his breed; he buys dilapidated vintage boats to renovate during the winter months 'to keep myself occupied'.

A tender can reach Shalfleet Quay at all stages of the tide except for one hour at low water springs. Boats up to five feet draft

Shalfleet Lake, one of the many Newtown creeks, has a sizeable stone quay and is a popular destination for yachtsmen going ashore in their tenders

can get there during three hours either side of high water, but will have to dry out alongside. There is a channel for another half mile to the mill outside Shalfleet village; however with no room to turn in the channel it is not recommended for yachts, but an inflatable can make it and ground on a muddy slip beside a footbridge, *416 896*, over the creek where it becomes the mill stream. The quay is most used as a stepping stone to the New Inn, *414 893*, at Shalfleet, a fifteen minute stroll along a waterside path. Of a summer evening there can be a couple of dozen inflatables all tied to one ring on the quay. And no wonder, it is a pub in a hundred, with bits of it going back to Domesday; stone built with yard thick walls, low beams and rough furniture, it is altogether unspoilt, but improved by having a landlord who knows good beer and serves generous helpings of good, fresh food. An ex-fisherman who still has a fishing boat, his speciality is fish – lobster and crab in summer, sole, cod and plaice in winter – and all caught by himself or other locals. Recently he has started eel fishing inland, so by now he may be serving smoked and jellied eel. If you are not a fish fancier, the blackboard in the bar offers such other delights as poacher's pie ('don't ask what is inside'), honey-coated gammon and coarse country pâté. I got up from my stool with my belly full for £3.95.

On a less sybaritic note there are numerous trails along which to seek out the bird and plant life which abound all over the saltings and creeks of the Newtown river delta. It is the only area in the Isle of Wight where black-headed gulls nest, and early in the summer the saltings are thick with thrift which gives way to carpets of sea lavender and, later, sea aster. Butterflies in abundance add flitting colours and then, come autumn, the birdlife takes over as the great attraction. As the yachts migrate to their winter berths or storage, the godwits arrive to perform their descending aerobatics, and with them come the waders and the wigeon from the Continent. It is in the winter that Newtown river gets a new lease of life and, having enjoyed it in summer, it should be re-visited in January when the saltings will be crowded with grazing brent geese which every so often lift in ragged flocks to wheel and criss-cross in the sky before settling on a different pasture. That will be the time to go by the Yarmouth ferry and use the shelter of the Newtown Nature Reserve observation post, *421 909*. I can highly recommend Mrs Laird's bed and breakfast at Shalfleet House, *408 894*, a big rambling former rectory with panoramic views over the Newtown estuary. In the garden in 1986 her sons, after several years, were not yet half way through rebuilding with patient dedication and craftsmanship a fifty-two-foot gentleman's yacht of turn-of-the-century vintage. They found it in skeletal state in the mud on the east coast and low-loaded it to the Isle of Wight. When finished, and that will be many years yet, it will surely be a possession beyond price.

Beverley Brook

London A–Z

I have met men in places as diverse as the Arctic, Ireland and the Isle of Wight who lapse into nostalgic memories at the mention of the Beverley Brook in London. They remember it as the adventure land of their childhood, as a place for country rambles only a few minutes' walk from their urban homes. The nostalgia is justified for Beverley Brook is still, for most of its eleven-mile course through London, a country stream running between well wooded banks which are the habitat for a wide variety of wild life.

It rises underground in New Malden having been put into a pipe when the area was being developed, and does not appear above ground until it reaches Beverley Gardens by Worcester Park Station. From here on there are Beverley Gardens, Street, Crescent and Road all the way to Putney where it empties into the Thames. For the next two miles it needs the A–Z street map to follow its course as it spends a lot of time hiding behind houses, running through private sports grounds and a corner of Malden Golf Course. It first comes into full view as it flows under the Kingston By-Pass, the A3, by the Coombe Lane flyover. The dual carriageways of the by-pass are here called Beverley Way South and North respectively. From there the Brook snakes for four miles through the western edge of Wimbledon Common with a footpath along both banks. This is a delightful walk through an area designated as a Site of Special Scientific Interest by the Nature Conservancy Council. There are several footbridges which enable one to cross from side to side to vary the view. The most common trees are silver birch, oak, horse chestnut, witches broom and hawthorn with its blossom in May and red berries in autumn. Lords and ladies, or cuckoo pint, dog rose, meadow buttercup, lesser celandine and soft rush bedeck the way. Surveys have listed eighty species of fauna covering many species of bird and butterfly and, visiting the water from the common, foxes and badgers.

On the east side the 1,100 acres of Wimbledon Common rise to a height of 200 feet, and several paths and rides from the brook join up with those which criss-cross the common. The first of these cuts through the middle of Caesar's Camp, an early Iron Age hill fort of about 300 BC with an external diameter of 950 feet. Unfortunately, this can only be viewed through iron railings to keep walkers off the golf course which has destroyed the wilderness of the place and reduced the significance of the fort to a fairway hazard; at least a golf course is better than a housing estate. In 1875 the proprietor of the land on which the camp is sited cut down the scrub oaks – there are a few left today – and started to level the banks and fill in the ditches with the intention of building houses. Before he had completely destroyed the site the Wimbledon and Putney Commons Conservators obtained an injunction restraining him from using the only available road across the common for other than agricultural purposes. That put a stop to his plans.

A relatively modern building on the high point of the common which does give great pleasure is the windmill built in 1817 by a Roehampton carpenter called Charles March for the Lord of the Manor, Earl Spencer. It was a corn mill of unusual hollow pot design which worked until 1864. Restored in 1975, it now houses a museum of windmills that is open on Saturday and Sunday afternoons from early spring through to late autumn. After a three-quarter-mile walk up Stag Ride from Beverley Lane, the path beside the brook, the tea-room under the windmill is a welcome facility. The soft earth paths along the brook are much favoured by joggers and those out on training runs. Children, and grown-ups too, have fun swinging over the brook at the end of ropes tied to high branches.

At the north end of this four-mile walk the brook goes under the A3 to re-appear in Richmond Park just inside Robin Hood Gate. If you want to change from walking to riding, horses can be hired at the stables by the gate for exploring the bridlepaths of the common. In the park the brook looks particularly pretty running between a guard of honour of weeping willows for just over a mile to near Roehampton Gate. There is a path along the west bank, but on the east is the boundary fence of the public golf course

Beverley Brook, a country stream running through London, is particularly pretty in Richmond Park

which was opened on 9 June 1923 by the Prince of Wales, the late Duke of Windsor, who was born nearby in White Lodge, now the Royal Ballet School. The course was laid out in an area of the park which had never been open to the public, known as Crown Meadows. The idea of a public golf course in the park was put forward by a consortium of golfers to provide facilities for the artisan class who could not afford, or were not admitted to, private clubs. There was some debate over the project, and at first King George V was reluctant to give his consent, but was persuaded when it was explained that he would be affording his poorer subjects the opportunity to play.

Saltings of Clamerkin Lake off the Newtown river which form part of the local nature reserve

Sea lavender carpets the saltings of Clamerkin Lake on the Newtown river nature reserve

Boats moored in the deep channel off Hamstead Quay, Newtown river

One of the raised wooden walkways which form a network over the Tollesbury saltings off the Blackwater estuary

A mud berth on the Blackwater estuary at Tollesbury where time has stood still

Heybridge Yacht Basin at the entrance to the Chelmer and Blackwater Navigation with a cement reproduction Norwegian pilot cutter in the foreground

Small cruising boats moored alongside the Chelmer and Blackwater Navigation

Across a hill from Beverley Brook are Pen Ponds which are primarily a bird sanctuary but coarse fishing is allowed by permit. They are not managed as a fishery but get re-stocked from time to time. The inhabitants include large carp, which are rarely caught, pike and eels which are also found in the ditches which empty into the brook. The most attractive feature of the park is its herds of fallow and red deer. The former take their moisture from the water content of their food and dew; red deer like water and will walk down to the brook to drink when there are no people about. The Richmond Park rut starts early in October and lasts for about six weeks. This is a most interesting time to visit the park as the older stags collect together their harems of hinds and then spend much of their time in combat with the younger stags waiting on the sidelines to kidnap a hind for themselves. There is a lot of roaring, charging and skirmishing, and the clanking sound of horns locking together as they try to throw each other off balance in a form of head wrestling. The peak of this activity is at dusk; the night is given over to mating so the visitor is unlikely to witness that.

After leaving the park the brook is lost behind houses for a moment and then runs along the bottom of Paleman Common, a few acres in extent and probably the smallest common in London. From there a footpath follows the brook for a short distance before veering off towards Richmond Road West. But it is a fruitful distance in autumn when the bramble bushes beside the path are heavy with blackberries – a rare harvest in London. To get there after leaving Richmond Park through Roehampton Gate, go up Roedean Crescent, turn left into Bank Lane and over the footbridge at the end. The next time Beverley Brook is open to the public, as it were, is across Barnes Common before it flows under five streets of Barnes Village to Barn Elms. To wear a pair of wellies and walk in the stream, which is no more than a foot deep, is an eccentric way to walk through Barnes passing under five bridges and along the sides of peoples' gardens. Barnes Green, with a willow framed duck pond and sit-outside pub, is the nearest thing to a country village to be found in London.

After running through the village the brook emerges with Barnes Common on its south bank and Barn Elms playing fields on its north. The common is quite wild and overgrown with paths no more sophisticated than sheep runs, and in its midst is the derelict Barnes Cemetery, a place full of Victorian angels with their heads knocked off. The undergrowth is rapidly taking over and roots are uplifting stones – a melancholy, contemplative scene which makes one realise how soon we must all be forgotten. Beverley Brook joins the Thames a quarter-mile away at Ashlone Wharf – now used by Sea Scouts and a Boys' Club – on Putney Embankment, alongside the rowing clubs which line the river bank to Putney Bridge. At this end the brook brings the countryside into the heart of London within a three-minute walk of the No 22 bus to Chelsea and beyond.

Tollesbury Saltings

OS 1:50,000 Sheet 168 and 1:25,000 Sheet TL 81/91

A deep keeled yacht had to be extracted from the mud at the top of the tide – if she stayed there another day she would be neaped and it would be getting on for a fortnight before they could get her out – but Mouse, the local shipwright, and his mates opined: 'It's too wet to be working out there today'. They certainly do not cultivate ulcers in Tollesbury.

Out there a November drizzle was obliterating the landscape and the saltings were not looking as fascinating as they do when the sun shines. The only sign of life was a man pushing a wheelbarrow full of coal along a narrow, wooden walkway to feed the stove in his boat. In the distance the distinctive honk of brent geese could be heard as they lifted off the saltings in front of a fast flooding tide to feed on a low lying field inland. There would be no activity down by the water that day, so I walked up to the village square with its plaster-and-brick fronted houses and took shelter in the village church of St Mary the Virgin to study what is called 'The Seafarers Window'. This depicts in stained glass three famous yachts that have contended for the America's Cup and the schooner *America* which first won the Cup in a race round the Isle of Wight in 1851. The window also shows a number of traditional east coast craft – a Billy Boy, an unusually ketch-rigged sailing barge, a 'Stackie' which was a barge specially built to carry stacks of hay and straw on deck for the stables of London, and a Tollesbury oyster smack rigged in the 1920s fashion.

The window itself is fifteenth century but the glass is comparatively modern, having been given by a Mr Hasler of New York as recently as 1963. The America's Cup challengers illustrated are the schooners *Cambria* which contended in 1870, *Shamrock II* in 1899 and *Endeavour I*, the first challenger of Sir Thomas Lipton. Men of Tollesbury crewed in fifteen of sixteen British contenders, and the last *Shamrock* and the two *Endeavours* were skippered by Captain Ted Heard, a recent ancestor of Gayle Heard, the local sailmaker. Another curiosity in the church is the font which bears the inscription: 'Good people all I pray take care, that in ye Church you doe not sware As this man Did'. An entry in the church register for 30 August 1718 explains it all: 'Elizabeth daughter of Robert and Eliza Wood, being ye first child which was Baptised in the new Font: which was bought out of five pounds paid by John Norman who some months before came drunk into ye Church and cursed and talked aloud in the time of Divine Servis, to prevent his being prosecuted for which he paid by agreement the above said five pounds'.

The chapel of St Peter-on-the-Wall at Bradwell was built in 654 and is the oldest church in Britain still in use

The church stands at the highest point in the village, which is the last one on the north shore of the river Blackwater in Essex. Across the estuary is Bradwell-on-Sea and nearby the site of the old Roman fort of Othona. It was across the ruined gatehouse of the fort that Saint Cedd, who brought Christianity to Essex in 654, built his chapel of St Peter-on-the-Wall, which is the oldest church in Britain still in use. Better – or worse – known today is probably Bradwell Atomic Power Station which dominates the entrance to the Blackwater as St Cedd's church never did. In Tollesbury's church there is a small window depicting St Cedd, holding in his right hand a model of the chapel of St Peter. It is a very long detour by road via Maldon and Southminster, but only a short trip by water, to visit the real thing. As the most ancient and interesting place in the vicinity, it is well worth making the trip.

From the end of the last century until the 1930s mud berths in the saltings at Tollesbury were the winter homes of many of the great 12-metre and J class yachts, and the village home to their paid hands who earned more in the summer months racing in the Solent or taking their masters' yachts to and from the Mediterranean than they could from their winter fishing. A log of yachts wintered in Tollesbury shows that several were 100 feet or more in length, and one steam yacht was 168 feet. There were boats in the twenty-seven to thirty-eight-foot range, but they were a minority with fifty to sixty feet being the average size. Almost without exception every owner, even one with a boat of twenty-seven feet had a professional skipper, although some looked after more than one boat. No doubt there were plenty of likely lads around to help out when more owners wanted to go sailing than there were skippers to go round. In 1900 one Zachariah Lewis was listed as skipper of five yachts! More than half the skippers shared only about eight family names, the Frosts being the most prolific providing twelve skippers in a space of twenty-five years. There were several Rices, Lewises, Pages, Carters, Potters and Heards, all village names which are met with today; which is why everybody calls the local shipwright Mouse (no one uses his surname, and most of the time they do not immediately remember it). In a village with a handful of indigenous names and several members of a family sharing the same Christian name, nicknames have become the norm.

The main architectural feature of this muddy backwater is a row of four three-storey weatherboard sail lofts which stand on concrete stilts on the waterfront. The largest yachts, those over 100 feet long, used the ground floors, smaller yachts the first floors, and the local fishermen had the use of the attics. The upper parts are reached by ladders and at high springs water covers the road in front of them. Visitors who are ignorant about such matters as tides have more than once returned from a walk along the sea wall to find their cars under water. The sail lofts are now

These three-storey weatherboard sail lofts which stand on concrete stilts are the prominent achitectural feature of Tollesbury

owned by a charity called Fellowship Afloat, one of which they use as their offices; and they also own 147 acres of the saltings with all the mud berths. The Fellowship is a non-denominational Christian youth organisation whose activities are centred round *Memory*, an old Thames sailing barge used as a dormitory, an old fishing smack for cruising, as well as a number of dinghies and sail boards. They provide life-on-board experience, cruising, dinghy sailing, wild life studies, fishing and arts and crafts activities for church and school groups and individual youngsters referred to them by the welfare and probation services. They are very practical, their activities fairly rugged, and they are recognised by the Royal Yachting Association as a teaching establishment. Their staff is a helpful source of information on local conditions and on the flora and fauna of the area. Boating folk with any feeling for mother nature, and those who enjoy a journey into the past before the days of marinas, should be more than grateful to the Fellowship Afloat. As long as they own the saltings and part of the waterfront there is no possibility that this unspoilt nature reserve and living museum of bygone boats will be 'improved' by developers.

There are two ways of exploring the Tollesbury saltings and the several surrounding creeks and marshes. One is on foot along the network of raised wooden walkways over the muddy pools and squidgy hummocks of the saltings, each leading to a communion of boats sitting in the mud alongside a rickety landing stage. For a more encompassing and slightly elevated view of the whole area there is a public footpath along the ten miles of sea wall which makes a circuit round all the creeks between Shinglehead Point, *990 105*, and the village of Salcott. The same footpath, heading in the opposite direction, takes you to Maldon at the head of the Blackwater. Looking across the saltings at low water, spinneys of masts can be seen growing out of the mud. Then as the flood comes the creeks, gutways and channels start to fill, prising free a hundred hulls from their glutinous holes. Eventually there is as much water as saltings and everywhere there are boats seemingly floating on the landscape.

Bowsprits and clinker hulls in their mud berths at Maldon; the treeline on the horizon marks the course of the Chelmer and Blackwater Navigation

A small boat, preferably with an outboard which can be tilted, is the best vehicle for navigating the gutways which vein the saltings. An inflatable out of the back of the car is particularly ideal as it can go further into shallower water and be man-handled when you stick in the mud – as you surely will. Neap tides are best for going to the uttermost ends of the creeks, at the heads of which can be found the decaying remains of wooden wharves to which small coasters and sailing barges brought coal, timber, bricks and manure, and took away grain and stacks of hay and straw from the surrounding farms. Neaps occur early morning and evening, and springs around the middle of the day. With an inflatable you would have three hours either side to go more or less where you pleased, but only near the top of the tide can you land anywhere other than at a slip or hard without having to plough through mud. With a draft of two feet you have an hour either side of high water close in to the shore, but longer out in the channels. There are many boats in the saltings and creeks with five-foot or six-foot draught, but they need a high spring to float out. Any boat with a keel or a reasonable draft is regularly neaped.

The saltings shelter a very varied collection of craft, ancient and modern, but mostly the former. A boat looking like a top-heavy converted harbour launch is actually a sixty-year old Broads cruiser which has been there for twenty years. The present owner has taken her as far away as King's Lynn in the Wash and down into the Medway. *William and Emily* is a fishing smack which was built in Tollesbury and is known to the locals as *Odd Times* because she was built between other jobs using mostly scrap materials. The Fellowship use her for coastal cuising. For Old Gaffer buffs there are plenty of smacks and bawleys now used for private sailing and lots of old-time bowsprited yachts. Among the hulls which serve as floating cottages and will never sail again

Tollesbury Hard – a mix of indigenous fishing boats and local tenders

is a 1904, 12-metre. About a third of the boats are motor craft of all sizes, from a 150-foot minesweeper, an ex-RAF sixty-foot air-sea rescue launch and an MTB, down to a naval pinnace and small cabin cruisers and day boats of every age and shape. Among the oldest is *Plain Kate*, an ex-motor cruiser used by the Fellowship as an annexe to *Memory*. The original owner had her built on barge lines with her engine right up in the bows, immediately aft of which he had a large workshop, and the wheelhouse was astern of a saloon deeply upholstered in leather; so her engine controls and the prop shaft ran from the front to the back of the boat.

All year round the tide line is populated by water fowl and waders according to season. Among the residents are oystercatchers, shelducks, cormorants, redshanks and of course gulls. Summer sees the arrival of terns, buntings and warblers; winter is the time for dunlins, knots, and brent geese whose massed flights over water and marsh are most spectacular. On the shore the plant life starts at the water line with bladderwrack, a little higher up marsh samphire, and then on the knolls which are only occasionally submerged sea purslane, sea lavender, thrift, sea aster, eel and cord grasses. The Fellowship saltings form a triangle bounded on the north by Tollesbury Fleet, and the sea wall on its east and west sides. Only twenty-seven of their 147 acres are used for mud berths, the rest they keep untouched as a nature reserve. A room in one of the sail lofts is equipped with fish tanks and microscopes for the visiting youngsters to study the marine life.

Tollesbury has held onto its charm and interest by virtue of being at the end of a road which goes no further, is not part of a trippers' circular tour, and neither the village nor the foreshore offers any obvious facilities or entertainment for visitors. With the exception of a very few plastic boats, the saltings and their mud berths look today exactly as they did forty or fifty years ago, with many of the boats even older than that. As there are no facilities for visitors, so also there are none for boat owners. Everything needed on board – food and drink, water and fuel – has to be carried along the narrow plankways raised on stilts. A few owners live on their boats all the time, very many more spend their weekends and holidays aboard. For every boat that ever goes out there are as many serving out their remaining years as houseboats, but they are no less characterful for that.

There are two distinct types of owner on the saltings. The recluse who will quickly go below as you approach and keep an eye on you through a porthole – there are few windows on Tollesbury craft – until you go away. And there is the sociable type who will stop wielding a scraper or brush and entertain you with a complete history of his boat since the days when it was raced by a lord, saved a company of men at Dunkirk or was used to make annual passages to the Riviera. His wife might rather have a garden, but she does not want to become a boat widow so stoically helps in the never-ending restoration, and may very well invite you on board for a cuppa; on some boats at the right time it may be a generous offering of 'plonk'. That is the atmosphere of the place. When the wind blows across the saltings there is no shelter, and when it rains everything becomes clammy inside and slippery outside. It is a way of boating with which our grandfathers were familiar and for which, unless they were rich, there was no alternative. Today there is, and the people on the saltings are now a rare but distinguished breed of masochists. Lying in a deep ditch surrounded by mud does not appeal to the majority who prefer to get their views of local life from the pontoon of a marina or from the bar of the nearest sailing club or yachties' pub.

Surprisingly, for all its old-world, scruffy quaintness, Tollesbury does cater for the technology-wise, creature comfort-loving sailing type. It has both a first class marina and a cruising club with its own indoor swimming pool. This complex together with its boatyard – basically for hauling out and laying up – and a chandlery is happily visually separated from those other parts already described. Not that the marina is an eyesore or anything like that. Occupying a hole scooped out of the mud with a half-tide sill (with a depth of seven and a half feet at mean high water springs and five and a half feet at high water neaps), it is largely hidden below the sea wall which provides visitors with an amphitheatre from which to look over the smarter collection of boats lying to the pontoons. The marina covers seven acres at the head of Woodrolfe Creek, *968 104*, which forms the east boundary of the Fellowship saltings, and has accommodation for 240 boats with a maximum draft of seven feet lying afloat. The Cruising Club is a private operation owned by the Goldie and Waterhouse families who built the marina, but is affiliated to the RYA. It is open seven days a week during the season, but is closed on Tuesdays from September to May. There are a bar, restaurant and hard tennis courts; also showers, baths, a washing machine and drying room for those coming in from the sea. Honorary temporary membership for the day is linked to visitors' daily mooring rates.

Continuing beyond the marina there is a breezy walk for two miles along the top of the sea wall round Tollesbury Wick Marshes and the north shore of the Blackwater estuary, opposite Bradwell Atomic Power Station, to Mill Creek, *970 090*, due south of Tollesbury village which can be reached along a footpath, making the walk a complete circuit. Out in the deep water off Shinglehead Point coasters, tankers and car ferries are usually going busily about their business. On the inside of the sea walls there is a borrow dyke for drainage of the reclaimed land. The name 'borrow' means what it says, the dyke being excavated with the earth used to build the wall. The water in it is brackish, a mixture of fresh water draining off the marshes or water meadows and sea water seeping in through the drain culverts during the flood tides. The slopes of the sea walls are covered with a carpet of vetch, and club rushes and reeds grow in the dykes where families of coot are wont to swim in naval formation. Redshanks are likely to chirp angrily until you are well past their nest sites, and shelducks take off with an amazingly fast wing flap. If the tide is out the oyster-catchers will be strutting about on their pink legs while their orange bills jab up and down. Skylarks may be singing above, while butterflies, yellowhammers and bullfinches add to the darting colours. It needs only a moderately keen eye to fill these wet wildernesses with life.

Mill Creek is now a muddy, drying out little creek of no significance, but it once had pretensions to becoming a big port for the east coast. In the event it was Harwich not Tollesbury which became the port, and rightly so if you look at the topography of the two places. It was all very much the dream of a Mr Arthur Charles Wilkin who had such fabulous crops of strawberries that he decided to go into jam making. Eventually, in 1885, he opened his jam factory at Tiptree – the name will be familiar – and built a railway from the main line at Kelvedon, *863 192*, through Tiptree to the water's edge at Tollesbury where he had a pier built one-fifth of a mile out to sea so that ships could lie alongside at all states of the tide. The pier was purposely destroyed during the last war for obvious reasons, and all that remains today is a hard and some foundations of the little station. The line of the railway is now difficult to follow, and the only substantial memento is an old water tower, *957 108*, on the northern edge of Tollesbury. The line did quite well for a time, carrying shellfish up to join the main line and so on to the London market, and of course jam both inland and for export. Inevitably it was dubbed 'The Jam and Winkle' line and, by all accounts, it was a most friendly business with train drivers willing to stop anywhere to give a lift to a housewife with her shopping or a man with his tools.

Going north out of the village up Back Lane and then west along Old Hall Lane bring one to Old Hall Farm, *957 123*, and Old Hall Marshes, the RSPB's reserve and its most costly purchase at £780,000 in 1984 for 1,134 acres of unimproved grazing marsh, salt marsh, grassland and two little islands. Old Hall Marshes were owned by a Brigadier Colvin and maintained as one of the best known shooting estates in the country. The marshes are very undulating because of old creek systems and have been grazed by sheep and cattle for 500 years. They were bought by the

Tollesbury saltings on the Blackwater estuary where the scene has not changed in 50 years

RSPB because of their international importance as a roosting, feeding and nesting area for a wide range of species, especially large flocks of wintering brent geese. Re-seeding of grassland within the reserve will alleviate the pressure of geese grazing on farmland outside the area.

The main tool of management is cattle on the rough grazing within the sea wall. In the first year of ownership when the reserve was very much undergrazed almost all the young redshanks which were hatched died of pneumonia. It rained every day throughout the spring, and in the long grass the young birds had no way of getting out of the wet and into the sun to dry. On any shooting estate, after a good shower of rain, you will see the pheasant sitting around on the road drying out. Cattle provide the short grazed sward which is ideal for certain waders and wild fowl, for instance lapwings which like an open aspect and make no attempt to hide their nests. Cattle are mobile mowers and much better than sheep or goats because they are very selective feeders and, therefore, there are grass species which they will not eat, so they leave tussocks of these growing which are ideal for nesting. At the same time the RSPB have to be careful not to overstock – the difference between one beast and three per hectare is ten per cent, and sixty per cent of nests lost underfoot.

In the early summer of 1987 a census by the warden and his staff came up with 400 pairs of skylarks, 182 pairs of meadow pippets, 120 of reed buntings, 190 of reed warblers and 100 pairs of sedge warblers. In its first year the reserve had 2,000 watchers, and in 1986 there were 5,000. That was before any facilities or restrictions, apart from keeping to public footpaths. Now the western end of the reserve is being developed with a car park, proper laid out walks of about two and a half miles and hides giving good views but leaving most of the area a wilderness without humans. The sea wall walk is seven and a half miles long, but visitors are discouraged from walking its skyline where they stick up like sore thumbs, as the warden Peter Gotham put it. He says that people have got to be organised in the country as they are in the towns: 'You have accepted parking meters and double yellow lines because in the towns you need discipline for society to work. Here we need discipline in order that the reserve remains a reserve. We want to attract rare birds, but they are generally fairly shy and do not like people so we cannot have them wandering all over the place; also we cannot mix people and cattle because we cannot trust our visitors 100 percent not to throw clods around, chase our cattle and leave gates open. Visitors will be encouraged to use one end of the reserve and leave the rest a wilderness area'.

There is no entrance fee, and there are no plans to try and keep non-members out – with a public footpath circling the reserve on top of the sea wall it would be impossible anyway. It is quite feasible to sail up Old Hall Creek and Salcott Channel, on either side of the reserve, which would allow good viewing of waders on both banks, particularly in late summer and early autumn when a lot of migrant waders use the saltings. The problem is that a boat would have to go up on a tide and wait through an ebb and half a flood to see anything. It would be a long sit on the mud and would mean keeping still and quiet on board. Only at the top of the tide, and springs at that, would there be any worthwhile view from a deck over the sea wall and across the marshes into the habitats of the singing birds. Of course the whole of the Essex and Suffolk coasts are indented with estuaries, creeks and guts where a pair of binoculars add a dimension to boating which is not to be had in the more developed yachting centres of the south coast. For a final description of this intriguing place I would quote a local resident, Mr Brian Birkin, who told me: 'I do a lot of fishing at night when there are no yachts about. When the moon shines on the saltings, or in the early morning light before the sea mist comes in, it is all just beautiful. Words could not paint the picture; a camera would not do it justice'.

Chelmer and Blackwater Navigation

OS 1:50,000 Sheets 167/168

Under an Act of 1793 the penalties which can be imposed for causing damage or obstruction to the Chelmer and Blackwater Navigation include transportation. The Act has never been repealed, but you can be certain that causing wilful damage to the canal banks today would not procure for you a free passage to Australia. However, this legal curiosity is one of the many things which make the quaint and little known waterway which connects Maldon in Essex with Chelmsford well worth exploring.

The canal starts at Heybridge Basin across the Blackwater from Maldon and can be entered through the sea lock during the one hour before high water. The period immediately following high water is reserved for locking out, and then the gates are closed to conserve water. The first half-mile of the canal is well known to East Coast yachtsmen as the home of a motley collection of boats, mostly rather ancient, which line both banks. The village has provided a large car park with direct access to the towpath which becomes crowded with sightseers during summer weekends. And there is plenty for them to see – modern yachts in from the sea for a few days, Thames barges, part-converted fishing smacks, and once proud pre-war yachts waiting for the restoration which never seems to be finally accomplished. It has long been a favoured fitting out berth by those with dreams of sailing away forever and a day to coral isles and palm fringed shores. A few make their dreams come true, but the many 'For Sale' notices show that most do not.

Among the big boats there are usually a few small outboard driven cabin cruisers which never go out through the sea lock, but spend their lives on the thirteen miles of willow-lined navigation, part river, part canal, which runs through the gentle Essex countryside. There is a charge for using the sea lock at Heybridge related to the size of the boat and a mooring fee of ten pence per foot per week. A licence is required to navigate through the locks above Heybridge, and permanent moorings alongside the river or canal beyond the first lock cost nine pence per foot per week. So it is almost certainly the cheapest inland waterway there is. However, the navigation is not available to the majority of boats which come in from the sea because, although it is broad and the locks will take vessels of sixty-foot length and sixteen-foot beam, draught is limited to two feet – making it the shallowest navigation in the country. Also there are eleven locks in the almost fourteen miles length, all unattended; gate keys are issued on payment of a deposit. The charge for casual users with outboards is £1 a day, £3 a week, but such short-term use is not encouraged and requires some special pleading with the office! It is best to use a boat which is light enough to be portaged round the locks as the proprietors (it is a privately owned navigation) do not take kindly to a small boat using 50,000 gallons of water to go through *each* lock! If your boat is too heavy to carry you are expected to wait until you can join a convoy of regular cruisers, and they are only likely to form up at weekends and during the school holidays.

The navigation is ideal for the occasional day of tranquil rustic boating or walking. Remote from road, except where three bridges cross the water, and going through no villages, the flora and fauna are undisturbed, making it a perfect location for nature study; it is used for this purpose by the local schools. With a towpath along its whole length, it can be taken in sections on foot, and very pleasant it is too with occasional coarse fishermen to chat to (they fish for roach, gudgeon, perch, chub, bream and carp up to twenty-four pounds, with some good specimens of tench) and plenty of grassy banks on which to rest and absorb the utter peace. The village of Heybridge Basin which grew up around the sea lock into the canal did not exist until the navigation was started in 1793 and it developed along with the canal trade. The Old Ship public house, *873 069*, formerly the Chelmer Brig, dates back to the 1790s but was rebuilt in 1858. The lock-keeper's house was built in 1842, and two cottages nearby are dated 1822. In its heyday the tidal basin accommodated sailing ships of 300 tons which brought timber from Scandinavia and coal from Tyneside.

Today it is entirely a yachting scene with a high proportion of old timers with their tan sails and bowsprits leaning every which way in the mud when the tide is out.

Until about twenty years ago there was a certain amount of boat building and barge repair work being done at Heybridge Basin but now, although there are still a couple of old shipwrights in the village, the last boat to be built was in 1982 by Holt & James, the local yard. She was a thirty foot oyster dredger, the *Ostrea Rose*, a totally traditional craft which, when finished, looked as if she had been built in 1882. James Macmillan, one of the partners, explained to me the Micawber-like economics of building wooden boats these days. 'You have got to like doing it because you will never make any money out of it, although every time you think you will make your money on the next one if the order comes quick enough. Of course the deposit on the next boat is really paying off the last bills of the previous one'.

The yard is the only one in the country which still makes wooden mast hoops, bands of wood fitted round a sailing boat's wooden mast to hold the luff, or leading edge of the sail, close against the mast while allowing it to be hoisted and lowered. They are now found only on very old boats or those built to an old design. Traditionally a sail is 'bent' to its mast hoops using tarred twine, called marline, which is two strands tightly twisted together and very weather resistant. The edge of the sail is seized to the hoops by passing the marline several times through grommets and the hoops. Modern boats have metal or plastic tracks which the sails run up and down like curtains on a rail. Making hoops which are complete and yet can be put round a standing mast must, I thought, need some skill. James Macmillan thinks not. 'We thought there was a skill, but we have come to the conclusion that it is pure luck in the end. We have tried every technique we could think of to make it a skilful and successful operation, but every time we have ended up with more firewood than mast hoops. We use ash and have found that it is fairly critical how it is cut into staves, as is the steaming time and the rate at which the staves are bent. Each end is scarfed and then the stave goes into the steam pot for twenty-five to twenty-eight minutes. We have a bending machine which we made ourselves on the principle of the gadget used for taking tyres off car wheels. One end of the steamed stave goes in and a team gently bends it round and fastens the ends with a screw while it is still in the mould. Then when we take it off we hold our breath while we wait to see if it is going to give way or not. The screw can be taken out so the hoop can be put round a mast like a split key ring and then the ends rove with a copper nail'. Their hoops go all over the world and are proving a better proposition than building boats.

Looking out of his office window I wondered about a strange green boat sitting on the mud looking very derelict except for a beautifully polished wheel standing proudly on the decaying deck. 'That', said James Macmillan, 'is one of the lost causes. It was originally out in the East where it went round the fishing junks collecting their catches. At great expense it was shipped home and the owner rigged her in a rough and rudimentary way. Since then all he has been able to do is set up a nice steering wheel. One day she will be stuck in the mud till she rots away because for some inexplicable reason the predicted tides are getting lower each year and soon we will not be able to haul out a six foot draught boat'. James Macmillan does not come from a long line of local boat builders, but is a 'foreigner'. He came to live on a boat in the canal in 1970, commuting daily to a job at the Home Office in London. In 1973 he opted for early retirement and with his partner, Arthur Holt, took over the yard. 'A "foreigner" is anyone who has only lived at Heybridge Basin for twenty-five years or less. The true locals are the basiners who have lived all their lives there and belong to one of the few village families. Those who have come to live on their boats in the canal basin cannot by definition be basiners'.

A long straight artificial cut runs from Heybridge Basin one and a half miles to Heybridge village which is virtually a suburb of Maldon. It also developed with the opening of the canal and the siting in 1811 of Bentall's ironworks, *858 080*, beside the navigation which supplied it with ore and coal. Their warehouse, built in 1863 by the road bridge over the cut, is a scheduled industrial monument. A public footpath from the centre of the village leads to one of the original brick bridges, *846 080*, of the 1790s. A little way upstream are the only 'waterfalls' in Essex! They are in fact a series of weirs at Beeleigh Lock, *839 084*, where the Chelmer and Blackwater rivers are joined together by a cut to form the navigation with excess water pouring into the tidal reach of the Chelmer. Another original brick bridge, a disused lock, an older canal arm built in 1792 to serve Langford Mill, a stand of willows and an extensive waterscape make this a picturesque and practical point from which to study the engineering of this waterway system.

Five miles and three more locks upstream on what is now the canalised Chelmer river you reach Paper Mill Lock, *776 090*, the 'half way house' along the navigation in bargeing days. This is a unique site of canal archaeology; not restored, museum-ised or developed with restaurants and souvenir shops as is Stoke

Paper Mill Lock, a unique site of canal archaeology, looking today as it did when it was built at the end of the eighteenth century

Bruerne on the Grand Union Canal, but looking today much as it did when it was built. Beside the lock is the bothy, a small brick building where the bargees used to sleep; opposite are the stables where their horses spent the night at two pence per animal including their feed. The bothy is now the registered office of the Company of Proprietors of the Chelmer and Blackwater Navigation Ltd, where they keep the company records going back to the minutes of the first meeting of the Committee on 15 July 1793 and the books of correspondence from the days before carbon paper when every letter, in or out, was painstakingly copied in copper plate writing into a ledger. On the walls are photographs of the horse-drawn barges which took timber to Chelmsford up until 1960, after which a diesel barge was used. Commercial traffic ceased in 1972 after 180 years, and since 1975 the navigation has been kept open for amenity use.

Proposals to make the Chelmer a navigable river from the sea to Chelmsford were first mooted in 1677, then again in 1732 and 1765, but an Act was not passed for the making of a navigation from Colliers Reach (now the Heybridge Canal Basin) to Springfield in Chelmsford until 1793. At that time some 10,000 tons of goods and 5,000 tons of coal were being transported annually by rough road over Danbury Hill into Chelmsford, and it was quite obvious that this could be done more easily and economically by water. John Rennie was appointed the principle engineer for the project, but he was already fully occupied building canals all over the country and only visited the Chelmer and Blackwater site five times. His sole design contribution was to supply drawings of his locks for the Stowmarket Navigation for the resident engineer, Richard Coates, to copy. Starting in October 1793, the work employed fifty men and took three years and eight months to complete at a cost of £52,000. It is a very broad navigation and the eleven pound locks, which lift the water seventy-six feet eleven inches in its thirteen miles, measure sixty-eight by seventeen feet each.

The years 1797 to 1845 were the most profitable in the navigation's history, with 1842 being the peak year when 60,000 tons of goods were carried. Between 1846 and 1865 the tonnage carried remained constant, but tolls had to be cut to compete with the Eastern Counties and the Maldon-Braintree railways. After that the company declined as a navigation, but it survived by selling some land and later from the planting in the 1860s of cricket bat willows along the canal banks. When these came to maturity they helped to keep the company solvent and continue to do so today, together with a contract to supply water to the Essex Water Authority for their reservoir at Hannington. It is for this reason that strict control over the opening of lock gates has to be enforced.

The Navigation Company owns some 2,000 willow trees which are felled after about twelve years, providing they are in

The Navigation Company owns some 2,000 willow trees which are felled after about twelve years and used to make cricket bats

good condition and have grown tall and straight. To ensure a good straight trunk without branches, shoots are lopped off every spring. The trees are felled by the willow specialists, J S Wright & Sons of Great Leighs, who pay in the region of £50 for a tree with a straight trunk of at least ten feet and free of knots. The optimum size for a tree's girth at chest height is fifty-six inches or over – there is no such thing as a bat willow which is too big. The optimum height is determined by a bat length, which is twenty-eight inches. So in ten feet of clean uninterrupted straight grain there will be four bat lengths, and with a girth of sixty inches, it is possible to get ten bats per bat length. The trunks are sawn into two foot four inch lengths which are then split lengthwise into wedge shapes, or clefts, which are the rudimentary shapes from which the bats will be made. These clefts are rough sawn to the final shape of bat blades before being waxed and stacked ready for delivery to Stuart Surridge, the famous bat makers, where, among other processes, they are put through a two-ton press which so compresses the wood fibres that a blade will take a heavy blow from a hammer without denting. Wrights process about 125 trees a week from local estates and their own plantations, as well as those from the navigation. Not all the willows are used for making cricket bats; the firm has another speciality – wooden balls for coconut shies in fairgrounds. These balls are a standard two and a half inch diameter and, being made of willow, are so light that they will only rarely knock a coconut off its stand! They make 25,000 such balls a year and, from time to time, the coconuts as well; these are made of elm with a coconut matting jacket fitted round them. They also use off-cuts of the light but strong willow to make blanks which go to an artificial limb factory to be carved into artificial feet.

From Paper Mill Lock a converted canal narrow boat *Victoria* runs scheduled pleasure trips over the May and August Bank Holidays and is available for charter at other times. She can accommodate a dinner party of twenty-six while cruising, but up to forty-eight for a buffet and drinks party. For a small cabin cruiser keeping to the speed limit of four miles per hour and allowing time for working all the locks, a return cruise from Paper Mill Lock – which is the only launching site along the canal – to Chelmsford in one direction or to Heybridge in the other will take about eight hours. There are no fuel supplies or other services along the way, but Little Baddow, an exceedingly pretty village with a twelfth century church, is but a mile's walk from either Paper Mill Lock or from Little Baddow Mill Lock, *759 084*, further upstream. Downstream from Little Baddow Mill the lock

The spindle operation in the manufacture of cricket bats; the willows from which they are made grow beside the Chelmer and Blackwater Navigation

The winding mechanisms of the hatches by the mill house at Little Baddow on the Chelmer and Blackwater Navigation

opens into a mill pond which mirrors a white late-Victorian mill house beside the tinkling water of a weir. It stands on the site of an earlier mill burned down in 1893. Going on up the canal there is the prospect of Danbury Hill, *779 052*, the highest ground thereabouts at 365 feet above sea level. It is conspicuous, being topped by a church spire.

The navigation takes an artificial cut to by-pass the site of Sandford Mill, *737 062*, which once had four pairs of grinding stones and its water power was augmented by a steam engine. In 1924 Chelmsford acquired it for a water works which now extracts two-million gallons of water daily from the canal. By the cut Bundock's Bridge, built in the 1790s, takes the towpath under its arch. Barnes Mill, *726 064*, a late eighteenth century weather-boarded building, has been converted into a country house with picture windows and tailored garden and is hardly recognisable for what it was. The lock into Springfield Basin in Chelmsford had been completely vandalised when I last saw it, and the basin was full of shopping trolleys. There has been much talk of turning it into a marina, but nobody has backed the talk with money. Anyway there is no great need to do anything because boats can go up to, and turn round at, the radial gates at King's Head Meadows which is closer to the town centre anyway.

The Chelmer can be navigated beyond Chelmsford by canoe or inflatable boat as far as Little Waltham where, getting weedier and shallower, it goes on to its source above Great Dunmow, a town with a timbered guildhall and a pond where the first lifeboat tests were made in 1785 by Lionel Lukin. It is, however, better known for the Dunmow Flitch, a side of bacon awarded to couples who can prove to a mock court that they have enjoyed conjugal harmony for a year and a day. Childhood dreams of emulating Sanders of the River or some intrepid explorer seeking the source of the Zambesi can be recalled by taking a boat, light enough to be portaged, over the rollers in Chelmsford for an eight-mile voyage up the river Can into the hinterland of east Essex! Or at least go as far as Writtle, three miles by water, a village with Tudor timbered houses, Georgian brickwork and many varieties of pargeted plaster work around a green and a pond. Here it was that Marconi set up his transmission aerials when he opened his first wireless workshop in Chelmsford in 1899.

River Stour

OS 1:50,000 Sheets 154/155/168/169

Every year in May a small flotilla of boats cruise under oars the length of the river Stour from Sudbury to the sea at Cattawade. The distance is only eighteen miles, but it takes two days of rowing and a lot of humping and heaving through undergrowth round fifteen sluices, and some bottom-scraping and bow-hauling over the shallower stretches. This energetic exercise, which anybody with their own rowing boat or canoe is at liberty to join, is organised by the River Stour Trust to assert and maintain the right of navigation granted by Queen Anne in 1705. Barge traffic to Sudbury ceased in 1911, the locks have since disintegrated and the water level has dropped several feet. But the Act *'for making the river Stower (sic) navigable, from the town of Manningtree in the county of Essex, to the town of Sudbury in the county of Suffolk... which will be very beneficial to trade, advantageous to the poor, and convenient for the conveyance of coals, and other goods and merchandise, to and from the said towns... and will very much tend to the employing and encrease (sic) of watermen and seamen,* (nothing new about job creation!) *and be a means to preserve the highways...'* has never been repealed.

Commercial navigation is no longer possible, but the right does allow for a little enjoyable pleasure boating – a leisure amenity which could be expanded. When the Anglian Water Authority was formed in the 1960s they decided it would be very convenient if there was no right of navigation and argued that because it was no longer exercised commercially it had lapsed. For once a statutory body did not have it all their own way; the River Stour Trust was formed to fight them and the case went to the House of Lords who ruled against the Authority. In 1973 the Authority struck again with a bye law forbidding all motorised craft on the Stour except for a short stretch between Sudbury and the weir, *881 386*, at Henny Street, along part of which a tripper launch already operated and rowing boats could be hired. The Authority maintained that the rights did not include motorised vessels because barge traffic had always been horsedrawn. In fact there had been steam dredgers and at least one steam barge on the Stour in the last century and, for proof, the hull of a steam barge was recently dug out of the mud, its prop shaft and stern gear intact, and is now going through the long process of restoration by the Trust. Once again the Trust objected and managed to get a Court of Inquiry, but this time they lost. So their annual cruise has to be done by muscle power; it is always made during the close season before the fishing starts in June so as not to upset the anglers – not that they have any right to object, and legally should lift their rods when a boat passes. As far as the Stour is concerned they will have paid the riparian owner for access over his land to the river bank, but have not paid to actually use the river. Before leaving the subject of navigation I must caution that you need a licence from the Authority in Colchester to put a boat on the water.

The Stour is tidal from Harwich to Manningtree, a distance of nine miles, and at high water it becomes a mile and more wide, and at low water the channel is still half a mile wide off Parkeston Quay, *235 328*. By the time it gets to Mistley it has shrunk to fifty yards, after which, as far as a boat is concerned, the water runs out altogether and the approach to Cattawade, *102 330*, and the fresh water reaches is blocked by acres of mud. It is doubtful if many of those who do sail up the Stour know that they could, theoretically, continue on up the fresh water river all the way to Sudbury if they took to their dinghy. The way in is over an incline of rollers beside the barrage at Cattawade – a sop to the legality of navigation – which is why the trip could only be made in a very small portable boat. To attempt to row all the way to Sudbury would be a Herculian task, but a day trip from Cattawade up as far as Dedham is quite feasible and takes in Flatford Mill and Dedham Vale, the very heart of Constable country. The channel from Mistley to the barrage will only float a boat for about ninety minutes either side of high water, therefore a cruise up the Vale and back is only possible when there is a morning and evening high tide, which is just after neaps. It can, of course, be done at any time with a trailed boat from a convenient patch of ground beside the summit of the roller slipway.

The river here winds its way across open marsh and water meadow past Brantham Mill, where Thames sailing barges once called, and through the remains of Brantham Lock, *093 334*, which used to be the tidal limit. After Judas Gap, another barrage, the river starts to be tree lined and the marsh land gives way to sloping fields. Very soon Flatford Mill, *077 332*, comes into view, and through the trees you get a glimpse of Willy Lot's cottage. The mill, largely red brick with white-painted weather boarding, is a great tourist attraction although it has been very much 'improved' over the years and is leased by the National Trust for residential courses to the Field Studies Council and is not open to the public. Willy Lot's cottage is very recognisable as the one in the corner of Constable's *Hay Wain*. The lock at Flatford is the only one on the Stour in working order, having been restored by volunteer labour. It was re-opened in 1975, and a boat can be locked through on application for the necessary keys to the Misses Richardson in a nearby cottage. Like other Stour locks, it was designed to take a barge forty-five feet long and ten feet wide and has the characteristic lintel over the gates at each end.

A feature of Flatford is the sixteenth century thatched cottage which used to be a tea-shop but has been refurbished by the National Trust as a museum with a modern glass and timber tea-room erected beside it! John Constable's sketch book of 1814, now in the Victoria and Albert Museum in London, includes several small sketches for his painting *Boat Building at Flatford*. The dry dock, which is shown in great detail and which belonged to his father Golding, was excavated by the River Stour Trust in collaboration with the National Trust and it will be used as a dock for hiring rowing boats. A barge was found under the silt but its back was broken so it had to be extracted piecemeal; its place is being taken by the restored steam barge. A later sketch by Constable shows a sluice gate which allowed the dock to be flooded to float out a completed barge. It was emptied through a pipe which went across the river bed to emerge beyond the embankment on the other side where, when the plug was pulled, the water drained into the water meadow below. In April 1987 two divers located a ten-foot missing section of the cast iron pipe which had been laid in sections with the cone shaped end of one being pushed into the next and the joints sealed with lead. A repair was made by threading a plastic pipe through the whole length of the cast iron one, at the same time bridging the gap. With the dock drained its brick floor was exposed and the wooden posts of the grid on which the barge hulls were supported.

At the top of Flatford Lane in East Bergholt the Kings Head pub, *078 344*, used by generations of Stour lightermen, has a good display of photographs in its public bar of the river's commercial days. Constable was born in the village and married the parson's daughter. The parish church of St Mary-the-Virgin dates back to 1350 and is faced with some beautiful examples of East Anglian flintwork. Its tower, which is incomplete, was begun at the expense of Cardinal Wolsey in 1525, but work on it stopped when he died five years later. So, instead of a bell tower, there is a bell cage in the churchyard, erected as a temporary measure in 1531! Inside are five bells, the oldest dated 1450. It is the only cage where the bells are rung by hand applied directly and not by rope and wheel.

For the three miles from Flatford Mill to Dedham the river runs through open fields with trees literally growing out of the banks and in places forming arches over the water. On this stretch you will not have the river to yourself as rowing boats can be hired at Flatford Mill and Dedham. Dedham village has some lovely old buildings including a fine Queen Anne house with a sundial on the wall where the ancestors of the American General Sherman lived. The church is a noble example of the Perpendicular style and was built in the year that Columbus landed in America. It features in several of Constable's paintings. The lock at Dedham now performs no more useful function than to provide a small waterfall when the river is in spate and it is awkward to carry a boat round it, but not impossible. It would indeed be worth the effort to row up the next one and a half miles, if suitably attired and with cheque book in pocket, to lunch or dine at Le Talbooth, *042 335*, a timber framed house beside the river with its own landing stage – although I doubt if their clients ever arrive that way. The hotel part of this establishment, known as Maison Talbooth, with its coronet-topped bed drapes and sunken circular baths with gold fittings, is three quarters of a mile away – the walk between bedroom and restaurant is supposed to be good for you. There are footpaths along both river banks from Le Talbooth to Dedham and thence to Flatford Mill, after which one keeps beside the river to Cattawade. So there are plenty of walks at this end of the Vale through pastures, under trees and finally out across marshland. Dedham, as I have said, is about as far upstream as most people will want to go by boat. The other popular boating reach is between Brundon Mill, *864 423*, above Sudbury, which is the head of navigation, down to Henny Street.

The Stour rises at 380 feet above sea level somewhere near the edge of an old airfield on Wratton Common by Western Green.

Flatford Mill on the river Stour was immortalised by Constable and is a great tourist attraction although not open to the public

The weir at Henny Street on the Stour marks the end of the last short stretch of river which can be navigated under power

Wissington Mill, on the river Stour, which stands at the end of a long straight reach has been converted into a magnificent private residence

The start of a leafy walk beside the Stour from the park at Clare which leads to the ruins of an Austin Friars friary

A magnificent view of the broad Conwy valley looking downstream from the 1,000-foot vantage point of Llangelynin Old Church

A heron stands watching for its prey
on the mud flats of the lower reaches
of the Conwy river

For some way it is little more than a drainage ditch, but gets stronger at Wixoe after it has been fed by two tributaries. On one of them is Steeple Bumpstead which has a toytown size Moot Hall, dated 1592, and opposite is the vicarage where Edith Cavell worked for five years as a governess. Martha Blewitt, who was a licensee of The Swan at the road junction outside Wixoe, died in 1681 after outliving her ninth husband, and in a house across the road a Robert Hogan outlived his seventh wife to die in 1796. This bumper crop of marriages is celebrated on a tablet in the parish church at nearby Birdbrook. Stoke-by-Clare was the site of a Norman Benedictine priory which is now Stoke College. Clare, the next village a mile downstream, has had a market since the time of William the Conqueror and its buildings have something to show for every century since. A miniature country park has been laid out round the base of its Norman tower which stands on a 100-foot-high Saxon motte overlooking the village on one side and the Stour on the other. There is a short walk under the trees along the river bank past the remains of a priory of the Austin Friars. The tower is all that remains of a great castle with buildings, gardens and vineyards covering twenty acres. It accommodated some 250 people and hundreds of horses. There is much to be seen in this little town and a good starting point could be the Swan Inn which was an alehouse in the fifteenth century when it was called Le Swan. The carved inn sign of a chained swan wearing a crown and the arms of England and France was made very early in the fifteenth century and is extremely well preserved. The ancient house by the church, built in 1473, is decorated with very fine examples of the East Anglian craft of pargeting or decorative plasterwork. It is now a local history museum, but at one time came very near to being sold for dismantling and shipment to the USA! On Clare common earth banks and ditches quite clearly mark the layout of an Iron Age fort built some time between 55 BC and AD 55.

A gently sloping green backed by pink washed thatched cottages, overlooked by a magnificent church with jutting stair turret, is what one first sees of Cavendish when arriving from the west. The main street of this affluent looking village has some venerable inns, antique shops and the headquarters of the Sue Ryder organisation. But its big novelty hidden away behind the church is Cavendish Manor, a fifteenth century wool merchant's house with vineyards planted in 1972 by Basil Ambrose, a character very much to the manor born. The idea of having his own vineyard came to him at a wine tasting: 'I looked into my glass and thought: Could I grow my own wine on my own land and put it on my own table for my own guests? There had been a Roman villa in the village so there must have been a vineyard. If the Romans could do it perhaps an Englishman in the twentieth century could do it'. His vines, 10,000 of them which came from Alsace, were planted by hand, and when that was done he had about doubled the acreage of vineyards in England at that time. In his third autumn he got a light crop followed by three successive good growing seasons which gave his vines a fine start in life, and he was soon taking prizes at home and abroad.

Cavendish shares the Stour with the smaller village of Pentlow on the Essex bank with its very fine mill surrounded by beautiful lawns. Two miles on downstream the Glem flows into the Stour, which at that point has developed into a complex of little lakes in a woodland setting which is very pleasing. Since Wixoe the Stour has run alongside the A1092; now it takes a sharp turn south to accompany the A134 into Sudbury, but first it is joined by the Chad Brook that passes through Long Melford, which has been described as the most impressive single thoroughfare in Suffolk, and I am sure it is. Nearly all its buildings are of architectural interest with many of them washed in Suffolk pink and other muted colours. A number of good quality antique shops provide an atmosphere of wealth, and for the tourist there are two stately homes. Melford Hall is a Tudor mansion with its original panelled banqueting hall in which Elizabeth I was entertained in 1578, but there are also Victorian bedrooms with displays on Beatrix Potter. The former moat is now a sunken garden, and there is an unusual octagonal Tudor garden house, the windows of which survey the ten-acre village green. Kentwell Hall is another moated Tudor mansion which still remains a family home. It hosts several special events, foremost among them an historical re-creation of Tudor domestic life, and an open air theatre season in August.

The most magnificent sight of Long Melford is Holy Trinity Church. It was built, as were many other churches in East Anglia, by men who had made their money in the wool or cloth trade and wanted to spend it on a memorial to the glory of God – and perhaps to themselves as well. Regardless of their small congregations, the churches were made great. Completed in 1484, Holy Trinity has the proportions of a cathedral. Its Lady Chapel is peculiar in having an indoor cloister around the worshipping area which gives the effect of a small chapel encapsulated within a bigger one. Among its seventy-two windows a mediaeval glass shows Elizabeth Talbot, Duchess of Norfolk, kneeling in prayer, and one is immediately reminded of Lewis Carroll. It is said that

The south side of the magnificent Holy Trinity Church, Long Melford, built in the fifteenth century with money from the wool and cloth trade

Long Melford's Holy Trinity Church has the proportions of a cathedral. Its Lady Chapel has an indoor cloister around the worshipping area which gives the effect of a small chapel encapsulated within a bigger one

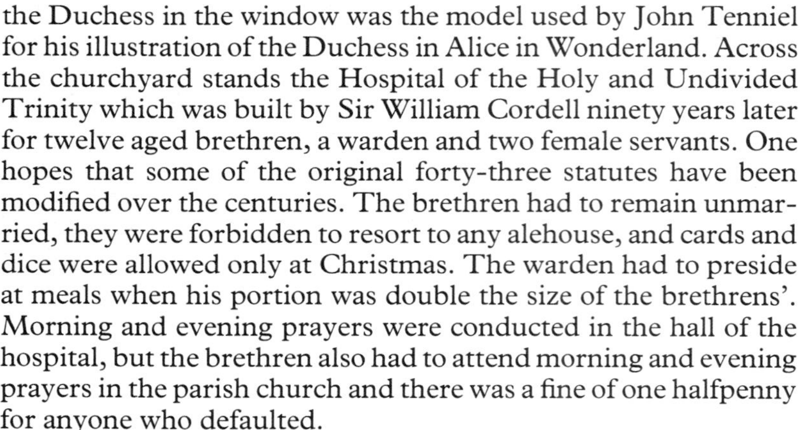

the Duchess in the window was the model used by John Tenniel for his illustration of the Duchess in Alice in Wonderland. Across the churchyard stands the Hospital of the Holy and Undivided Trinity which was built by Sir William Cordell ninety years later for twelve aged brethren, a warden and two female servants. One hopes that some of the original forty-three statutes have been modified over the centuries. The brethren had to remain unmarried, they were forbidden to resort to any alehouse, and cards and dice were allowed only at Christmas. The warden had to preside at meals when his portion was double the size of the brethrens'. Morning and evening prayers were conducted in the hall of the hospital, but the brethren also had to attend morning and evening prayers in the parish church and there was a fine of one halfpenny for anyone who defaulted.

There is a four-mile walk from Long Melford to Sudbury starting at the lane opposite the Bull Hotel, along the left bank to Liston Mill and a picnic site by the river at Rodbridge Corner, *856 436*. This is the start of the Valley Walk along two miles of dismantled railway line to Ballingdon on the outskirts of Sudbury. The path passes two mills – a small one at Borley, *856 430*, and, very worth a visit, the big white-painted Brundon Mill, *865 423*, with moss-dappled tiled roofs and a weir cascading into a sylvan mill pond, the whole site surrounded by woods. From there an alternative route would be across water meadows to Sudbury's green, known as The Croft and the home of a large colony of assorted ducks. I have explored this section of the river in a small inflatable with an electric outboard and a crew of children – a mini adventure which they thoroughly enjoyed forcing a way through reeds and tunnels of overhanging branches. Through Sudbury there are two long riverside paths. One starts at The Croft and passes the weir which controls the mill race to the Mill Hotel. This very big mill-turned-hotel has an internal revolving water wheel as a feature of the dining room. The route ends where the tail race enters the Stour behind the Boathouse Hotel, where rowing boats can be hired and from where a tripper boat operates. Another footpath from the Mill Hotel crosses the river to join the Valley Walk, from the end of which the way continues along the old railway track on the other side of the A131 and over a railway

Behind the mill in Nayland is Fen Street where each house has its own footbridge over the mill race

Brantham Lock approaching Cattawade. Public footpaths beside the water only exist in short stretches and have to be hunted for on the OS map. Since the Stour is a navigation the best way to explore it is in a small boat, one or two sections at a time. There are launching sites at The Boathouse, Ballingdon Bridge, Sudbury; Friary Meadow, Sudbury; The Granary, Sudbury; the Swan Inn, Henny Street (with permission); the Recreation Ground, Bures; beside the Bell Bridge, Nayland; off the public footpath by the mill at Stratford St Mary; The Boathouse or the car park at Dedham Bridge; between Flatford footbridge and the lock, or below the lock which is difficult but possible; and finally at Cattawade barrage. No doubt many landowners would give permission to launch off their land if asked, but the right of navigation does not give any right to use river banks, which are private property.

River Conwy

OS 1:25,000 Outdoor Leisure Sheets 16/18

Up on the boggy moorland called Migneint at a height of 1,488 feet the overflow from the small Llyn Conwy trickles – or pours, depending on the rain – through an iron grill to drain into the peaty soil. Such is the ignominious start of the river which, only twenty-five miles away, meets the sea in a noble estuary a mile wide and guarded by Edward's great castle at Conwy. It begins as a wet streak hardly worth putting on the map, but such is the rainfall on this frontier of Snowdonia and the sponge effect of the peat, that within a few hundred yards it has become a proper mountain stream, and before a mile is making a big display as a multiple-cascade waterfall, *781 444*. This, the first of many falls, is beside the B4407 where it meets the private road to the lake. For the next few miles the river hurries downhill swelling perceptibly every minute as it is fed by innumerable streams. It enters Ysbyty Ifan, its first village, already a broad river. From 1284 to 1974, when Mr Heath and Mr Walker made all those local government name and boundary changes, it was the boundary between Caernarfonshire and Denbighshire, so the village had two parish councils and was represented on two different county councils. Now the whole of the river Conwy and all its tributaries bar one minor stream are in Gwynedd. An old lady in the village told me that before 1955 when electricity for the village came from a turbine generator driven by a water-wheel fed from the Conwy, there was not enough power to light both the cottages and the chapel, so in winter the cottages were subject to power cuts during evening services. For the same reason the women had to take in in turns to use their electric irons.

My informant suggested that I should talk to Huw Selwyn Owen, the poet. I found him making a pair of coffins, for he is also the village carpenter. He gave me a concise history of Ysbyty Ifan, which means Hospital of John. In about 1190 a hospice of St John of Jerusalem was founded for travellers on the site of the village which was on one of the pilgrim routes to Bardsey Island. It was granted the right to give sanctuary, which was later extended to take in the surrounding countryside, by Llywelyn Fawr, Llywelyn the Great. By the fifteenth century the right of sanctuary had got out of hand or, as Mr Owen put it: 'It became a centre for bandits and murderers who had fled from wherever they had carried out their misdemeanours and the law couldn't touch them. They plundered and robbed and no one was safe within about twenty miles of here. Eventually they were driven out of the area by one Meredith ap Ieuan, the founder of the house of Gwydir whose castle stands on the left bank of the Conwy opposite Llanrwst'. Then the village settled down to mind its own business with farming and slate quarrying as the two occupations. The slate quarries closed down in the 1930s, and by the 1950s the chapel congregation had dwindled from over 400 to less than 150. It was Thomas John Roberts, the miller, who realised during the war that unless life was made easier and brighter the young people would all leave the village and it would soon die. He decided to bring some light into their lives, and installed a turbine generator in his mill at a cost of £150. He charged the villagers half-a-crown per quarter per lamp, or seven shillings and six pence for four, but since his own power source was free water there was no restriction on how much of his electricity they used. The mill building is still there, as is the overshot water-wheel. The mill race came from a mill pond behind a dam higher up the river built by Mr Roberts' grandfather and reached the wheel down a wooden trough, of which only a truncated bit remains. The river bed here is made of large tilted shelves of smooth rock so the water cascades over dozens of shallow ledges and swirls like liquid amber between the rocks for it has only just left the peat.

From Ysbyty Ifan the Conwy wanders down a widening valley along its rocky bed to reach the main A5 London–Holyhead road and there it turns and runs northwards beside the road to Betws-y-Coed. It has now left the wilderness of moor and hill farms to travel through wooded gorges flanked by fine houses and gardens. It is not easily seen from a car on the road, which is narrow and busy with very few lay-bys. It is better followed on foot, and in winter when in spate it is noisy and angry, bashing its

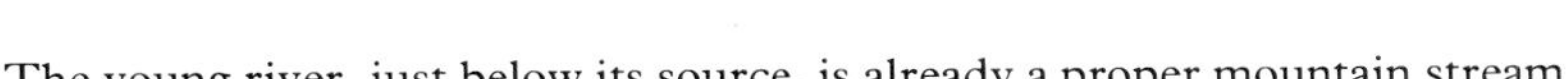
The young river, just below its source, is already a proper mountain stream

By Ysbyty Ifan, its first village, the stream has swollen to a broad river

way over rock and boulder. Come winter's snow and ice this bit of Wales becomes an Alpine fairyland – in fact there is a stretch just before Betws called the Fairy Glen which is dramatic and photogenic at all seasons. But first there are the Conwy Falls, *808 535*, split into two by a massive pinnacle of rock; the water pours over a flat top into an eighty-foot chasm where it boils and whirls before sorting itself out and flowing on. Although the drop is almost vertical, there are ledges and protruding rocks on the way down so that it would seem quite impossible to shoot these falls in a canoe and live. I had always believed that it had never been done until one winter weekend in 1986 I happened to arrive below the falls just in time to see a canoeist come cartwheeling down and survive. It was the best missed picture of my career. The falls can be reached by walking up from the gorge of the Fairy Glen or through a pay turnstile beside a café at the junction of the A5 and the road signposted to Penmachno. The Conwy is a salmon river, but not above those falls!

A few yards beyond a woollen mill by the river Machno is Roman Bridge, *807 529*, a thin sliver of moss-covered stone arch without side walls high above the river in the ravine below. It is not Roman, but very old anyway. The Machno Falls beyond Roman Bridge are attractive without being impressive. The water tumbles in and out of rock pools until at the last moment it plunges into a dark hole under a total canopy of trees. Penmachno is a village of grey stone and darker slate, and the home of Mr Boon, North Wales' last basketmaker. He uses rattan cane from the tropics, willow from Somerset and rushes from Holland for making and repairing chair seats. His cottage is his showroom, and he works in an outbuilding, which was the slaughter-house, on the banks of the Machno in which he soaks bundles of cane and willow to make them supple for use.

Instead of going back to the A5 and its heavy summer traffic, take the narrow lane which carries on beyond the Machno Falls, dropping steeply through thick woods to a stone bridge, *796 541*, over another Conwy tributary, the Lledr, which runs through countryside very reminiscent of parts of the Lake District with fell-like hills criss-crossed by stone walls. To see it at its best climb the hill to Dolwyddelan Castle, *721 521*, variously thought to have been the birth-place of Llewelyn the Great or to have been built by him in the thirteenth century. From its crenellated tower – the crenellations being a nineteenth century embellishment – there are long views up and down the valley with its backdrop of mountains. Perched on its crag above the river, the castle has a bleak foreboding air on days when storm clouds scurry low, and it is easy to imagine how it must have concentrated the minds of any marauding tribe with ill intent. It was one of the

Dolwyddelan Castle, commanding the Lledr valley, is thought to have been either the birthplace of Llewelyn the Great or to have been built by him in the thirteenth century

strongholds of Llewelyn's grandson, Llewelyn the Last, during his struggle against Edward I who took it in 1283. This beautiful glacial valley has been saved twice from vandalism in recent years; the first time when the Central Electricity Generating Board decided against using it for a vast pumped storage scheme, and the second time when plans were mooted, but not followed through, to construct a main north–south trunk road through it.

No sooner has the Lledr emptied its fast-flowing mountain water into the quieter Conwy than its other mountain tributary, the Llugwy, joins in at Betws-y-Coed. This has been a popular tourist resort since mid-Victorian times and shows it. Once picturesque in a grey way, it is today awash with colour from petrol stations, cafés, postcard stands and sheepskin rugs dyed in bilious colours. The crowds go a mile up the Lledr to queue at the turnstile to Swallow Falls which have nothing to do with swallows; the English name is the result of faulty translation. In Welsh it is Rhaedr Ewynnol meaning foaming waterfall, not *wennol* which is swallow. And foaming it is as it hurtles into a deep hollow heavily shaded by trees. The Llugwy has the highest source at 1,787 feet of all the Conwy tributaries, and is the one which rises nearest to Snowdon. No wonder it rushes down over spectacular cataracts and falls. The British Canoe Union advise that the Conwy is normally only practical from Llanrwst four miles downstream of Betws, but the Harbour Master at Conwy assures me that canoe parties all the way from Capel Curig Army Training Camp, well up the white water Llugwy, frequently arrive on his doorstep. Capel Curig is *the* climbing centre for North Wales with excellent climbing shops, and Plas y Brenin National Mountaineering Centre which started life as Snowdonia's first mountainside hotel in 1790. One of the finest views of Snowdon and its associate peaks is from the high ground, *718 579*, behind the centre looking down the length of a long lake, Llynnau Mymbyr, which starts and ends with a waterfall. From that point Llanberis Pass is five miles down the valley.

Llanrwst is an ancient town first mentioned in history as Gwrgystu where a battle was fought among the princes of North Wales in AD 954. Here the river is wide, fast-flowing and shallow over a boulder bed, and is spanned by a very elegant bridge designed by Inigo Jones and built in 1626. The parish church of St Grwst stands a little back from the grassy river bank where the townsfolk can stroll and look across the water to the many-tiered Snowdonian mountains. In Gwydir Chapel attached to the church is the large empty stone coffin of Llewellyn-ap-Iorwerth, Prince of Gwynedd. It has no lid, and what happened to the body nobody knows. This little chapel, also designed by Inigo Jones, is full of curiosities including the spurs of one Jenkins, a local outlaw, a sort of North Wales Robin Hood. Across the river is Gwydir Castle, formerly the seat of the Wynn family who were in their time paramount in the area. It is more a collection of domestic buildings assembled over generations than a castle in the military sense; both house and gardens are open to the public. From here a high-level forest walk follows the river back to Betws. Llanrwst has always been an important market town, but in the past it also had a number of small industries being noted for its clogs and boots, and from the seventeenth century for its harp makers. During the Civil War Charles I arrived in Llanwrst while on the run from Cromwell and the local people, being of the Royalist persuasion, helped him – and themselves – by providing him with a boat and sending him on his way down the river to Conwy from where he made his way to Chester.

There are no boats in Llanrwst these days and barely enough water to float one. But I had, for a long time, had the desire to see just how far one could get up it in a small boat following in the wake of the paddle steamers which made trips up and down as far as Trefriw before the last war. My base for the expedition was not beside the river but 1,000 feet above it at a house called Garnedd-Wen at Llangelynin on the slopes of 2,500-foot Tal-y-Fan, possibly the most remote guest house in Wales. From its doorstep there is a wide panoramic view over the walled town of Conwy, its castle and the broad estuary that it guards. For my purpose it was an ideal place to watch for the right weather before making my trip up river, and from a vantage point nearby I could look far up the vale of Conwy, spread out below like a three-dimensional map. Tom Morris, the owner, takes people pony trekking along the hilltops on the western edge of the Snowdon range overlooking the Vale of Conwy. His sheep and ponies graze on the hillside around Llangelynin Old Church, of very primitive design, a good 900 years old but still in use. It was on a drovers' road over the mountains, and parts of two walls still remain of the inn which was attached to the church. Up until the eighteenth century the inn was used by slate workers from quarries further up the mountain as well as drovers. In those days there were quite a few houses around the church, but there is almost no sign of them now. The inn was also a hostel for the sick who made the long steep walk to the church to wash in or drink from the Holy Well in a corner of the churchyard. It was reckoned to cure typhoid which was then rampant.

There is rarely any living proof of the efficacy of Holy Wells, but for this one I have found two witnesses. First Tom Morris told me that some years back he started to lose his hair; his doctor told him this was quite natural and nothing could be done about it. In a spirit of experiment rather than faith he started rubbing water from the well onto his head. Today in his seventies, he has a good head of hair with no sign of baldness. In the village of Henryd in the valley below Mrs Roberts told me how, thirty-one years before, her twelve-year old son fell prey to Huntingdon's Chorea. The hospital doctors sent him home saying there was no more they could do, so the little boy asked his mother to wash him with the holy water. 'I filled bottles with water from the well, warmed it up and washed him all over. He was soon much better and the problem never came back'. Unfortunately he is not alive to confirm his mother's story as he was killed in a road accident in his twenties. But she has newspaper cuttings of the time about the miraculous cure. Tom Morris and I had long discussions about the well. Was it faith alone that brought cures, or was it trace elements with medicinal properties? After all there had been lead mines in the area until recently, and where there is lead there is arsenic and other chemicals.

The distance up the tidal reach to just below Llanrwst is only eleven miles but, depending on tide, wind and the amount of rain which has fallen on the mountains, the Conwy changes from a broad expanse of water, in places a deceptive half-mile wide with somewhere below its surface a deep channel, to a river of mud veined with hopeful looking channels. These mock you with bumps of mud which bury your propeller, beds of weed which cocoon it and shingle banks which dent and bend the blades. Most of these channels turn out to be cul-de-sacs, and when you try to escape by getting out to wade and tow you are liable to fall into a pothole. It is very much a question of going up on the flood and down with the first of the ebb; and if the trip is to be enjoyed to the full you need a spring tide when high water is soon after midday to get ashore for lunch. But it must not be too long a lunch as the river empties very much faster than it fills, and if you are not away within the first hour of the ebb you may run out of water at the other end. I am talking about a cruise in a craft doing three to four knots at the most under its own power, not a fast runabout. You also want a nice day when the sun shines and the air is clear as the scenery for most of the journey is of distant mountains which are dramatic in good light, but which become amorphous smudges in haze or grey light.

Eventually the day came when high tide at Conwy was at 12.30, and one hour twenty minutes later it would reach Tal-y-Cafn six miles up river, roughly half way to Llanrwst and as far as motor cruisers and ski boats normally venture. It is a popular stopping place because of its two pubs – the Ferry Inn on the west bank with a landing stage, waterfront garden and massive saloon bar, and the Tal-y-Cafn Inn on the other bank for those who prefer to talk and drink away from the sound of outboards in a

Inigo Jones's bridge over the river Conwy at Llanrwst can no longer be reached by boat

The steamer quay at Trefriw is now hardly visible, but the tea pavilion is still there as is the brick and stucco building alongside it which once served as a bath house

more intimate setting. It has no landing place but is reached by a Bailey bridge. If Tal-y-Cafn is missed there will be two hours of flood to complete the remaining five miles of the journey, leaving time to go ashore at the other end.

I launched my inflatable boat at the slipway next to the boatyard beneath the back wall of Conwy Castle, just upstream of the three bridges, at nine in the morning to allow plenty of time to watch the bird life and make a couple of stops on the way up. For most of a tide the water sluices through the bridge arches in a wicked looking jet stream causing weird back eddies and whirlpools off the slipway. Once into the stream itself you are shot up-river for a good 100 yards before things calm down. On the ebb, of course, the worry is that if the outboard were to stall you would be taken very fast under the bridges and out into the estuary, and then it could be a mile or more before you came up against a shore. For the first four miles the river winds in broad stately sweeps through the flat pastoral floor of the valley with very green fields edged by pebble beaches which extend to steep slopes of glistening mud as the water runs out on the ebb. Conwy Castle was lost to sight after the first bend and the scenic cruise began. Ahead lay a wide expanse of water diminishing in perspective to meet the backdrop of the Snowdonia massif to west and south.

The first site of interest above Tal-y-Cafn is the little mediaeval church of St Mary at Caerhûn, half hidden in a small plantation atop a hillock rising from the flat west shore. It is worth going ashore and plodding up the hill to take a closer look. The side walls of the nave are thirteenth century and the most modern parts are probably sixteenth century. It is a long, low, dark church very carefully looked after and in regular use although a long way from any sizeable village. What makes a visit here doubly interesting is the fact that the church is in the middle of the site of the Roman fort of Canovium built by the Libyan general Agricola about AD 77. It is sited on the military road over the mountains from Chester to Segontium, now Caernarfon. The layout of the fort is visible in aerial photographs, but it needs a trained eye to discern much of it on the ground. There was a Roman quay at the foot of the hill, and with a very large amount of luck your boat might actually lie alongside what remains of it, but you would probably not recognise the odd few stones for what they were. After this the left (east) bank becomes steep to and wooded while the flat ground on the right is a patchwork of water meadows hidden for the most part either by dykes or beds of tall reeds. If you lift up your eyes you will see, beyond the immediate flatness, the high wall of mountains marching south with the river, its face incised by steep forested valleys each with its mountain stream flowing into the river.

After passing under a footbridge by Plas Maenan one comes by a sharp bend in the river to the grounds of Maenan Abbey which was built to house the Cistercian monks displaced from Conwy Abbey in 1283 when Edward I decided to build his great castle and garrison town there. The few remaining stones of the abbey lie in the gardens of the Maenan Abbey Hotel. From that point on the scenery changes sides. The river moves over to the west and sidles up to the steep hills which come alongside, while water meadows now spread out to the east. I found the site of the old steamer quay a short way downstream of Trefriw, but if I was to make Llanrwst I would have to hurry on. In fact it was not possible to reach Llanrwst, only the Gower footbridge a half-mile before the town. At that point the river runs only inches deep over a wide shoal of boulder and gravel – it looks more like a filter bed than a river, and by the footbridge and at intervals up to and beyond the town are 'Private, No Boats' notices. Strangely, they all face upstream and so cannot act as a warning to intrepid sailors coming up from the sea.

There is barely a trace of the steamer quay other than a line of overgrown dressed stones, but on the bank above were two intriguing buildings. One was a wooden house, in style much like a cricket pavilion, which was originally the tea-room which catered for trippers off the boats. As they came up on the flood and went down before the ebb got going passengers only had a half-hour ashore, hardly time to walk into the village and back, so the tea-room had a captive market. On inquiring I was told that the lady who lived there had died a month earlier. The other building of brick and stucco was at one time a bath house. Between the wars a German doctor ran a form of health hydro in what is now the hotel above. He had his curative water brought down in barrels by horse and cart from a spring in a mountain cave to the bath house where guests from the hotel, now the Princes Arms, went to soak away their ills. With the declaration of war the doctor was interned and the location of his spring has been lost – locals think a rock fall must be hiding the cave entrance. I have heard that the property has been sold at auction and that the buyer will probably demolish the tea pavilion.

Returning to Conwy I found that the water had run out faster than I had anticipated and the slipway was high and dry beyond a barrier of jagged, mussel-encrusted, seaweed-draped rocks. It was still only September, the season had not ended, but it was dark by the time the boat had been painfully hauled over the rocks and stowed in the car boot. It had been a long day for a short but very scenic journey.

River Kent

OS 1:25,000 and 1:50,000 Outdoor Leisure Sheet 7 and Landranger Sheet 97

Before the coming of the steam engine the swiftly running rivers of upland Britain provided the vital water power for much of our industry. The river Kent on the eastern boundary of the Lake District, which falls 2,000 feet in twelve miles, was typical of such rivers having, by the end of the eighteenth century, no less than ninety water-mills along its course. Together with mills on its tributaries, the area of the river Kent supported more manufacturing – largely bobbin, paper, textile and snuff – than would, at that time, have been found in and around Birmingham. By the middle of the last century when steam power had made many industrial water-mills redundant, there were still fifteen in business beside the Kent. Now there is only one which works – not as a museum, but grinding tobacco to make snuff.

The Kent is born of a waterfall at Hall Cove, *441 095*, which drains the high, marshy ground below the old Roman road called High Street, that runs from Ambleside to Bougham reaching a height of 2,719 feet at its summit, *441 110*. At first the Kent starts as a mountain stream in a hurry rushing from its source at 2,300 feet between the steep fells of the Kentmere Valley to almost sea level just before the old wool weaving town of Kendal. From there on it strolls through softly rounded countryside of narrow lanes and sheep farmland to become a part of the landscaped scene of Levens Deer Park, before dissipating itself across the expansive mud flats of its estuary in Morecambe Bay. You can walk from north to south down its valley through 120 million years of geological history; volcanic rock in the high fells, then limestone, grit and slate and then more limestone and softish shale which, being subject to erosion, provided the east-west passes for the old packhorse routes. Near the estuary the flattened valley is overlooked by limestone scars or cliffs which make superb viewing platforms over southern lakeland and Morecambe Bay. It is a walk which could possibly be achieved with great effort in a long day, but certainly the wild part from Staveley to its source or just below is a comfortable day walk for the reasonably fit.

The pub sign of the local inn at Staveley, showing an eagle hovering over an infant, is the crest of Lord Derby, Earl Strickland, one of whose bachelor ancestors fathered a child by a servant girl. As a ploy by which he could take his natural son into the family home he had the infant placed in an eagle's nest where it could be conveniently found by an estate worker. On the 'discovery' of the child he adopted it as his own and made him his heir. The Eagle and Child is a good pub; they do bed and breakfast, and their car park is the last place where it is practical to leave a car before walking up the Kentmere Valley. Photographers who do their own black and white printing will be more than familiar with Kentmere photographic paper which is made in Staveley. The business goes back to 1902 when the two owners of the chemist shop, which is now Boots in Windermere, decided to cash in on the burgeoning lakeland tourist trade by starting what is thought to be the first 'High Street' developing and printing service in Britain. The rapidly growing popularity of taking snapshots, and the increasing number of amateur photographers who wanted to make their own prints, also prompted them to get into the business of making sensitised paper. For this purpose they purchased the old cotton mill at Staveley which had been built in 1785. They used the water wheel to turn a turbine to make their own electricity until the present directors made the momentous decision to stop using it and go onto the mains in 1972 – just in time for the miners' strike! Water for the paper coating process was never taken from the river but from wells. The River Gowan, little more than a stream and only about six miles long, forms an attractive 'canal' through Staveley before joining the Kent. Even that small tributary once provided water for its own seven mills.

Going upstream, the last weir curves gracefully across the river alongside Barley Bridge, *470 987*, by the mill. Over the bridge the road leads to a footpath along the east bank which, after a couple of miles, joins the Dales Way which continues beside the river until Burneside when it turns aside, *506 960*, to go to Yorkshire. The Kent above the weir runs fast over a boulder-strewn bed and is hemmed in on both sides by trees; most delightful in spring when the senses are amused by the sound of rushing water and the sight of spring flowers under freshly leaved trees. The road up the valley crosses over from the left to the right bank at Scroggs Bridge, *467 994*, after which it starts to distance itself from the river, and they do not meet again until Kentmere village. For a walk close beside the water go on up to Ullthwaite Bridge, *456 012*, cross over it and take the footpath through the woods of Kentmere Hall to Kentmere Tarn and beyond. The bridge is a scheduled historic monument.

The tarn, a half-mile-long strip of lake in the path of the river, is of recent origin, replacing a very much larger lake – the Kent Mere – which was drained in 1840 to reclaim land for farming. In the event the land was not much good, most of it remaining too swampy, and the flow of the river was disturbed so that the mills downstream were short of water in dry periods, which was one of the reasons for building the Kentmere Reservoir up near the head of the river. The reservoir's industrial benefit soon waned as improved transport made coal available to steam power and, one after the other, the water-wheels stopped turning.

The beginning of the electrical age in this century called for insulation materials, and one was found in the dried up bed of Kent Mere in the form of diatomaceous earth which consists of billions of minute fossil remains of diatoms – microscopic unicell algae with siliceous cell walls. They were sea creatures, but the shore of the tarn today is 450 feet above sea level! In 1955 two fourteen-foot dug-out boats, thought to be Viking, were excavated from the bed of the mere. The better preserved one is now in the Maritime Museum at Greenwich, and the remains of the other in Kendal Museum. It was about this time that the 'mining' ceased and a sheet of water mysteriously appeared, gradually expanding to form the present Kentmere Tarn. The road proper ends by Kentmere church where there is space for a handful of cars to park. Late arrivers then park wherever they can without appreciating the needs of country life – in gateways, in passing places, and on the verges so that the dust cart, the milk and fuel tankers are blocked, as would be an ambulance or fire appliance. Calls for more parking places are usually met by local objections that this or that place is an area of very fragile ecology, and anyway no one wants the valley scarred with car parks. What may have been decided upon by the time this is read is a barrier at the Staveley end of the valley which can be closed when necessary. This is, of course, a problem throughout the Lake District, and everywhere where people want to go en masse. The trouble is that they nearly all want to use their wheels and not their feet.

The church at Kentmere, *456 041*, is dedicated to St Cuthbert who was a monk at the abbey in Melrose in the seventh century. Widely respected for his spirituality, he chose the life of a hermit on Farne Island, but in 685 he was called from his reclusive life and, reluctantly, accepted the Bishopric of Lindisfarne. He only lived for two more years, but in that short time exercised a considerable ministry throughout the north of England. Some time after his death in 687 the Norse raids started on the east coast, and the monks of Lindisfarne were afraid that his grave would be robbed and his body destroyed so they exhumed his coffin, enclosed it in an outer one of lead, and travelled with it around the north of England and Scotland trying to keep one step ahead of the invaders. His final resting place is not recorded, but there is one theory that the monks wanted to get his remains to Ireland but that they lost them in the river Duddon on their way to the sea. Many of the churches dedicated to St Cuthbert are said to be on sites where his body was rested on the journeyings, and Kentmere is well placed to fit that assumption, being on a main packhorse route until the coming of the turnpike roads. If the story has any truth in it the monks may well have brought his body over the Nan Bield Pass or down from High Street then followed the Kent southwards to get to the coast.

Outside the church stands an ancient yew tree held together with plough chains which, some locals will try and convince you, was planted when St Cuthbert's body was at Kentmere. That is nonsense, but the tree could well be some hundreds of years old; it is still sound, and was given a clean bill of health by a tree surgeon in 1986. Kentmere Hall, *451 042*, is a private farm with a substantial ruin of a defensive pele tower built in the fourteenth century. It was formerly the home of the Gilpin family, the most famous of whom was Bernard Gilpin born in 1517. He was a Protestant divine who got on the wrong side of Queen Mary, or at least the Catholic authorities, and was summoned to London where he would almost certainly have been martyred, but he had an accident on the way. By the time he had recovered the queen was dead and affairs swung back in his favour. Known as the Apostle of the North, he spent a lot of his personal fortune on the care of the poor and educating people in the community.

You can walk along both sides of the upper Kent to the reservoir, both routes starting as farm roads before becoming footpaths only. Up the west side the path passes by Hartrigg Farm, *456 060*, which works in tandem with Kentmere Hall and is the last and most isolated in the valley. The parish of Kentmere,

One of the magnificent views from Scout Scar near Kendal in Cumbria

The river Kent is at its loveliest where it wanders through Levens Hall Deer Park before reaching its estuary

This water wheel of the snuff mill on the river Kent is still used to drive the 200 -year-old machinery

From Sandside, the Kent estuary, whose treacherous quicksands and tides took many lives when people crossed the sands in the days before railways and proper roads

Sizergh Castle near Levens Hall, owned by the National Trust, should be visited, if only for the vivid colours of its Virginia creeper

The quarry road down beside the river Sprint in Longsleddale was paved in the 1930s but is now used only by walkers

The hurrying river Sprint looking downstream from Cleft Ghyll near its source at the head of Longsleddale

Kilnstones farmhouse on the river Sprint, was used in the sixteenth century as a hostelry for packhorse drivers

On the approach to Kentmere Reservoir the steep mountain sides are littered with the spoil from disused slate quarries

which encompasses the valley for seven miles above the church to Nan Bield Pass, *452 097*, and two miles below down to Millriggs Farm, *458 023*, has a population of about ninety, many of them incomers, whereas there were once 400. The valley is dotted with farmhouses, but today there are only five working ones made up of farms which have amalgamated with at least two of them under joint ownership. It is mainly hill farming, sheep and beef cattle. Leaving out the hilltops, the parish is nowhere more than a mile wide. On the approach to the reservoir the steep mountain sides of Ill Bell and Hollow Bank Quarter are littered with the spoil from slate quarries dug into the rock face. The quarries on either side of the river are joined by a causeway along the top of a man-made waterfall over an escarpment of spoil. High up on the east bank a cave gives access to a gallery leading via a steep scree slope to an inner chamber dug out of the slate, as big as the nave of a good size church.

Between the point where the newborn Kent joins the reservoir, and Lingmell Gill tumbles into it, there is a nice spot under a rowan tree, *445 084*, to sit and eat your lunch before walking back along the east bank of the river. On the way the path runs through the 'grounds' of Tongue House, *452 068*, a once fairly substantial stone farm house now a shell with the remains of an ancient settlement beside it which was first discovered in 1969. This sad ruin gives walkers an excuse to rest while they speculate on what it would cost to buy and renovate. Just before reaching Kentmere again a footpath, *465 050*, to Stile End climbs over the fells 1,200 feet to Longsleddale, through which runs the Kent's nearest

The river Kent through Kendal has been tamed with embankments and weirs to prevent flooding

The new Shambles in Kendal; originally the houses were built round yards with narrow entrances which could be closed at night against marauding Scots

neighbour and tributary, the Sprint, the subject of my next chapter.

It is a very different river Kent which flows through Kendal where it once had its own way and frequently caused heavy flooding. Now it has been tamed with embankments and weirs and has to behave itself however much rain falls in the mountains. As far as climbers and walkers are concerned the town is known for its mint cake, a quick-energy food which is carried in almost every backpack and forms part of the survival rations of Marine Commandos in the Arctic. From the Middle Ages, almost the entire population was engaged in the wool industry, particularly a cloth known as Kendal Green. The houses were grouped round courtyards, now known as yards, with narrow entrances which could be closed at night against the depredations of the marauding Scots. The wool merchants had their businesses on the east side of the main street, Highgate and Stricklandgate, with premises going down to the river, where stone steps and stands for washing the woollen cloth can still be found. Production amounted to some 300 laden packhorses a week.

The oldest residence is the Castle Dairy, 1564, near Stramongate Bridge where the roads from Shap and Sedbergh meet. The dairy is also a very self-conscious, but extremely good, restaurant run by two ladies. Booking is absolutely essential, and even a few days in advance may not be enough. A deed dated 3 February 1626 records the sale of a tannery beside Stramongate Bridge for eight pounds and four shillings and an annual rent of two shillings and four pence. The site, with its ample supply of fast-running river water, remained a tannery for the next 250 years. Today it has a more savoury smelling use as a riverside restaurant which opened recently after sympathetic restoration and decoration. Opposite Miller Bridge, the next downstream, and on the corner of Lowther Street is an interesting secondhand book shop; then over Nether Bridge, the last before leaving the town, is Romney's House where the artist died in 1802. It is open to the public insofar as it is now a bed and breakfast house.

The best way to get a quick understanding of Kendal's history, especially the development of industry and farming in the area, is to visit the Museum of Lakeland Life and Industry at Abbot Hall next to the parish church. Farmhouse rooms and workshops of different periods have been recreated with great realism, and there is an abundance of everyday artefacts, all presented in contexts which have minimised the need for intrusive labels. A most excellent museum which rightly was the first winner of the Museum of the Year Award. The church of The Holy and Undivided Trinity is the widest parish church in the country with five aisles in a width of 103 feet. It dates from the early thirteenth century, and inside there is a fragment of an Anglian cross *c* 850; but more impressive are the fifteen angels who watch you from the high ceiling. The corona over the nave altar commemorates Gilpin.

A huge pestle and wooden-sided mortar at the water-powered snuff mill south of Kendal

South of the town the Kent meanders round the four-acre site of Alavna, a Roman fort built of stone and thought to have been occupied from about AD 90 to 340. Tucked into the next bend in the river is Gawith, Hoggarth & Co's snuff mill, *513 903*, which has been grinding tobacco leaf since 1885. Before that it was a marble polishing mill. As far as can be proved from records, a water mill has turned on that site since the twelfth century. The mill building stands a little way to the side of the river and is fed by a mill stream through a mill pond which has a dam and double sluice gates to regulate the flow under the wheel. The mill is built of Westmorland limestone with a floor made of marble which was not suitable for other purposes because its surface was defaced by a large number of fossils.

There was only one man working at the mill when I last visited it, John Powley, and it was his sixty-third birthday so he may be retired by now. He told me that he grinds tobacco leaf from Malawi, Zambia, Zimbabwe, Canada, Brazil, India and Korea. He also does the basic blending at the mill. 'The leaf arrives from the warehouse and I mix up a rough blend depending on how it is going to be ground; wet or dry. If it is to be dry it has to be prepared in a drying room and then ground in the ball mill, a rotating drum with steel balls in it, which is the most efficient way of grinding but it is very noisy. It takes ten to fifteen hours of continuous running before it is ground fine enough. The other way is to grind the leaf wet with pestle and mortar which gives a nice silky finish. Either way certain salts are added, including common salt, and one or two more to bring out the natural bouquet of the tobacco. After that I sieve it to take out any lumps that may be left, and then it goes from here to the factory in town where they add the essential oils and scents. There are a hundred different snuffs – lemon, bergamot, honeysuckle, wallflower are just some of them'.

The drive from a single shaft off the water-wheel is distributed to the grinding machines, which are all over 200 years old, by a series of pinions, bevel gears and belt drives with amazing tolerances and all thickly coated with brown tobacco dust. Pestles the size of bowling pins rumbling round cone-shaped mortars – some with smooth wooden sides, others of cast iron with ridged surfaces – add to the cacophony of slapping belts, clanking gears and metal balls tumbling inside their steel drums. The whole scene could have been invented by an early Victorian Heath Robinson, but it works perfectly – and the power is all from the one water-wheel. But what happens in a dry summer, I asked? 'We have never stopped', John Powley told me. 'As long as there is water coming over the lip of the weir, and there always is, the wheel will turn. I may not be able to run all the machines, but I can always run some'. The wheel produces between eighteen and twenty horsepower, depending on how much water is let through. It is made of wood (iroko now but it used to be teak) and the spokes last about thirty years, the flat blades – which are called buckets – between ten and twelve years.

In the fields across the river from the snuff mill lies the dried up bed of the northern section of the Lancaster Canal which was closed and drained between Kendal and Stainton by the British Transport Commission in 1955. The towpath, which starts from Canal Head in Kendal near the gas works, is still a public right of way and provides a pleasant country walk alongside the Kent passing several bridges, now spanning dry land, until it turns east at Hincaster, *509 850*. From Stainton, *521 854*, there is water in the canal as far as Tewitfield where it has been strangled in a culvert for the benefit of the M6 motorway, and the flight of eight locks badly damaged. From there on south it remains a navigation and is used by pleasure boats as far as Preston with access to the sea via a canal branch to Glasson Dock. The first gunpowder mill, *508 877*, in the north of England was built in 1764 beside the river near Sedgwick, and a footpath from the canal towpath leads to the very overgrown ruins. Half a mile downstream further signs of another gunpowder mill can be found. It was the plentiful supply of ash which made the best charcoal for gunpowder, as much as the water power of the Kent, which decided the location for these gunpowder mills. Production continued until shortly after the First World War, by which time dynamite was being used instead for blasting in mines.

Before entering Levens Deer Park the Kent tumbles down rapids beside a salmon leap, *508 865*, with a viewing platform built above the water on one of the concrete piers of the bridge which carries the new Kendal motorway link-road over the river. Although the Kent has always been a salmon river, a disease almost entirely wiped out the stock a few years back and it may be a long time yet before Kent salmon return to spawn in significant numbers. There are still trout and sea trout, but it is too fast a river for coarse fish. The Kent is at its wildest where it races between the high fells, and at its loveliest where it wanders through Levens Deer Park alongside a mile-long avenue of ancient oaks.

Two footpaths run the length of the deer park, one on each side of the river and both starting at Levens Bridge, opposite the entrance to Levens Hall. Most visitors only walk a little distance along the riverside, usually being more interested in the hall with its garden and sideshows, so the far end of the park is more likely to be deserted and there is a convenient way in at that end over a stile, *506 863*, a mile up the minor road going north out of Hincaster. The river skirts the gardens of Levens Hall, which are

Above Garnett Bridge, here seen from the viewpoint on the A6, is the valley of Longsleddale with the backdrop of snowcapped Harter Fell beyond

useful if I want to do any alterations; it's one committee less to go through'. Places like Garnett Bridge look delightful and timeless to us who only pass through, but to those who have lived a lifetime in them the changes of the last twenty-five years have been traumatic. 'If you look at the house next door what do you see? A small whitewashed cottage with little rooms and little windows, but its value has gone up from £440 to £75,000 since they built the motorway. A friend begged me to buy Bridge House for £4,000 a few years ago; I didn't, and now it is worth over £110,000. I have seen almost the whole village sold bit by bit for £10,000; today it must be worth millions. The old Westmorland farming stock have gone and instead we have the gin and tonic types; they have integrated quite well, but our lovely dialect has gone; it is taught out of the children at school and by television.

'If I speak the local dialect no one knows what on earth I'm talking about except those in the geriatric hospital where I do voluntary work; the nurses haven't a clue. When a sister who had come from London told an old lady who had forgotten her reading glasses to get someone to bring them in, she was quite foxed when the old lady looked up at her and said: "Ah but wars I gahn to git to gah and lait em?" By which she meant: "And who am I going to get to go and find them?"'

Longsleddale is an easy valley to explore, with no very steep parts and, perhaps unfortunately, there is a road suitable for cars for two-thirds of the way up as far as Sadgill, *483 057*. It is only seven miles from Garnett Bridge to the derelict workings of Wrengill Quarry and the man-made waterfall, *473 085*, which is the start of the Sprint. The waterfall is fed by Wren Gill and a dozen other un-named mountain becks. Both sides of the Sprint can be walked, by the tarmac road on the east bank as far as Sadgill or by the old road on the other side which is now more a track, which also stops at Sadgill but was probably the more important packhorse route in olden days. There is no prettier sight along the way than Bridge End, *511 000*, where a short causeway of stones, perhaps the relic of a clapper bridge, leads onto a wooden footbridge across the water in front of a neat, white house set among trees. From there a track leads over the fells to Staveley. A little further on and another bridge, but just flat planking, carries a road to Kilnstones, a farmhouse built in the sixteenth century as a hostelry for packhorse drivers; but a dwelling is known to have existed on the site since 1263 when records describe it as a corn mill, and later it became a fulling mill working for the wool merchants of Kendal. There is some fine oak panel-

A weir on the river Sprint above Sadgill, Longsleddale.

After Sadgill the river runs over gravel flats, rare in the Lake District, meandering in great loops and flooding after heavy rains to leave temporary ox-bows

ling inside the house, and the main room or hall was originally lit by five mullioned windows, but all save two were walled up when the tax on windows came into force in 1695, which imposed on a window only a foot square a sum equal to what an ordinary worker would earn in a week. The whitewashed, rough cast façade of this stone house is a typical local treatment used to further weatherproof the walls. A tumbling white water stream on the fell behind the farm acts as a marker and provides the owners with continuous water music.

Across the valley Yewbarrow Hall, *504 026*, is a seventeenth century farmhouse with a fifteenth century pele tower, now used as a dairy. Although large, with walls six feet thick, it is not a perfect example as it has at some time been truncated and given a gable end on one side. The parish church of St Mary, *501 029*, half way along the valley, comes as a bit of a surprise in so isolated and sparsely populated a place. But it must be remembered that while today only two or three farmers are working the valley, there used to be dozens, and there were water-mills too which have all gone and the population dwindled. Although old in parts, St Mary's is largely a mid-Victorian renovation and is not very exciting. At High Swinklebank Farm, *494 043*, look out for the big barn with a projecting balcony which is peculiar to Lakeland farms. Sadgill, where the road ends at a low arched packhorse bridge, could be mistaken for a very small hamlet, but is in fact a sheep farm with a range of very solid outbuildings which once made up three farms. The whole makes a pretty scene with the bridge in the foreground and the high crags of Shipman Knotts rising up behind. The farmhouse does double duty as the local Mountain Rescue Post. To the left of the bridge a seventeenth century farmhouse known as Low Sadgill is skirted by the south-going track off which the old packhorse road branches away to Kentmere.

Soon after Sadgill the bottom of the valley opens onto gravel flats, which are rare in the Lake District, and the river starts to meander in great loops, flooding after heavy rains to leave behind temporary ox-bows. But soon the valley steepens dramatically and the fells close in again. From here on it is more exciting to leave the quarry track and take to the rough ground beside the water as the river is now an almost continuous cascade of white water in a rocky gorge, with every so often a miniature waterfall gouting from a restricting fissure into a deep, crystal-clear rock pool. As the gradient increases walking becomes rough until the final great cascade below Wrengill Quarry. The quarry site itself has that dark satanic look of all abandoned slate workings, and what remains of cottages, sheds and a tub railway look as if they will tumble further at any moment. Perhaps not a safe place for the heavy footed to walk about. The quarry road, on the other hand, is well preserved, thanks to Uncle Mathew's work in the 1930s. Hairpin bends help to reduce the gradient, and the stone pavé set at an angle to the slope certainly makes the walk back a pleasure.

We must be grateful for the loveliness of this short valley, for twice it came near to being spoilt. In 1845 there was a proposal to make a reservoir on its flat floor above Sadgill, a vandalism which was only abandoned after they had counted the cost of the Kentmere reservoir. Then there were those buckets that might have trundled back and forth in the sky. To those recently come to know Longsleddale it has a secret which it does not reveal. Below the surface of this idyllic dale there is another waterway flowing through pipes and tunnels; it is the subterranean aqueduct carrying water from Haweswater. The scars have long since healed so no one need know it is there.

The Sprint cascades over the Falls below the old slate quarry at the start of its headlong rush down Longsleddale

River Esk

OS 1:25,000 Outdoor Leisure Sheet 6

The most stimulating first sight of Eskdale is from the western side of Hardknott Pass, above the great Roman fort, *219015*, which lies in plan view on the mountainside. From there you look down on the valley shared by woods and sheep farms with their patchwork of pastures bounded by the high green fells. The river Esk is discernible by the trees which line its banks. The only straight line in the picture is the horizon of the Irish Sea in the far beyond. Roman troops posted to the fort would have arrived at the port of Glanoventa, a tidal lagoon formed by the estuaries of the Irt, Mite and Kent rivers. Seeing it today – a place only suitable for boats which can take the ground, which they have to do for long hours of every day – it is surprising that it could have served the Romans as a major port of equal importance with Chester. They completely ignored the Mersey, Ribble and Morecambe Bay. Their third port serving the Irish Sea coast was, equally surprising, Bowness-on-Solway which was also the most westerly fort at the end of Hadrian's Wall. Today it stands on the salt marshes without a vestige of shelter and with a tide which rushes in and out like an express train.

One can only surmise that the coasts and foreshores were very different 2,000 years ago and that Glanoventa, which is now called Ravenglass, was accessible at all states of the tide with a reasonably deep water anchorage; it was definitely a little further inland to the east of today's village. Now, what water there is at Ravenglass lies behind extensive sandbanks which only half cover at high water and through which the river Esk maintains an extremely narrow and shallow channel. A few local yachts berth there to spend half their lives sitting on the mud. But once a year in July Ravenglass becomes an important yachting venue when the fleet of boats competing in the Three Peaks Race put in there for the run to the top of England's highest mountain, Scafell. The race, which started in 1976, is a sailing and running endurance test in which the yachts race from Barmouth in Wales to Fort William in Scotland, and en route a pair of runners from each boat must disembark first at Caernarfon for a twenty-four mile return run and 3,560-foot climb to the summit of Snowdon. They land again at Ravenglass for a thirty-two mile run and 3,210-foot climb of Scafell Pike, and at Fort William they scale Ben Nevis, 4,406 feet, and a seventeen mile run to the finishing line. With the backing of *The Daily Telegraph* during its first ten years, the event now attracts a fleet of over thirty boats.

It is at Ravenglass that the race is often lost and won, or as one skipper put it: 'For many of us the race starts all over again at Ravenglass. You can arrive there five or six hours ahead of the next yacht and than have to wait that time for the flood tide to get you in, by which time the others have caught up with you. So you all start again'. Equally frustrating for keel boats which get in on time is when the two runners come down to find there is not enough water left to get out. Multi-hulls and boats with lifting keels can occasionally get in and out on one tide, but their runners have got to be up Scafell Pike and down again in about four and a half hours. The average time is five and a half to six hours. Incidentally, the record time for the entire race up to 1987 was three days three hours fifty-seven minutes, set in 1985. Looking at the map it would seem feasible for the Scafell section to be routed up the Esk valley, there being footpaths alongside the head of the river and its tributary, Little Narrowcove, which lead to the summit. But that is not the way the runners go; in fact they go well to the north round the top of Wast Water.

Locally the Three Peaks Race is a one day wonder; the Ravenglass and Eskdale Railway is the permanent attraction. It was built as a three-foot gauge railway between 1875 and 1876 to carry iron ore seven miles from the Nab Gill mines above Boot in Eskdale. The mines failed in 1882, but the railway struggled on carrying local goods and tourists until 1912, when it was closed as unsafe. In 1955 Mr Bassett-Lowke of toy train fame came to the rescue and organised its conversion to fifteen-inch gauge, which it is today, to carry scale model locomotives and rolling stock. After that it had several owners until, in September 1960, it was auctioned off for £12,000 to the recently formed Ravenglass &

Hardknott Castle, a Roman fort, stands in plan view on the mountainside with the high fells above and a patchwork of pastures in the valley below

Eskdale Railway Preservation Society which had raised the money through a national Save the Little Railway campaign in the media. It now operates a local commuter service all the year round, and is a major tourist attraction from spring into autumn.

Despite its name, the railway does not run through the Esk valley until near the end of its journey. On leaving Ravenglass it runs north-east alongside the river Mite and the steep to, north side of Muncaster Fell. It comes down into Eskdale at Eskdale Green, *145 998*, two and a half miles before its terminus at Dalegarth Station, *174 007*. The Esk makes a sharp hairpin bend from the inner end of its entrance channel at Ravenglass to run due south before turning north-east past the grounds of Muncaster Castle, which has a renowned rhododendron garden and an early fourteenth century pele tower which are open to the public from Easter until the first Sunday in October on Tuesday, Wednesday, Thursday and Sunday afternoons. The main building is a private residence. If travelling by car the river can be joined at Muncaster Bridge, *113 964*, on the A595, and just past there a minor road, Birkby Lane, runs close by the river for about five miles to cross it at Forge Bridge, *149 995*, just out of Eskdale Green. This route gives intermittent views of the water, a continuous view of Muncaster Fell, and far away to the north-west glimpses of the Scafell massif.

Half-way along at Knott End there is quite a surprise – a tarn, *134 977*, with little peninsulas and islets looking as pretty as a picture and too good to be true, and it is not marked on the map! It is a man-made three and a half acre waterscape created by Bill Arnold and stocked with brown, rainbow and American brook trout. Anglers can book day or evening rods, and tuition is given in roll and Spey casting by Hugh Falkus, a well-known game angler and author. Fishing at Knott End is obviously more for the sport than the pot; one regulation says: 'The daily kill limit is one brace. Anglers must release all other fish *unharmed* (their italics) – by running a hand down the leader and removing the hook with the fish in the water. Anyone not observing this rule may be requested to stop fishing'. With the rods spaced thirty yards apart in this relatively small tarn, there must be many fish that have been left *unharmed* many times – but I doubt if they would put it that way. In unexpected contrast to the fishing business is the Good Health Clinic run by Bill Arnold's wife Marie. In a miniature clinic in one of the outbuildings she offers remedial massage using infra-red, intra sound, ultra sound and magnetic pulse, and aromatherapy; she gives advice on diet and nutrition and dispenses homoeopathic medicines. A little way before Knott End a footpath leads to the far side of the river over Stocks Bridge and then accompanies it for a while before turning away to Eskdale Green. Further on the road itself runs right beside the water and there is an ideal spot along that stretch to have a picnic and, for children, a paddle where the water runs cool and shallow over smooth stones.

A riverside footpath from Forge Bridge makes a very pleasant walk through trees to sixteenth century Dalegarth Hall, *170 001*, the home of the Stanley family since mediaeval times. It was an Edward Stanley, High Sheriff of Cumberland, who proclaimed the Prince of Orange as King William III at Carlisle Cross in November 1689. It is a private house, but its distinctive tall round chimneys are easily seen from the path, which then brings you to the access stile to Stanley Ghyll and thence to Stanley Force, *174 995*, which falls sixty feet in a narrow gorge of black granite. The waterfall was not as impressive as I had expected; like all water scenes, it needs sunlight to give it sparkle and shape. Unfortunately, it faces due north and is only really well lit for a relatively few hours a year during those midsummer evenings when there is no cloud cover. It also needs plenty of rain to make it live up to its name of 'force', and midsummer tends to be a dry period. However, the walk up the ghyll is altogether delightful. It starts as a gently sloping, wooded glen with much oak, some hazel and rowan. After a short distance the ascent steepens and the way is partially blocked by literally tons of boulders washed down by floods in 1962, but they have left plenty of room to scramble round them. The torrent is now noisy as it tumbles down its rock course and the atmosphere is damp with airborne spray. It is a world of brilliant green sphagnum moss which holds water like a sponge, common liverwort and ferns. The path crosses the turbulent water over three wooden footbridges wedged into what has become a deep, dark, narrow canyon from whose steep sides trees, mostly rowan, miraculously grow out of the apparently solid rock. In summer the leaf canopy almost blocks out the daylight, and everywhere water trickles and splashes down from fissures. It only needs a hot day for the imagination to make it into a tropical ravine. From the third bridge one gets an oblique look at the falls, but it needs a climb off the path and along a narrow shelf to get round a slight bend for a full frontal view of the force.

To the right of the last bridge a very steep track goes up above the falls to where, in the middle of a veritable forest of rhododendrons, one comes to the bare stone edge of the sheer, flat, black, vertiginous wall of the canyon. The falls can only be seen by looking over the edge, and for that I would suggest it is best to lie on your stomach. The normal route to Stanley Ghyll starts from the railway terminus at Dalegarth where there is a very big car park. From there go 250 yards along the road to the schoolhouse, turn left down a lane and over Trough House Bridge, *172 004*. Downstream of the bridge a very deep pool has been chiselled out of the rock by debris carried along by the rushing melt water of a last Ice Age glacier – as have so many Lakeland gorges, ravines and deep pools. It is a picturesque geological scene which is somewhat lost on very hot days when it becomes an impromptu swimming pool and discarded clothing is draped over rock and bush. From the bridge the way to the force is well signposted.

Dalegarth terminus is a great place for steam buffs who can look at, and fondly pat, the locomotives as they stand patiently puffing beside the platform. Otherwise, in high season it is just another crowded tourist centre with its café, shop and booking office. Fortunately, the very obvious attractions of a steam railway running through beautiful countryside draw the tourists as a magnet does filings, which leaves the tiny hamlet of Boot, just up the road, reasonably uncrowded at most times. One can say that Boot is unspoilt, a huddle of white, stone cottages close enough together, and the one lane narrow enough, to deter parking by all but the most uncouth – and they are soon asked to move. Customers of the Burnmoor Inn (seven bedrooms) have use of a car park tucked away almost out of sight. Parts of this pub date back 300 years and, although the present décor is alien to its age, it has retained some of its old character. Anyway, the décor goes unnoticed when the place fills up with climbers and walkers, who look so much more in keeping with the countryside than the car borne sightseers. After a walk along the tops they are a hungry crowd and Tony Foster, the landlord, keeps a good kitchen.

He looks a rather urbane gentleman who might in the past have managed a superior hotel or restaurant. Not so; in the past he was a shepherd. If you should happen upon a time when The Burnmoor is quiet – difficult in the summer – and Mr Foster is in the mood to join you, then you will have the chance to be a wiser person when you leave. His knowledge of Lakeland, and Eskdale and Wasdale in particular, is not only encyclopaedic but, if the word is acceptable in this context, grassroots. As well as shepherding, he is skilled at drystone walling and told me that he found it very therapeutic. 'You have to have a certain artistry perhaps to be a good wall worker. You must know exactly the stone you want and pick it up from the thousand lying at your feet. You can be out on a wall all morning and you are throwing stones down and getting very annoyed because none of them seem to fit. You go home and have your lunch, come back and every stone goes on right. You have a different feeling in you'. I know only too well what he means, having spent many a morning trying to get a first paragraph right and then churned out pages in the afternoon.

The basic construction he describes as: 'One on two and two on one. Like laying bricks, you have to break your joints. The larger stones go on the bottom so the wall rises from about two feet wide to eighteen inches. It is really two walls with small stones filling in between. At a certain height it is prudent to put a stone that goes through one side to the other to lock your wall. The wall should be capped so that it is rather proud and there is a projection which the sheep hits if it tries to jump over. The capping stones must tilt in harmony with the lie of the land. The average height will be about five and a half feet, but some go up to six feet, to deter the athletic Herdwick ewes. Most walls were originally up to 200 years old at the start of the Clearances, which went on in Cumberland as in Scotland. They were built to divide the fields at a time when there was no wire netting and hedgerows would not grow like they do in the south. Also, it was a good way to clear fields of stones. If a few stones fall down it costs you nothing more than a couple of hours to put them back, and when it is a real, hell-fire gale the sheep and cows, and even man, can put their backs against a good stone wall and have shelter.' From him I also learnt the reason why hounds in the Lake District are always light and bright in colour. It is because horses are not used, so the hounds have to be watched on foot from afar. 'We try to breed them light so you can pick them out as they go across the fell, otherwise they would be as visible as little maggots'.

They say that no self-respecting farmer in Lakeland would be seen without his walking stick or shepherd's crook made by Arthur Irving of Bridge End, Boot. Now in his eighties, he still climbs an outside ladder every day to his workshop in the loft of a barn beside his cottage to make the sticks, which have a fame far beyond the fells. His tools are simple – surforms and files, a vice, brace and bit and hot water. His raw materials are mostly hazel, blackthorn when he can find it, very occasionally laburnum and sheep horn. He goes looking for good straight sticks in December and January when the sap is drawn, and combines that work with the pleasure of following the hounds. His more elaborate sticks have horn handles turned into a variety of shapes. 'I can turn horn over a fire, but if you don't watch it closely it takes all the nature out of it so I use boiling water which softens it so you can pull it out straight or twist if to any shape you need'.

From the pub the lane leads a short distance to a bridge over Whillan Beck and a water-mill which has been working since at least 1578 when, according to the Great Survey of all lands belonging to the Percy family who were Lords of the Manor, the tenancy was held by Robert Vicars and his brother Henry for eight shillings per annum. It is thought that a mill almost certainly operated on the site in the thirteenth century, possibly even in Roman times to supplement the supplies at Hardknott fort. The mill prospered in the hands of several families who all held it for many years until the 1920s when it was converted to drive an electricity generator. The village did not get mains electricity until the 1950s which, even so, was quite early for that area. Now restored to full working order it is owned by Cumbria County Council and has been open to the public since 1976, but it is nothing like as well-known as the railway or Stanley Force. In 1986 the then custodian, Pamela Swinson, told me that it was visited by fewer than 4,000 people between April and September. As her pay was linked to the number of people going in at forty-five pence a time I was not surprised that she was leaving for a better situation, even though the very pretty miller's cottage and garden went with the job.

I understand that figures have risen since 1986, and they deserve to for Eskdale Mill, as it is called, is a most picturesque and instructive site looking just as it always did – unencumbered by car park, souvenir shop and other so-called tourist facilities. Behind the mill a path takes you round the mill's water system from where a leat leaves the beck, just above a small waterfall, to supply a pond which has a sluice gate controlling the flow of water along a mill race carried in a wooden trough, from which it pours over the twelve foot diameter overshot wheel. Theoretically the overshot wheel is the most efficient type as it does not need a fast flowing stream, only an abundant flow. Breast wheels receive their water from a mid point round the circumference and undershot wheels – the cheapest to construct – are driven by the water flowing under them with the speed of that flow having a direct effect on the horsepower developed. There are actually two wheels; the second was added along with a second pair of grindstones in the middle of the eighteenth century, but only the original one now turns.

Corn is the generic term for most types of grain and usually refers to wheat, barley and oats. Wheat and barley would dry in the fields, but oats, which was the grain mostly ground at Eskdale Mill, holds more moisture and needs to be artificially dried. This was done by spreading it over perforated iron plates set in the top floor, known as the kiln, heated by hot air from a peat fire on the floor below. The dried grain was shovelled down a shute to a hopper and a feed shoe which was vibrated to shake it into the eye of the runner, or upper stone. The diameter of the stones was five feet, they were grooved so that they cut the kernel of the grain like scissors, and the upper stone was slightly convex to allow the grain to spread out from the eye to the circumference where it spilled into a 'box' then down a funnel to the lower floor. The stones did not actually touch each other, but were adjusted to leave a slight gap between them which determined the grade of the flour. This required the stones to be very finely balanced which, considering their weight and the apparent crudity of the wood and iron structure of the machinery, must have needed a very special patience and skill. Oats needed to be ground twice, the first time to burst the kernel from the husk, called skelling, and a second time with the stones set closer together to grind the flour.

A sack hoist powered off the revolving axle of the water-wheel was used to lift heavy sacks from the floor below. This hoist was controlled by an ingenious mechanism whereby a sack reaching the upper floor struck a plate which automatically threw the hoist out of gear and closed a trap-door under the sack. Among the many pertinent and interesting exhibits within the mill is a bowler hat. The miller always wore one as protective headgear and as a sign of rank when he went to the Corn Exchange and that, they say, is how the bowler came to the City and why it is always worn by those little fellows in the TV commercials.

At Eskdale the miller enjoyed peat digging and grazing rights on the moor above Boot and brought his peat down by horse and sledge. Most mills ended up using coke, but Eskdale remained peat-burning to the end of its working days. A good inn, venerable cottages, a maker of walking sticks and an unspoilt working water-mill together make Boot well worth visiting; but there is still more, much more, to explore. Over the packhorse bridge and beyond the mill vestiges of the Nab Gill iron ore mines can be very clearly seen. First there are what look like great streaks of pink paint running down the steep mountainside; they are the spillage of haematite, a sesquioxide of iron or, more prosaically, iron ore which was mined near the fell top. The name haematite describes the colour of the ore, haema being the Greek for blood. Then there are the still well-defined stone walled ramps of the self-acting inclined railway used to bring the ore down to the three-foot gauge railway which linked the mines to the main railway at Ravenglass. Wagons on two parallel tracks were connected

The walk up Stanley Ghyll in Eskdale is altogether delightful, starting in a wooded glen and ending in a steep canyon where rowan trees grow out of the apparently solid rock

The soggy ground around the little frequented Eel Tarn on the Eskdale Fells above Boot is decorated with fluffy fruiting cotton grass in May and June

Whillan Beck, between Boot and Gill Bank Farm in Eskdale, is a mile-long succession of waterfalls and tranquil pools

All the peaks of the 3,000-foot Cuillins can be seen from the sea as you enter Loch Scavaig

The anchorage in Loch Scavaig. The skipper going to fetch water from the 'Mad Burn' (All t a' Chaoich) at the foot of the Cuillins

by a long cable which ran round a wheel at the top of the incline. Loaded wagons running down under gravity pulled a string of empty ones up to the top to be loaded. After loading at the top and unloading at the bottom the process started again.

At the foot of the incline the layout of Boot Station, the former railway terminus with its passenger platform and loading bays, can still be traced on the ground. The wooden building on the platform, the only one along the line with a lavatory conveniently built over a stream, has gone but the shell of the stone mine building of the 1850s is standing. There is the window of the manager's office through which miners were paid, and on the other side of the room a view up the inclined railway to the adits, the horizontal entrances to the mines. Other parts of the building were a store, a drying room and a smithy. The work of the miners was always wet and they used hand drills, so a constant supply of sharp ones was essential to keep production going. Well away from the office and smithy are the stones of a low, round, thick walled shelter which was the magazine. Blasting was done by gunpowder before 1874 when Nobel's new dynamite was introduced after a convincing demonstration at Muncaster Tarn near Ravenglass. Before the railway the ore was transported by horse and cart at a cost of ten shillings a ton, which was a third of the profit gone. The railway brought the cost down to one shilling and nine pence a ton. However, the mines never lived up to their expectations, the ore was soon worked out and they closed in 1882. It was the end of a very long era – Iron Age man had smelted iron ore along the Esk, but he must have been very inefficient as his cinders are still working out absolutely full of iron.

A footpath up Boot Bank to the top of the iron workings crosses Eskdale Moor, an area of Bronze Age circles, to Burnmoor Tarn, *18 04* after which the pub at Boot is named. A continuation of that path goes all the way up to Scafell Pike. A more likely walk is across the top of the mines to Blea Tarn, *166 010*, a pretty stretch of water, and then back down the steep fell to the road at Beckfoot Bridge, *169 004*, over the Whillan just before it runs into the Esk. From there it is a half mile back up the road to Boot. Just before the bridge in Boot there is a gated farm road, which looks private but is public, running alongside Whillan Beck to Gill Bank Farm, *181 018*. It starts beside Boot Falls which, in my opinion, are far more picturesque and intimate than the accredited sights like Stanley Force because, except when the beck is in full spate, it is possible to walk about among them on slabs of rock with the water rushing and tumbling about you. Exactly which stretch of the beck constitutes Boot Falls is difficult to say because there seems to be no end. All the way for a mile to the farm there is a constant succession of cascades and little forces, rock weirs and white water rapids with here and there

The old carding mill on Whillan Beck by Gill Bank has been re-roofed but otherwise stands blind and neglected

The delightful and ancient hump-backed packhorse bridge at the meeting of Lingcove Beck and the river Esk

a tranquil pool. It is not possible to keep beside the water all the time and stone walls – which on no account should be climbed over – force you back onto the roadway at least twice.

A right of way through Gill Bank Farm takes you over a bridge to an old carding mill which still has its water-wheel, but its windows are boarded up – or were at the end of 1987. For years it was occupied by an old wood turner whose work was much admired. He died and the mill was burned so that only the walls were standing. It was bought by an American who re-roofed it and tried but failed to get planning permission to convert it into a home, so it now stands blind, forlorn and quite unattractive. The mill pool and race are almost lost in undergrowth and grass, but the weir still tinkles on. A few hundred yards upstream a lovely waterfall, or force, drops a sheer twenty feet into a deep pill known as Buck Pot, *181 021*. Back just before the farm a footpath turns off to the right to join an old peat track which winds up the fell to Eel Tarn, *189 019*, a little hand mirror of water with Harter Fell above it. The ground around is very soggy so walking means striding from one tussock to another. Not greatly frequented, it is typical of dozens of lonely pools to be found all over the high fells. It is decorated with flowering cotton grass in May and June and water-lilies from July to September, and birdwatchers could stay content there for hours. To go on up the track past Eel Tarn is a strenuous hike to the high tops over Great How and Slightside to Scafell. The other way is a downhill path to the Woolpack Inn, *190 010*, beside the road to Hardknott Pass. The inn is a popular base for walkers and climbers making for Harter Fell and Scafell.

A most pleasant walk from Boot to the Woolpack avoiding the road goes from Brook House, at the end of the lane up to Boot, down a track to Esk View Farm and thence to St Catherine's Church, *176 003*, on the river bank, a plain but neat seventeenth century granite building. From there a path follows beside the river a couple of miles to Doctor Bridge, *189 007*, passing on the way a pair of girders over the river by Gill Force. They are all that remain of a branch railway line from Dalegarth to an iron ore mine on the south side of the Esk. At Doctor Bridge the path meets a farm road going one way a few hundred yards to the main road just by the Woolpack Inn, and the other way through Penny Hill Farm, *194 008*, along the base of Birker Fell to the bottom of Hardknott Pass and Brotherilkeld Farm, *213 014*, which marks the start of the Esk as a mountain stream. Penny Hill Farm is a bed and breakfast house with a self-catering cottage attached. It has all the charm of a house built in 1731 with massive stone walls and wooden floors which slope every which way. The dining room, where one breakfasts at a table which would seat a dozen with ample room, seems surprisingly big for a farmhouse, but then Penny Hill Farm was originally an inn and beer house, when it would have been a public room. The farm was bought by Beatrix Potter who later gave it to the National Trust. It is a working sheep farm and when I stayed there Ralph and Margaret Jackson, the current tenants, were pretty despondent as they faced their second year of restrictions following the Chernobyl disaster.

From Brotherilkeld Farm to Lingcove Bridge, *227 036*, is a gentle two mile stroll into the foothills of the Scafell massif. The path keeps faithfully beside the river which, for the first few hundred yards, runs through a glade, but one is soon out on the open rocky fell by the young river, frolicking its way downhill between gullies, spilling out of rock pools and behaving in every way like the mountain stream it is. There is one good waterfall half way along the route and lots of miniature ones. Lingcove Bridge, a delightful and ancient hump-backed packhorse bridge named after the beck it spans, is a most satisfying destination. Just below the bridge the Esk comes rushing down a staircase of five falls, and above the bridge the short Lingcove Beck has its own moment of glory as it appears, as from nowhere, over a ledge to drop foaming-white down a sheer cleft into a boulder-strewn bed. Not until it has reached the bridge does it hesitate; for a moment it is quiet as it flows through a clear pool before taking a tumble into the Esk. The old packhorse route goes on beyond the bridge, but from there on the going becomes steep so there is no more strolling, but when the weather is set fair there is no reason why the fit and able walker should not follow it as it keeps beside the Esk and its numerous falls right to its source below Esk Pike at about 2,500 feet.

Loch Scavaig and Loch Coruisk

OS 1:25,000 Outdoor Leisure Sheet 8, The Cuillin and Torridon Hills

The sea was like ripple glass and there was barely enough wind to keep the ghoster filled. But the spring sun shone and the sky was blue as we lunched and lazed our way past the Point of Sleat and across the entrance of Loch Slappin to our anchorage for that night at the head of Loch Scavaig, *486 196*, which lies tucked right in under the 3,000-foot Cuillins on Skye. Always ahead of us were their twenty still snow-streaked peaks, and as the sun moved lower during the afternoon their every craggy detail was thrown into sharper and deeper relief until we were almost under them and, in an instant, the sun was blocked out. The inner recesses of the loch, being completely walled-in by the mountains, were in deep shadow when we dropped anchor, black walls rising from black water.

The final approach to the anchorage is dotted with rocks which remain just submerged or barely awash at low water, and the anchorage itself is in a pool behind an islet called Eilean Glas, with a rock sixty yards off its western end. The way in is between the islet and the rock in the centre of a sixty yard channel, and a course should then be kept along the line of sand on the bottom which can be seen by a look-out in the bows; it forms a light track between the blackness of the kelp-covered rocks either side. There are two fathoms in the pool and mooring rings on the shore and the islet, which it is wise to use because it is a wicked place for squalls which can hit Loch Scavaig unpredictably from any direction off the mountains. On the west side of the pool a tumble of waterfalls drops down the face of the mountain, and on the east side the fresh water from Loch Coruisk cascades over a great rock sill into the sea. On the islet a colony of seals watches with seemingly critical eyes as you drop anchor and furl sails. Everyone was struck by the drama of the place, some of us thought it was spookie.

One of the reasons for going to that anchorage is to row ashore to an iron ladder beside the weir-like sill and walk across the moraine barrier to Loch Coruisk, the most impressive example of a glacial valley in Britain. It is ringed by a nine mile horseshoe of gabbro peaks which are reflected in the dark water. The loch, 125 feet deep, has a wild and lonely foreboding, primordial aspect. Walking boots exchanged for deck shoes, we walked and scrambled along one side of the loch over layers of glacial debris. Huge chunks of black rock with the texture of sandpaper and called whale backs, which is what they look like, litter the sloping foreshore so you have to walk up and down them, and squelch through boggy ground between them, which makes it an exhausting walk, and being pestered by Highland flies does not improve matters. But it is worth every step for the awe-inspiring scenery, the solitude and the quality of the light which changes the rock from black to purple, then grey and back again to black as the sun sinks below the peaks with a final flare of bright light.

Not quite two miles long, nowhere wider than 800 yards and almost completely walled in by the Cuillins, it has a grandeur far above its size which is best appreciated not by walking round the shoreline but by making the effort to scramble up to the spot height marked 143 (metres) on the OS map, *493 196*. From there the surrounding Cuillins are seen in better perspective, and the scale and shape of Coruisk, pointing like a dagger at the heart of the massif, can be better appreciated. The first time I crossed the rock sill and stood looking up the loch I thought it would make an eminently suitable location for a James Bond film. The crew saw it, as do all climbers, as a direct route to the ridge of the Cuillin horseshoe. Carrying ropes and climbing shoes, they made a bee line for The Slabs, *47 20*, a forty degree incline of rock which leads up to the 2,300 foot Sgurr Dubh Beag, *465 204*. It can be taken at a scramble using hands and feet going up, but a rope is needed on the descent because if you move too fast you cannot stop. The Slabs are considered an easy route for a rock climber of reasonable skill, but not one to be attempted by those whose experience is limited to hill walking. With its twenty munroes – peaks over 3,000 feet – and black gabbro, a coarse crystalline

The best views of the whole Cuillin range are from Elgol on the east shore of Loch Scavaig

igneous rock which offers reliable hand and foot holds, the Cuillin massif provides some of the best climbing in Europe. The easiest peak is Bruach na Frithe, *461 252*, whose summit can be reached in about four hours from the base of its north-west ridge by scrambling rather than climbing, but otherwise most of the peaks require considerable climbing skill. The weather can be as difficult, with mists suddenly rising from the surrounding sea cutting visibility down from miles to feet. Landmarks vanish and, because of the magnetic content of the rock, a compass may tell lies and lead you into danger.

Loch Coruisk was, until early in the last century, a very secret place because high mountains and the corries which they embrace were looked upon with dread as being peopled by malevolent spirits. Then came the turnpike roads and the steamers, and people with more imagination than fear began to travel and to marvel. They returned home and, in words and sketches, endowed the places they had been to with a romance and glamour quite beyond the comprehension of the natives. Sir Walter Scott was one of the first publicists for the Isle of Skye, and after visiting Loch Coruisk by rowing boat sent off from the Lighthouse Commissioner's ship, he described it in *The Lord of the Isles*, to which Turner added his sketches, in the following verses:

> For rarely human eye has known
> A scene so stern as that dread lake
> With its dark ledge of barren stone
> . . . above – around – below
> Nor tree, nor shrub, nor plant, nor flower
> Nor aught of vegetative power
> The weary eye may ken.

One must assume that Sir Walter did not walk far around the loch side or, coming to the far end, he would have found the flat delta of the Coruisk river which is an oasis of green in an otherwise black world. Soon the Victorians, those few who could afford the luxury of holidays and travel, had put Skye high on their sightseeing list. But the Cuillins, magnificent and admired from a distance, remained a closed world to all but that, then, very rare breed, the mountaineer. The highest peak, Sgurr Alasdair, *447 207*, was not scaled until as late as 1873.

In 1835 the Reverend C Lesingham Smith tried to reach Loch Coruisk by boat from Elgol, but was thwarted by storms – it was probably the wayward winds off the mountains – so he decided to walk in with a forester who had taken quite a few people there before, none of whom had ever left the floor of the corrie. It was the forester who suggested they try a return route through Lota Corrie where he had seen deer climbing. By pushing and pulling each other up, with the Reverend much encumbered by his umbrella, they finally reached the highest crag, making them the first climbers of the Cuillins. From then on walkers and climbers started to discover Loch Coruisk, and eventually pleasure steamers were disembarking passengers in the anchorage for a quick look. The Caledonian MacBrayne boats still do, for a very brief twenty minutes or so on their weekly cruises.

Today the roads on Skye are made for motor traffic and quite a few tourists find their way down the long road to the dead-end at Elgol, *516 136*, on the east shore of Loch Scavaig from where they have a most wonderful panoramic view of the whole Cuillin range across the water – from nowhere else are they seen to better advantage. And there is Robby McKinnon who takes a few people at a time in his fishing boat over to the anchorage by Loch Coruisk. There are two ways in by foot, both requiring several hours of really hard walking and a bit of scrambling well beyond the taste or stamina of the average holidaymaker. So Loch Coruisk has still not been 'discovered' in the way that more accessible places have, and it certainly never gets crowded. Going in one's own or a chartered boat is, of course, the best way, as you then have a fully furnished and equipped base. The only shelter for people on foot is the Coruisk Memorial Hut, a climbing hut sited above the landing place. The log book inside makes interesting reading with some very succinct observations, particularly the one which reads: 'This is an ideal place for the beginner to come climbing and break his bloody neck'.

We returned to our boat only when it was getting too dark to explore any more to find that our skipper, who had stayed behind on anchor watch, had been gathering our supper off the rocks in the anchorage. That night we gorged ourselves on mussels. The next morning, after breakfast, the inflatable was used again to row over to the Cuillins shore to fill water cans from the Allt a' Chaoich, or Mad Burn as the locals call it because it roars down the mountainside in several directions at once in a succession of falls and pools. Since then a pipe has been most skilfully laid on the steep rock face to carry water from one of the pools to the Memorial Hut.

The thermal effects of the mountains on Loch Scavaig can bring some big surprises. It is possible to stand on the summit of a Cuillin peak in mid-summer almost suffocated by the still, hot air and watch a yacht tacking in a strong wind blowing across the loch towards the heated massif, while further out to sea sailing boats are having to motor in a flat calm. Our own exit that morning was a demonstration. As soon as we left the anchorage we shot into the loch like a cork out of a bottle with our port rail well under. It lasted all of five minutes, and then we were becalmed. For half an hour we drifted around hunting for enough wind to fill a sail, but in the end had to use the engine to get out of Loch Scavaig.

The most established route for walking to Loch Coruisk is from the Sligachan Hotel, *486 298*, at the head of Loch Sligachan, a route pioneered by Victorian climbers. While being par for the course for mountaineers, it is a heavy seven mile slog for the ordinary walker. The most tedious section is from Sligachan to

The most established route for walking to Loch Coruisk is along the valley of the river Sligachan, a seven-mile slog

the pass between Sgurr Hain (1,364 feet) and Druim Hain (1,038 feet), from which one gets a first sight of the loch. It is a good two hour walk over boggy, boulder-strewn ground with fords across innumerable becks draining into the river Sligachan which runs beside the path for most of the way. It is then downhill to the south-east end of Loch Coruisk.

A shorter much tougher way in is from Camasunary, *516 187*, an empty bothy maintained by the Fell Walkers Association and the Mountaineering Club of Scotland. It is a very rudimentary shelter for those who need it. Nearby are two buildings occasionally occupied as a holiday home. Camasunary can be reached by a track up the side of Loch Scavaig from Elgol or across the peninsula from the Elgol road just south of Kirkibost, *545 172*. From the bothy the path starts across a dead flat piece of ground to the river, which flows into Scavaig from Loch na Creitheach, which has to be forded since a bridge, *510 188*, built by the army, was recently washed away; but there are some naturally placed stones which can be used when there is not too much water. After rain you need to find shallower water upstream. Either way it means getting water over the tops of your boots.

The track skirts the base of Sgurr na Stri between fifteen and thirty feet above the water. It is a well trodden way, but very up and down, across boggy ground and over chunks of scattered rock – dreadful walking in the wet, laborious when dry. The eventful part comes when almost in sight of Loch Coruisk. Known as The Bad Step, *495 192*, this is a vertical slab of rock dropping straight into the sea. There is a natural traverse across and up the slab which gives a good foothold, but handholds have to be found above. This is the point at which walkers often decide that discretion is the better part of valour and turn back mightily disappointed. In fact, it is a traverse which does require some experience of rock climbing, particularly if carrying a heavy backpack – and no one should venture into even the foothills of the Cuillins, or any wild country, without carrying an emergency supply of food and survival gear in case the worst happens and they are be-nighted.

Ordinary country walkers, and even fell walkers, would do well to double their first estimates of the time they will take on any one leg of the expedition and, unless they have climbing experience or a very competent climbing companion with them, should keep to the relatively flat floor of the valley. However easy it may look to scramble up the rock faces, these mountains are full of blind alleys which, once up, can be very difficult to get down. The trip by fishing boat may seem tame especially if, like most visitors, you do no more than sit by the nearest end of the loch to eat your sandwiches. But at least the family can be safely taken that far to experience an incomparable scene, and not become so exhausted that they are fit for nothing next day.

Loch Laxford

OS 1:50,000 Sheets 9/15

It would be invidious to say that Loch Laxford is the most beautiful loch on the west coast of Scotland, but it does have the distinction of being almost the remotest and, therefore, little known and unspoilt. It has only two small communities of a dozen or so souls, no shop, hotel or pub and no road round its shores. Apart from one public telephone, it is bereft of all amenities, and if it were just another loch it would not be worth the long journey almost to the northern tip of Scotland to see it. But it is very beautiful with an intricate shoreline, thirty islands and skerries and a rich variety of wildlife. The north shore is a wilderness of grey and pink gneiss broken up by scores of fresh water lochs and lochans; an impenetrable country to all but the toughest walkers. A car could just manage the first four miles of a track leading off the Ullapool-Durness road, after that it is three more miles on foot to John Ridgeway's adventure school at Ardmore, *209 513*, where young and old pay to sail, canoe, climb, walk and camp in a harsh environment either for the sheer fun of it or as a character building exercise, depending on whether it was their idea or someone else's to go there. For an adventure school the setting could hardly be better; it is sited on the shore of an inlet off Loch Laxford looking towards mountain ramparts dominated by the peaks of Cranstakie, Foinaven, Arkle and Ben Stack.

The south shore is rather more civilised with a single steep narrow approach road with passing places linking its two communities of Foindle and Fanagmore (where the public telephone is) to the outside world. On and around the loch and its islands are some thirty different species of birds, a heronry, common and Atlantic seals, porpoises and otters. To get the full flavour of Loch Laxford you need binoculars, a boat and a companion with local knowledge of the waters and the wildlife. Two of those needs are supplied by Julian Pearce who takes visitors on a nature trail by boat round the loch and gives a running commentary tailored to the knowledge and interest of his passengers. He will either keep within the loch or, if preferred, go outside and around Handa Island Nature Reserve whose Torridonian sandstone cliffs and stacks are home to an estimated 60,000 pairs of assorted sea birds. His nature cruises start from the pier, *178 498*, at Fanagmore, normally at 10am, noon and 2pm on weekdays during the summer. He will sometimes make an evening trip when the sun has lowered a little, giving more shape and depth to the rocks and a better light for photography. Working on his own for himself he is amenable to suggestions.

Loch Laxford faces north west at the receiving end of the full brunt of Atlantic storms, and it is many millenia of Atlantic gales which have given the islands and shorelines their complex and photogenic shapes. Fanagmore, however, is among the most sheltered anchorages in Britain, tucked into the high land, totally protected from the north, west and south and only exposed to the east from across the narrow width of the loch. Julian Pearce's first 'port of call' round the loch is Foindle which has a stone harbour so far up inland that at low water it is high and dry and looks like a sheep fold. It is about the size of one too, with just about enough space for two small fishing boats to lie to its walls. Next comes Weaver's Bay, *20 48*, where boats used to moor to pick up wool from the crofts. The big iron eyes in the rocks which took the mooring ropes are still there, but the crofts went at the time of the Highland Clearances. A narrow channel passes behind an island called Port á Choit, the home of a seal colony and, when I last saw it, a lonely yacht. At the head of the loch, Laxford Bay forms the narrows to Laxford Bridge, *237 468*, the junction of the roads to Ullapool, Durness and Lairg, the A894 and A838. The signpost at the bridge is more laconic; it just says 'North' and 'South'. Wolf Rock (Eilean an Eireannaich), which has a spot height of sixty-three metres on the OS map, *191 505*, guards the entrance to Loch á Chadh Fi which is Ridgeway's fiefdom; at least Julian was not inclined to sail in and disturb him. From the main loch the masts of his sailing boats can be seen above the rocks and there was smoke rising from his smoke house – he has his own fish farm. The rock is so named because it is the last place in Scotland where a wolf was killed, they say. Eilean Ard is a big island in the middle

Eilean Ard, the big island in the centre of the loch with a heronry on its steep north side, is here seen from above Fanagmore

of the loch opposite the entrance to Fanagmore and any yacht sailing into Laxford should keep it on their starboard hand all the way round into Fanagmore. To pass between the island and the mainland risks a tangle with a lot of outliers. The heronry is on its steep to north side.

A sea tour of the loch must be followed by a look at it from the high points around Fanagmore and Foindle – they are the only two places where the road goes anywhere near the water, but then some stiff walking is called for. On my way to a superb viewpoint at 400 feet north of Fanagmore I came across an old lady cutting the peats. Although I spent several minutes photographing her from a distance, she affected not to have seen me and never for a moment straightened her back or ceased her labours. Afterwards, over a dram, Alec Macaskill, a crofter and the youngest man in Fanagmore (at that time he was seventy-eight; the only other man was in his eightieth year), told me that I had been photographing his sister who was eighty-three. 'She saw you', he said, 'but she didn't let on because she was afraid you might stop her from doing her work'. He had another sister of eighty-one in hospital in Inverness, but he was hopeful; his grandmother had lived to 100

Turning peat above Fanagmore; it is left out to dry during the summer and then taken home for winter fuel

after working hard all her life. '120 years ago she was employed planting out trees, working a twelve-hour day for four pence a day'. He lives in what had been the teacher's house forty years ago, and the schoolroom next door is now used on alternate

Alec Macaskill, a crofter, and at seventy-eight the youngest man in Fanagmore

Sunday evenings for services when the minister comes over from Scourie, six miles away.

His family have always been crofters; his father kept sixteen head of cattle, a pair of horses and sixty sheep. 'I got rid of all the cattle and horses some time ago, but I still have sheep. This is the best of pastures and it produces the finest mutton because the sheep are heather fed; they have a grand flavour. It's young heather. We burn the old stuff in the spring and they eat the new heather which takes two years to grow before we burn it again'. He looks after eighty sheep with one dog, and when he is gathering them in will walk ten miles a day over rocky hill terrain. When he was a young man, he told me, there were plenty of fish – lobsters fetched twenty pence a pound as against today's £6.50. The loch was full of herring too. 'The fishing went on from November to March, and I remember in 1928 with our small boat of sixteen feet or so we fished 1,500 crans of herring, and a cran is 750 fish. The catches went by motor bus from here to Lairg and then away by train. That year we were making £58.19.2 each for a night's work – it was a fortune. But we never spent it; we looked for a rainy day. There was plenty of wild salmon too when I was young. We were netting them in the loch, taking them ashore, splitting them open and drying them in the sun. Then they were packed into barrels to wait for a boat which came into Fanagmore to take them to the market in Stornoway on Lewis. And Stornoway was sending them to London!'

Wild salmon are rare in Laxford these days, but there are many thousands in the loch in fish farms which may do a lot for local employment but their floating cages and festoons of orange buoys have completely ruined several of the finest views. Fish farming has become an eyesore on so many Scottish lochs that if it expands much more their beauty will be totally destroyed. There has always been plenty of trout for the pot in the fresh water lochs in that part of Scotland, but today they all belong to angling clubs and even the locals have to pay for their fishing like the incomers and visitors. The land round the loch from above Fanagmore down to Laxford Bridge is owned by a Mrs Balfour, and the other side, except for a bit round Ardmore, is owned by the Duke of Westminster – 800,000 acres in all which he maintains solely for sport. 'Mrs Balfour is a very nice lady', says Alec Macaskill. 'She doesn't keep all her land for sport; she gives it all to us, the crofters, to do with it what we like'.

From Fanagmore a road runs over a hill to Tarbet on the west coast where a boatman will take you a mile across the water to Handa Island. A footpath crosses its centre and another goes round the cliff tops on the western side and back to the landing place passing all the best places for observing the bird life. The whole route covers three miles, some over very wet and muddy ground, and will take two and a half hours or more depending on how much time is spent watching. In the centre of the island you pass ruined crofts which were inhabited until 1848; here are great skuas or bonxies, which are like a big brown gull with white wing flashes, and sometimes the more delicate Arctic skuas. Puffin Bay, *135 487*, does not have many puffins but there are plenty of gulls and fulmers, guillemots and razorbills, and grey seals in the water. The Great Stack, *132 488*, is Handa's spectacle. This plug of rock rising 300 feet out of the sea is almost encircled by vertical cliffs, the tops of which provide a viewing platform round three sides. In summer some 12,000 birds nest on the Stack, each species keeping to its own level like theatre-goers in the gallery, balcony and stalls. Guillemots occupy the broader lower ledges, kittiwakes with their horrible screeching voices next on the narrower projections, and near the top are razorbills. The grass top knot is the habitat of the burrowing puffins, the most comic and colourful of birds. Continuing westabout, the path passes by a great blow hole set well in from the cliff edge which, at that point, is 400 feet high. When the Atlantic swell pounds the cliff face below a geyser of water shoots up through the hole. This area is thick with gannets, razorbills and a few shags. Spotted heath orchids are common, and in July and August bog asphodel lay a yellow carpet on the wetter ground.

On the way to or from Loch Laxford do try and arrange to make a diversion to Upper Badcall, *15 41*, to look out over Badcall Bay and wonder. At your feet lie 365 islands in about four square miles of water, one for every day of the year, and a superb sight in the setting sun. Another diversion which requires a lot of heavy walking is to Britain's biggest waterfall, Eas a Chual Aluinn, *280 277*. A track leaves the A94, *238 284*, three miles north of Skiag Bridge, or two miles south of Unapool, skirts the south side of Loch na Gainmhich, continues through Bealach a Bhuirich (Roaring Pass) to another little loch and then follows a stream south east until it plunges over Leitir Dhubh (Dark Cliffs). Go on just a little further to a heather covered slope from where you get the best overall view of these 600-foot falls. In a dry period they may be disappointing because then they break up into a succession of falls dropping from ledge to ledge. When in spate the effect is of one continuous torrent of water. The lazy way to see this spectacle, but at some distance, is to take a boat trip which runs from Unapool to Loch Beag at the head of Loch Glencoul from where the falls are seen up the valley about a half-mile distant.

Loch Roag

OS 1:50,000 Sheet 13

John Russell, a yacht charter skipper with a deep knowledge and love of the waters of the Highlands and Islands of Scotland, once invited me to join a cruise which would include a visit to what he called 'the jewel of the Outer Hebrides' where, hopefully, we would spend a day or two while waiting for a favourable wind to take us out into the Atlantic to St Kilda. John's jewel was Loch Roag on the west coast of Lewis. It is really two lochs, East Loch Roag and West Loch Roag, separated by the jagged mass of Great Bernera island but just made one by a narrow strait between island and mainland. The whole is a superb cruising ground in its own right which could well occupy a week as there are so many compelling reasons for going ashore, and that means walking which takes time. Unexpectedly for a place so far away and thinly inhabited, it does have a network of narrow but good roads so it can equally well be explored by car.

The east coasts of the Outer Hebrides are mainly rocky, steep to and bleak, but with many sheltered inlets. The west coasts facing the Atlantic are far more exposed, have few places in which to shelter, a low seaboard and large white and silver strands backed by sand dunes. The shoal sand blows inland to form dunes which the locals have dressed with seaweed to produce fertile and beautifully drained soil which has become colonised by herbs and grasses making the most wonderful pasture, the next best thing to Alpine pasture, with thousands of flowers in season. It is the same with Loch Roag; the West is nearly all sand beaches lapped by transparent green water, sands bigger and better than any child would dream of – smooth, clean and virtually deserted. The East Loch by comparison is totally rocky with lots of shelter, and the high ground overlooking the sea is richly endowed with archaeological sites. Great Bernera, which divides them, has no shape that can be described, its shorelines torn to tatters, and inland it is so broken up with lochans that it is almost more water than solid ground. There is nothing bland about the waters of Loch Roag; wherever you look a multitude of islets and skerries break the surface and the view – even seawards they seem to have been scattered almost to the horizon.

Unless you are so fortunate as to arrive here from the sea, it will be by car from Stornoway fourteen miles across a wild moorland landscape. On reaching the road junction at Garynahine, *237 317*, the choice is between turning west for a long journey on a narrow road to the sandy beaches, or continuing up the main A858 to Carloway near the mouth of the East Loch. Along the Carloway road are the forty-eight standing stones, *213 330*, of Callanish, thought to have been erected some 4,000 years ago in the late Neolithic – New Stone Age – period. Why they were erected, what purpose they served, has never been agreed, but there are theories galore. They stand on the bleak Lewis moorland, a most inhospitable site but one which gives them dramatic

The standing stones of Callanish were only uncovered in 1857 when the accumulated peat was removed

prominence. Fascinating to study close to, they are most impressive seen on the skyline from an anchorage, *210 328*, in the loch below. It was from there that I first saw them before climbing up onto the moor to wander among them. In the centre is a two-chambered cairn surrounded by thirteen stones from which lines of other stones radiate – five to the south, four to the west, four to the east and an avenue of nineteen stones a few degrees east of true north. One or two other small stones are dotted about and there may well have been many more in the past which have been taken over the centuries for building purposes. What is fascinating to consider is that in the seventeenth century peat had accumulated over the land surface to a depth of six feet completely covering the smaller stones. For thousands of years until 1857 when Sir James Matheson, the Laird of Lewis, had the peat removed, they may not have looked anything other than a few stones sticking out of the ground. Today the tallest stone, the central megalith by the cairn, stands fifteen and a half feet above the ground and its weight is estimated at between five and six tons. Perhaps their most noticeable characteristic is that they are the only megalithic structure set out in the form of a cross. Within a small area around Callanish eleven other megalithic sites have been found. Scattered over the moors, it would be difficult to give written directions to each one, but here are the grid references for the seven which are accessible and worth visiting: *222 326*, *225 327*, *230 304*, *234 299*, *247 303*, *164 342* and *215 350*, the last being a single stone on the edge of Breasclete.

Further up the road there is an hotel with a bar, plain and cheerless, but an oasis in its way because there is no other within an hour's drive. On my last visit they had run out of food so I was directed to the Post Office in Carloway where, in the post mistress's kitchen, I was served a modest meal from her deep freeze. Beyond Stornoway, Lewis is no place for the sybarite. Shortly after the hotel a track on the left of the road to Doune Carloway passes the broch of Dun Carloway on a hillock 150 feet above the loch. What is a broch? Again, no one knows for certain because although brochs seem to be defensive towers they nearly all lack the one necessity of a place liable to siege – a well. There are ruins of some 500 of them scattered around the Highlands and Islands, and the one at Carloway is by far the best preserved of those in the Western Isles. These massive towers were cone shaped with flared tops, similar to the cooling towers of atomic power stations. Dun Carloway has double drystone walls with a stairway spiralling between them leading to galleries within the cavity. The overall diameter at the base is forty-seven feet, and a segment of the double walls still stands thirty feet high with the stairs sufficiently intact that I was able to climb them, bent double, but fearing that the un-mortared walls might collapse on me. I need not have worried; varying in thickness between ten and twelve feet, they have stood for some 2,100 years. It is interesting that drystone building techniques were much the same 100 BC, in the assumed broch building era, as they are now with the use of large slabs of stone laid crossways to bond together the inner and outer walls. Access to the ground floor inner courtyard, which must have been roofed over at one time, is through a stone corridor only two feet eleven inches wide by three feet six inches high with a recess or sentry box at its further end, so only one person at a time could possibly have entered the broch, and then in a stooped and vulnerable posture. The ground floor is ringed with chambers, as were the galleries above. This magnificent example of a broch has been in state guardianship since 1887, but as recently as 1870 there was 'a respectable looking family living in the ground floor' according to a contemporary writer.

The Iron Age broch at Carloway, 150 feet above the loch; it is possible to climb the stone stairway to two galleries between the remaining walls

In the streets of the crofting township of Carloway you will often see bolts of Harris tweed lying on the ground outside the

Harris tweed is still woven on machines which use hand and foot power; once it was women's work, but now it is a full time industry for men

weavers' houses waiting for the daily lorry to pick them up and take them to the mills where the cloth is washed to soften it and pull the weave together. Weaving was once women's work, but has now become a full time industry for the men and about 600 looms are at work in Lewis and Harris. They are fairly modern machines, that is not more than thirty years old, and are all worked individually by hand and foot power. A weaver will make a small amount of cloth to sell direct to anyone who knocks at his door for a fraction of what it would cost on the mainland. But the bulk of his production is for the mills who supply him with the wool and their instructions as to design. The biggest market for Harris tweed is the USA and Canada, so the fortunes of the Carloway weavers fluctuate according to the value of the dollar.

Carloway has a small fishing harbour with a stand pipe from which visiting yachts may draw water, but as it comes out of the tap the colour of strong tea it is more acceptable for washing up than for drinking. The harbour is actually in Loch Carloway just inside the entrance to East Loch Roag, and it would be quite feasible to drop anchor near the entrance, row ashore to a beach and walk up to the broch. When I first visited Loch Roag John Russell anchored in the narrows, *14 40*, between the north end of Great Bernera and Little Bernera, which is uninhabited except for grazing cattle. That time we went ashore on the smaller island from the yacht, but on other occasions I have driven to Bosta at the tip of Great Bernera, pumped up the inflatable and rowed across. By the anchorage the rocks have gathered a covering of sand which by midsummer becomes a carpet of flowers so you do not know where to put your feet. It is a steep walk to the centre of the island for a spellbinding vista. A necklace of white sand crescents adorns the shoreline offset by a crystal sea supporting two dozen green islands. On the east side of Little Bernera a walled graveyard and small roofless church cling to the side of a hill which slopes down to another sandy bay. It has long been a graveyard for the people of Loch Roag and contains some fine memorial stones which reveal that the harsh life of a crofter was not necessarily a short one.

By boat it is a short passage from East to West Loch Roag between Great Bernera and Little Bernera, but by road it is a long detour round the head of Little Loch Roag, a narrow strip of water cutting five miles inland. On the east shore of the Little Loch and reached by a rough road over the hills is Scaliscro, an isolated pub and fishing lodge. It is run by a young fun couple, Cree Mackenzie and his wife Todag, and visitors are offered 'lots of lovely salmon and the occasional Arctic char from the surrounding fresh water lochs'. The way in and out of Little Loch Roag is through long narrows which most boats can only negotiate at high water slack. At other times there is a very fast tidal rip, especially on the ebb, with countless eddies and whirlpools which can put a boat into a spin for a long time if it does not get flung onto rocks first. To get his visitors in and out at times convenient to them rather than the tide and the turbulence of the narrows, Cree uses a fast high-powered trihedral hull craft which planes over the water. He has recently laid a visitor's mooring in front of the lodge in the optimistic belief that sooner or later some nerveless visitor will come for a drink the short, quick way through the narrows. It would have to be a quick drink as slack water lasts less than an hour, otherwise he faces a stop over of six hours before being able to get out.

All the way along the B8011 to the head of Little Loch Roag from spring into summer the locals will be out cutting their peat which is first stacked to dry, then taken home to store for winter fuel. Eventually the road leaves the lochside when you may either turn west into Glen Valtos and on to Uig, or take a sharp U turn over a little stone bridge to Valtos, a scattering of houses with a stone pier, which boasts a motor mechanic who overnight brought my outboard engine back to life. Beside Valtos is Traigh na Berie, a most beautiful mile-long sweep of white sand backed by rolling dunes where a few caravans can settle down in the hollows sufficiently hull down as not to spoil the view. Here children may play and safely swim. For the grown ups there is nothing to do but relax, soak in the view over Kyles Pabay to the two islands of Pabay Mor and Vassay and, after an evening meal cooked on the sands – for there is no restaurant or café – wait for the sunset. If they are as fortunate as I was in mid-June the sky will be a blood red dome at midnight slowly fading to give way to the loom of dawn. At the southern end of the dunes a stream comes down from a small loch, *110 355*, in the hills. On this stream are the traces of four Norse-type grain mills which were worked by horizontal water wheels, a type of mill used on the islands from the time of the Norse occupation to almost 100 years ago. Those at Traigh na Berie probably went out of use about 150 years ago.

Taking the route through Glen Valtos you arrive at Uig Sands which, at low water, turns a landlocked bay into a three-square-mile playground. It was here that the famous Lewis Chessmen, seventy-eight ivory pieces belonging to at least eight chess sets, were found. The story goes that a cabin boy jumped overboard with his captain's chest containing the pieces. For some reason he was murdered by the locals, but they did not want the chest or its contents so they buried them. A crofter who found them much later took them to the manse where the minister said: 'How dare you have those idols, give them to me'. Taking them off him he sold them to the British Museum for £25. The manse, built in 1783 on the north shore of the bay, is today a country house hotel called Baile na Cille owned by Joanna and Richard Gollin, two young incomers. It is a place for peace and quiet, furnished and run like a private house, and there can be no hotel anywhere with a beach of its own so big. They do not own the beach of course, but they do have a private path down to it and you are more than likely to have at least a square mile of it to yourself. They have converted the stable block so that they have a total of ten bedrooms, and were very candid in telling me that there was a local story about a mad minister who committed suicide in the stables. He was Mr Watson who, at the time of the split with the Church of Scotland, went over to the Free Presbyterians and as a result had no congregation but his housekeeper. But in his mind his congregation grew, and every time he sent his returns to Edinburgh he increased their number until eventually he had an impossibly huge congregation. Edinburgh sent a message of congratulations on winning so many people for the church and saying that one of the Elders would arrive to share in worship the following Sunday. Poor Mr Watson took the letter into the stables and there hanged himself.

On the hillside behind the hotel Mr Will Macleod, the shepherd, is often to be seen tending his flock; on Sundays he will be in church tending his other flock as the Reverend Macleod. The grounds of the hotel border an ancient burial site in which the most recent tombstones are over 100 years old and all but concealed by thigh high grass and nettles. They represent only the top layer of graves, with three more below them going back 1,000 years. The graveyard is surrounded by good arable land, far too valuable in an island which is half barren rock to be used for burying people. So the site was never extended; instead every time it was filled up sand was brought from the beach and stacked on top of the graves to start another layer so that it is now a little hillock beside the sea. Curiously only men lie there and they were all buried with their feet towards the sea. Their womenfolk were given a more sheltered place inland.

Lough Neagh and Lower Bann

OS 1:50,000 Sheets 14/19/20

The Irish giant Finn McCool had a terrible temper, and in an argument one day with an English giant he lost his cool, scooped up a handful of Ireland and threw it across the water. But it fell short of its target and landed in the middle of the Irish Sea; it is now called the Isle of Man. Of course, that is but one of umpteen stories credited to the legendary McCool, being based on the similarity in size and shape between Lough Neagh and the Isle of Man. The truth is that Lough Neagh has its origins in the pre-glacial Tertiary period some sixty million years ago, long before giants were thought of. Volcanic lava poured all over the north east of Ireland covering much of what is now Ulster and hardened into basalt to become the Antrim Plateau. The great weight of basalt caused stresses in the earth's crust which sagged to form a large basin into which rivers poured their waters giving birth to Lough Neagh. It was at least twice as large as it is today, but over millions of years sediment from the rivers reduced it to its present size of a mere 200 square miles with an average depth of forty to fifty feet, apart from a 100 foot trench at its northern end.

Nevertheless, it can take pride of place as the largest lake in the British Isles and the second largest in Europe. But big is not always beautiful, and Lough Neagh can look particularly bland with no nice wooded islands breaking its surface, as they do on other Irish lakes, and no mountains, or even much in the way of hills, to reflect in its surface. Look out across this lake and all you see is a vast expanse of water with nothing on the horizon; it looks as the sea does when you stand with your back to the land – and, except when a storm is raging, the sea is not much to look at until it meets the land. It is the cliffs and the strands, the bays and the creeks, estuaries and little harbours which fascinate us about the sea. And so it is with Lough Neagh. Its sixty-five mile coastline reveals a number of enchanting bays and beaches, a diverse catalogue of flora, a mass of birdlife rich in every season, a quaint and thriving fishing industry and plenty of sites and buildings of historic interest. There are yacht harbours so it would be possible to explore these shores by boat, but it would mean long hauls across featureless water which can kick up very nasty. If it were not for the cost and logistics involved in trailing boats across the Irish Sea, Lough Neagh could have become a popular international playground and race-track for offshore-class powerboats, whose afficionados would appreciate the elbow room and the scarcity of sailing boats to get in their way.

Antrim is a convenient base for touring this area. It is near Belfast's ferry port and only along the road from Aldergrove Airport, and there is a marina on the outskirts of town at the mouth of Six Mile Water. The most impressive structure is in Steeple Road; this is a fine round tower, 100 feet tall and in perfect condition. Nearly 100 round towers in various stages of ruin are to be found all over Ireland. They were always built beside a church or monastic building and it is most likely that they were used both as belfries and as refuges from Viking raiders. Their Irish name, clogtheach, means bell tower. The entrance doors were always above ground level, and access was by rope ladder which could be pulled up. They were all high enough to afford an early warning view of approaching raiders when the church treasure could be taken inside in good time. Hand bells were used for calling the congregation to worship, to warn the community of danger and to summon help. Some towers were built as late as the twelfth century so they must have had a continuing purpose after the Viking raids had ceased.

The Lower Bann, which flows due north to the sea at Coleraine, would be a good point from which to make a clockwise tour around the lough. It is the dividing line between the predominantly Protestant east side of the lough and the Catholic west. The A6 Antrim-Londonderry road crosses the estuary of the Lower Bann at Toome Bridge, *989 906*, the centre of the eel fishing industry, which I shall describe in detail later. The road south out of Toome to Knockaphort leads to a delightful stretch of indented shore at Long Rock, *996 855*, and The Three Islands where

Tarbet near Loch Laxford and the departure point for Handa Island Bird Sanctuary, which can be seen in the distance

Fanagmore on Loch Laxford is one of the most sheltered anchorages in Britain although the loch itself is open to the full force of Atlantic gales

Valtos, a scattering of houses on West Loch Roag, where there is a mile-long sweep of white sand – Traigh na Berie – backed by rolling dunes

The Giant's Causeway with its basalt cliffs and lava steps seen from a boat offshore

A quaint and thriving eel fishing industry continues on Lough Neagh based on the many natural harbours, such as this one on the Tyrone shore

wildfowlers keep their multi-coloured wooden boats in miniature creeks. From there the road runs east along the lough to Churchtown Point, *055 852*, with its ruined thirteenth century Cranfield Church (the name means 'wood of wild garlic') and St Olcan's holy well, the gypsum pebbles from which are said to protect a woman from death in childbirth and save a man from drowning. Randalstown Forest further along the shore is a reserve for fallow deer, red squirrels and water birds which can be watched from hides, but a permit to enter the reserve must be obtained from the Forestry Division of the Department of Agriculture. From the minor road which loops down from Randalstown back to Toome a lane, *070 885*, leads down a slope beside the forest to find one of the best panoramic views around the lough. With a deep bay going into Antrim, this is one of the few points from which you can see land across the water.

The river Main runs through the forest, dropping 200 feet in its last mile to the lough, making it popular with canoeists. Beyond it are the grounds of Shanes Castle, one of the very few overt tourist attractions around the lough. Here is a nature reserve with hides managed by the RSPB which is very much open to the public. From a station by the entrance gates a narrow gauge steam railway runs through the reserve to the ruins of the old castle, burnt out in 1816. Lord O'Neill, the present owner of the demesne, farmer and steam railway buff, lives in a neo-Georgian house of 1858 in the park. His step-father is Ian Fleming, the creator of James Bond. He succeeded to the title when he was eleven, and as a schoolboy at Eton went train spotting at Taplow station; he now drives his own train. His estate was requisitioned by the army during the war who left behind bits of a two foot gauge military line which became the basis of his present estate railway.

Down the east coast two miles offshore is Ram's Island with its stump of a round tower. It is a great sanctuary for song birds, particularly blackbirds, thrushes and finches; it is a pretty and musical place for a summer picnic. A boat can be hired at Tunny Cut on the coast north of Portmore Lough. My favourite spot is at the head of a narrow bay inside Morrow's Point which is found at the end of a lane from the village of Leansmount, *082 623*. Here, alongside water meadows, are the traces of an old quay and the largely intact first lock of the Lagan Canal, in what is called Ellis's Gut, *080 626*, which ran from Lough Neagh to Belfast. The canal cut still has water in it and can be followed on foot past several more derelict locks, at least as far as Aghalee, the village where John Lavery the portrait painter was born. Near the village the canal runs into a stretch called Broad Water, which is like a long thin lake, then becomes canal again for a mile before being brought to an abrupt halt just past Lady's Bridge, *160 618*. From there to Lisburn almost all traces of it have been obliterated by the building of the M1. This canal was the last section of a waterway linking the Shannon with Belfast; first by the Ballyconnell Canal, then across the southern end of Upper Lough Erne and again across country via the Ulster Canal to the south-east corner of Lough Neagh at Maghery.

The Lagan Canal from Belfast reached Lough Neagh in 1794. By 1889 the tonnage that it carried had risen to over 170,000 tons, a fourfold increase on the 1830s, and the net profit averaged £5,000 a year. Coal counted for two-thirds of the traffic being imported from Belfast and sent inland, a reversal of the expectation of the founders of the canal who thought it would be used to take coal from Tyrone after being carried down the Coalisland Canal, across Lough Neagh to the entrance of the Lagan Canal and so on to Belfast for export. Steamers towed lighters across the lough, but horses were used for towing on the canal, a haulier getting two pounds from the lighterman, who lived on board, to haul him from Belfast to the lough, a two-day journey. The last lighter delivered coal to the Island Quay in Lisburn in 1954 and after that the canal rapidly fell into disrepair. Today the towpath can be followed from the Molly Ward locks in Belfast for seven and a half miles to Lisburn past derelict locks and lock houses, miniature rapids, invading woodland and marshes, which make it a walk of interest to the naturalist.

Oxford Island, *045 615*, is the best-known nature reserve on the lough because it is only a five minute drive from junction 10 of the M1 from Belfast. With the Lough Neagh Sailing Club and a small yacht harbour it is a popular location for family outings. Up until 1846 when the level of the lough was first lowered it was a proper island, but since then it has been a peninsula. In its days as an island, cattle were driven across the ford, hence Oxford Island. The nature trail is one and two-third miles in length, going up, down and across the peninsula through a variety of flora and geology. The hides are really good, wooden structures with ample room for several people and perfect for observation or photography. A report commissioned by the Craigavon Borough Council recently listed 129 bird species throughout the year including one rare sighting of a storm petrel. The haughty heron is seen all the year round, and the pochard is the most common wintering species. The butterfly census listed fifteen species, which says much for the vegetation which runs to 188 varieties.

My own astonishment came when, emerging from a copse into an open patch, I saw before me a cloud of insects suspended just above the ground and scintillating in the sunlight against the dark background of trees. There were millions of them, whatever they were, and I had an immediate fear of being bitten a thousand times if I went near. I need not have worried. It was a swarm of Lough Neagh flies which were on the wing for a short moment of time to mate and lay their eggs on the water before dying. They are scientifically known as *chironomids*. A year after hatching they metamorphose into midges inside pupal cases which float up to the surface, when the adult midges break out and fly off to swarm and mate. During those few days of their life they do not feed and, therefore, do not bite, so providing a spectacle without trouble to us.

The next place to visit is Derrywarragh Island, a real one this time, at the south-west corner of the lough, which is separated from the mainland by the original outlet of the river Blackwater and by a cut which was the Lough Neagh end of the Ulster Canal. From this point the Blackwater is still partly canalised. The island, reached by a bridge across the cut, *924 636*, rises at its highest point to about 200 feet, where stands the ruin of The O'Connor's Stronghold, now reduced to a sliver of a stone tower about eighteen feet tall. For a small nephew it provided a tempting climb with a relatively high level view across an otherwise flat landscape. In fact, much of the surrounding area is fenland with peat and bogland ecology. The east side of Derrywarragh overlooks Coney Island, a National Trust jewel of rich green forest surrounded by blue water and, peeking out of the trees, a little white house which a year or two ago was waiting for a tenant who was prepared to live like Robinson Crusoe as the Trust caretaker. The public may take a boat from Maghery to the island and walk round its forest paths. The locals will tell you that emigrants from there named the beach outside New York after their Coney Island.

There have been several drainage schemes since the original one in 1846–58 which have changed the level of the lake so that in many places cattle graze on raised beaches; the best example of these is seen on the periphery of Derrywarragh. On the foreshore itself the lapping water has in many places left two to three feet 'cliffs' where the layers of silt left behind on subsequent lowerings resemble a cut layer-cake. The ground below the centre hillock is marshy and fit only for cattle, but with a pair of gumboots on it is an excellent area in spring and summer to study the variety of water-edge and submerged plants, which are also common elsewhere around the lough but not always so accessible. A little way back from the water the wet margin land is alive with darting dragonflies and butterflies. Many of the marsh plants are rare elsewhere in Ireland, but the Irish lady's tresses orchid is rare throughout Europe. It is pointless taking a car onto the island as the road, after a few yards, is really suitable only for tractors.

The river Blackwater is navigable for eleven miles inland through meadows for the first four as far as the M1, where there is eight-foot headroom under the bridge just after the junction with Coalisland Canal, *887 672*. A little more than two centuries ago Coalisland was the inland port for Ulster's only sizeable coalfield, and the canal was constructed at enormous expense to take the coal to the sea via Lough Neagh and the Lagan and Newry Canals. Iron works, forges and plating mills were built, but the whole project ended in economic disaster. The most interesting canal relics are some ruined arches at Drumreagh, *829 673*, and at Farlough, *819 673*, between Coalisland and Newmills. These are all that now remain of dry wherries, or inclined planes, up which barges were hauled on rails. They were the first structures of their kind and were later copied on the canal system in England.

Above the motorway bridge the Blackwater becomes even more interesting. Two miles on there is a slipway and boat moorings where it runs beside the 300 rolling acres of The Argory, an 1820 house which was the residence of the Magill-Bond family, substantial Armagh landlords. This is now a National Trust property and open to the public from April to September. Most interesting, and perhaps unique, is its acetylene gas plant for the domestic lighting. The gas is formed by water dripping onto a gaseous hydrocarbon powder, a messy process. People over sixty may remember the acetylene lamps which were common on motor-bikes and bicycles until the late 1920s.

Two miles beyond The Argory the river comes to the twin villages of Charlemont and Moy, the latter with a square laid out by Lord Charlemont in the eighteenth century, modelled on Marengo in Italy. During the eighteenth and nineteenth centuries the Moy Fair was one of the most important horse fairs in Europe. People tend to associate the Irish with their donkeys, whereas in fact the animal was little known in Ireland before the Napoleonic Wars when, at fairs like Moy, the country was denuded of its horses by the purchasing officers of the warring armies. To replace them great numbers of donkeys were imported from Spain and soon multiplied, becoming accepted as part of the Irish scene. On the Charlemont bank of the river is the derelict, narrow lock joining the Blackwater to the disused Ulster

Canal which once connected the Shannon and Lough Erne to Lough Neagh and the Lagan navigation. Soon after this point the river becomes impassable, being blocked by rocks just before the bridge at Blackwatertown, *840 524*.

Crossing over the Blackwater, from County Antrim into County Tyrone, the road is too far inland until Ballyronan in County Londonderry to provide many views of the water, but about every half-mile a lane runs down to the shore, usually to a natural fishing harbour; at Ballyronan it is a full scale yacht marina. The worthwhile diversions are to Ardboe Point, *968 756*, Newport Trench, *965 771*, and Salter's Castle, *952 823*. But first you will come to Mountjoy Castle, *901 687*, on a slight slope overlooking the lough. It is the ruin of a square fortress built during the 1602 campaign against Hugh O'Neill, Earl of Tyrone. It was taken and retaken by Irish and English in 1641, 1642 and 1645 and was again used as a fort by the forces of James II and William III. Salter's Castle further up, right on the shore, is the remains of a seventeenth century plantation house built by the Salter's Company of the City of London; all that can be seen now are a bawn wall with round towers and the gables. Before, and up to, the time of Elizabeth I the north of Ireland was in a constant state of rebellion, and near the end of her reign the estates of the O'Neills and O'Dohertys were made forfeit to the Crown. A commission was set up by Elizabeth in 1602 to define those lands and the rights of the rebels, which was followed by another commission by James I in 1606. Another rebellion and the flight of the Ulster chiefs in 1607 clinched the matter and enabled the king to declare that all their land was to be confiscated and parcelled out to settlers. This despite that, in Irish law, land belonged to the tribe and not to the chief. In 1611 the government started the settling, or colonisation, of the Province of Ulster which was to make Northern Ireland different from the rest of Ireland and to imbue the indigenous Catholic population with the bitterness they still have to this day.

Between 1603 and 1612 James I was guided by his chief minister, Robert Cecil, a confirmed anti-Catholic. It was in 1604 that the gunpowder plot, to blow up the king and parliament in the hope of establishing a Catholic government, was discovered. It gave vent to the persecution of Catholics and a great determination to populate Ulster with English and Scottish protestants. But initially the scheme did not work, and the government offered the city of Derry, the town of Coleraine and almost all of County Derry, in which was to be Salterstown, to the City of London. The Lord Mayor of London called upon the Livery Companies to provide the money to finance the plantation. The twelve principle companies raised £5,000 and the Irish Society was formed to manage the estates which were conveyed to them. Very soon a further £15,000 was required, but it was not forthcoming until some of the wardens of the companies had been committed to prison! The Irish estates were a continual drain on the companies' finances for many years, and they did not really settle down to enjoy the fruits of their investments, which eventually amounted to £60,000, until after their active part in the famous Defence of Derry and the granting of Letters Patent by Oliver Cromwell followed by a new charter issued by Charles II. Under the Irish Land Purchase Act of 1903 almost all the companies' estates were sold.

At Ardboe Point stands the best-preserved tenth century high cross in Northern Ireland. It is over seventeen feet tall and has twenty-two carved panels illustrating Biblical stories of the Old and New Testaments, from Adam and Eve to the Last Judgement. On the peninsula behind the cross, which gives good views along the lough shore, are the ruins of a sixteenth century church and a sixth century abbey. Newport Trench, a little over a mile up the coast, is a fishing harbour with a quayside pub and is the centre of the pollen or fresh water herring fishing fleet. This is a lovely flavoured fish found only in Lough Neagh and Lough Erne, but it does not travel well. It spawns on stony or gravel bottoms and moves in shoals; the small fry are much in demand for baiting eel lines. It is the eel which has made Lough Neagh one of the richest inland fishing areas in Western Europe, and certainly it supports the largest eel fishing industry of any country with an average catch of 800 tonnes a year.

Although found nowhere else in such abundance, eels are probably our most prolific fish; they are to be found in their thousands in all types of fresh water – lakes, ponds, reservoirs, rivers and canals – as well as in salt water harbours and estuaries. Since primaeval times they have provided a bountiful source of nutritious, high calorie food for the common man and his masters. The cathedral city of Ely is said to be so named from the ancient custom of paying rents in eels which, in mediaeval days, yielded the lords of the manor up to 100,000 eels a year. And there are many other places in Britain, such as Elmore on the Severn and Ellesmere on the Mersey, with names stemming from the local importance of eels. The Greeks treated them as a delicacy and the Egyptians deified them. It was the reverse in Rome, possibly because they were found in the city drains, and they are forbidden to Jews under the Levitical Laws for, being without scales, they are 'unclean'. In fact, they do have scales imbedded in their skins, but they are not easily distinguishable. They exhibit no signs of reproductive organs, and no one has ever seen them spawning, so that throughout history theory was piled on theory with innumerable false conclusions being drawn: they were born of dewdrops in May, said one ancient; they came from the entrails of the earth, said another; they were created spontaneously in the mud, said yet another. Pliny wrote that they rubbed themselves on rocks and their scrapings came to life, while Izaak Newton believed in their spontaneous regeneration.

It was not until as late as 1922 that the truth was conclusively proved and publicly stated by one Johannes Smidt, a Danish biologist. It is now known that they spawn at depths of 250 to 400 metres in the Sargasso Sea in the southern Atlantic. The eggs hatch in twenty-four hours into prelarvae five millimetres long. These grow into aspen leaf shaped leptocephallae which are carried on the currents of the Gulf Stream and the Atlantic Drift towards America and Europe. It takes these minute creatures about three years to reach our waters, by which time they have metamorphosed into glass eels or elvers, semi-transparent and between one and three inches in length. Some elvers, mostly the males, remain and mature in esturial waters, but the majority make their way up rivers turning from transparent to black en route. These migrations can be so large as to turn the water of a river black.

Eels spend most of their lives, from seven to fifteen years, in fresh water feeding voraciously, during which time they are known as brown or yellow eels from the colour of their bellies. Most will stay in a river, and some will wriggle overland on wet nights and dewy dawns to find other waters. For their overland journeys the eels are able to store water in a sac to keep their gills moist and allow them to breathe. They will eat almost any creature which is small enough whether alive or dead, and in a still lake they can smell a dead fish at 400 metres. Their favourite food is the spawn of other species which makes them the enemy of anglers, especially salmon and trout fishermen. Most of their feeding is done at night, and during the day they tend to hide. They are most active in the summer and become almost dormant during the coldest weeks of winter.

Having grown to maturity they will eventually get the urge to procreate, start downstream to the sea and eventually out into the Atlantic. These runs start late in the summer, reach a peak in September and October, with the heaviest taking place on wet moonless nights. At the same time as they make for the sea their bellies turn silver, their eyes become bright blue and protuberant, their guts shrivel and they stop feeding. In this bridal state they return 4,000 miles to the Sargasso Sea to spawn and then, it is thought, to die for no grown eel has ever been seen returning. Since they do not feed once out of fresh water, the migrating eels must carry their own energy reserves, which they do in the form of oil. European silver eels, which have the furthest distance to travel, contain twenty-eight per cent of oil by weight, making them a more valuable catch than the brown eel. Swimming about twelve miles a day, much of the time against a three knot adverse current, it takes the eels nearly eighteen months to reach their spawning grounds off the coast of Mexico. The female is known to lay up to 10,700,000 eggs, and although a large proportion are eaten by other species, those that survive to arrive as elvers in the mouths of Europe's rivers can be counted in tens of millions.

These days eels are caught by rod and line rather in the manner of angling for pike; by long lines with traces and baited hooks laid across a river bed or the floor of a lake; by simple eel traps similar to wire and net creels; or with fyke nets laid on the bottom. The latter look rather like the long keep nets used by coarse fishermen, but with two wings to guide the eels towards the net mouth. Silver eels are mostly caught in fixed traps which operate at night when they are running.

There are 210 boats actively engaged in fishing for eels on Lough Neagh, of which about eighty per cent are based on the west side. This bias has less to do with the distribution of the eels than with social history. For generations eel fishing was the only local work available to the mainly Catholic community on the west side of the lough. At one time a man would have fished for the pot with something over to sell, but in the seventeenth century Charles I granted the eel fishing rights on the lough to the Earl of Donegal, and throughout the centuries since then individuals fishing for themselves have been prosecuted. During the latter part of the last century and for the first seventy years of this the fishing rights were exploited under licence by commercial companies based at Billingsgate in London and exporting to Holland and Denmark. They used the full severity of the law to protect their monopoly and extract as much profit as possible from the fishing, the fishermen themselves being paid little more than a subsistence income for their efforts. From one generation to another they resented the profits from the biggest natural asset of Northern Ireland going to foreigners, but they, like so many in similar situations, were untutored, rugged individualists who could grumble but were incapable of organising themselves.

Then in the early 1960s they found an unlikely organiser and leader in Father Kennedy, a local parish priest. He re-organised their ineffective Lough Neagh Fishermen's Association and, single-handed, fought for the right of the fishermen to control and profit from their own industry. Once he had the fishermen, who had the nets, lines, boats and skills, behind him the 'foreign' interests knew that their days of easy profit would soon be over. Father Kennedy was going to settle for nothing less than complete capitulation and the handing over of the eel fishing industry to his flock. In 1971 it was all over; the complete share-holding of the Toome Eel Fishery (NI) Ltd, was acquired by the new Lough Neagh Fishermen's Co-operative Society Ltd, of which Father Kennedy was, and still is, the chairman. Today he presides with absolute authority over a two million pound a year business. He knows that Lough Neagh eels are the fattest, tastiest and best in the world, and if you want them you pay his price. If he had not taken Holy Orders he would have become a tycoon anyway. He takes no pain to conceal where his political sympathies lie, and I am certain that his thoughts are far more militant than his priestly mien suggests.

Follow any lane down to the west side of the lough and, inevitably, you will find a little harbour dug out of the foreshore with a handful of colourful eel fishing boats. Traditionally they are twenty-five feet long, clinker built with a high freeboard and fitted with an engine – and museum pieces some of the engines are, too. Charlie McIlroy of Ardboe was the last traditional boat-builder on the lough, but these craft are now made in fibreglass from moulds taken from one of his wooden boats, for which no royalties were ever paid.

Line fishing is the preferred method on Lough Neagh, although draught nets are permitted. Usually two men work a boat, which means that over 400 men are out fishing during the season from 1 May to late October, with June and July being the peak months. They are thought to be the main bread winners of some 200 families. Each boat carries four lines of up to 2,000 yards length with a hook every yard or so. The lines are prepared during the day with the hooks being baited with worm, perch or pollen fry, are set each evening and lifted in the morning when a Co-operative truck with special tanks and compressors collects the catches and takes them to Toome Bridge where they are graded, packed in ice and dispatched both by air and overland to Holland and Germany, with a small quota sometimes being allowed to go to London. The lines take about two hours to set and three hours to lift, and a reasonable night's haul for a boat would be 400 to 500 eels weighing between eight and ten stone. The most tedious part of the work is baiting the hooks and flaking the line on a board with all the hooks in straight rows so that it will run out smoothly and quickly from the boat. It is a laborious method of fishing, but traditional, and ensures that the lough is not overfished, which would seem impossible considering that at least twenty million elvers arrive in the river Bann every spring to make their way up the lough where they will spend up to fifteen years, which suggests a population of about 130 million. The elvers can get up the river on their own as far as the salmon leap at Coleraine which is too steep for them to manage, so the fishery company provides them with elver ladders made of straw ropes. It is a unique sight to watch millions of these translucent creatures swarming up their ladders looking like a cascade in reverse.

Left to their own devices it would then take them a further three years to travel the remaining twenty-three miles to the lough, during which time they would be at the mercy of many predators, and those that did make it all the way would be exhausted and easy prey to pike and other fish. So tanks are placed

Eel fishing on the Lough and the Lower Bann is a big export business. These wickerwork eel traps or sluices on the river are of exactly the same construction as those used in mediaeval times

Eel trapping on the Lower Bann is done at night; here, at dawn, the men are transferring the eels from a keep tank to bins for loading into tankers to go to Toome Bridge for grading and packing

at the top of the elver ladders from which they are decanted into lorries and taken by road to be put in the lough at various points around the shore. Those that survive to full maturity must eventually answer the call of the sea to spawn in the far away Sargasso Sea. Their only way there is back down the Lower Bann the way they came some fifteen years before, and it is this autumn run of silver eels which provides for a second and rich harvest at a time when the lough fishing is coming to an end. The wickerwork eel traps or sluices which form a zig-zag pattern across the river are of exactly the same construction as those built by the mediaeval monks who controlled the eel fisheries as Father Kennedy does today. There is no doubt now that this method of eel fishing has gone on for many thousands of years, since radiocarbon dating of sections of fishing weirs very similar in construction to those used today has placed them as pre-6000 BC, and parts of the foundation of the present structures are of mediaeval origin. Lough excavations have produced tools for impaling fish dating back to the same era.

The traps are made by interweaving willow rods about one inch in diameter between vertical stakes set in V formation to guide the eels to a narrow exit or venturi where a long net is set and kept open by the force of the current. The traps are connected by wooden piers which also support small huts where the fishermen can cat-nap and cook a meal during the night while they wait for the nets to fill. Work does not start until dusk as eels will only run in the dark, and the darker the night the better the catch. The best come on nights when there is no moon and a strong south or south-westerly wind. As the nets fill they are emptied into keep tanks set in the river to await the arrival of the Co-operative lorry at dawn.

The Lower Bann is a fully navigable waterway through which boats not exceeding ten and a half feet in height and five feet draught can make a passage from the sea through five sets of locks into Lough Neagh where some blue water boats winter. Near the head of the Lower Bann the river widens to form Lough Beg, a shallow water which is outstanding for its bird life. A feature of this lake is a church spire, *976 947*, prominent on the west bank; but you will look in vain for the church. The spire is no more than a folly built in the late eighteenth century by the Earl of Bristol, Bishop of Derry, who considered the view across the lake a bit dull. Coleraine, near the mouth of the river, is joined with the seaside resorts of Portrush and Portstewart, both centres of sea angling. Down by the river there is a marina and club which provide a good waiting place for the right weather for an inshore cruise along the Causeway coast. Whatever anybody may think of the Giant's Causeway seen from the land, they have seen nothing to compare with the awesome grandeur of the coast when viewed from a boat just offshore.

If coming from the sea the Bann should not be entered with

One of the five sets of locks along the Lower Bann which link Lough Neagh to the sea

strong onshore winds, or when swell is seen breaking on the training walls. When you do go in, keep nearer to the east wall then follow the well spaced perches up the river. It snakes across flat country for five miles to Coleraine, the channel kept clear to fifteen feet by the local dredger *Bar Maid*. There is very little tidal stream on the flood, and only about three knots on spring ebbs. The town quay, half a mile beyond the marina, takes coasters up to 2,000 tons trading with the Canary Islands and Cyprus. Having come this far and so near I must just mention a rather special drop of water – St Columb's Rill. This is a tributary of the river Bush which runs parallel to, and six miles from, the Lower Bann. And what is so special about it is its contribution to The Old Bushmills Distillery. It was the first licensed distillery in the British Isles, having been granted a license by James I in 1608 – so at least he did one good thing for Ulster. If you are not familiar with whiskey spelt with an 'e' I commend Bushmills to you, most especially their Black Bush. A near liqueur quality, aged in the wood for eight years, it is the finest 'uisge bheatha' (water of life), whichever way it is spelt. And if you are ever that way you may visit the distillery to be shown the malt mill, the mash tun, the great copper pot stills, the blending, and watch the coopers at work 'raising' the wooden casks in which the whiskey is left to mature – there will be 23,000 of them at any one time. Curiously all the wood is second-hand oak from old sherry casks.

Strangford Lough

OS 1:50,000 Sheet 21 of Northern Ireland

'The owner asks you to stay away from this part of the island because roseate terns are nesting'.

So reads a notice on one of Strangford Lough's islands, vital to the successful nesting of many species of wild birds, among them the oystercatcher, ringed plover and barnacle goose as well as both the sandwich tern, which is prolific, and the roseate tern whose numbers have declined in recent years. Similar signs are erected on thirty islands because Strangford Lough, while being one of the greatest bird sanctuaries in the British Isles with some 130 species of migrants including almost half the world's population of brent geese in winter, is also a very popular yachting water. In all there are seventy islands, a great many having miniature bays with inviting anchorages offering the temptation to go ashore, especially when there are restless children on board. Some twenty miles long and four miles wide, this north-south orientated inlet of the Irish Sea is encircled by a road which seldom loses sight of the water and has lots of little lanes looping down to all the interesting spots. But, for its fullest enjoyment, you do need a small boat; that way you will find even more hide-away nooks and crannies than can the man in his cruising yacht. If you do not have one there are sailing cruisers and day boats for hire.

It was as crew on a cruising yacht coming in from the sea that I first made the acquaintance of Strangford Lough – I still consider that is the best way to visit it – and only later did I fully explore its shores and hinterland on wheels. So it is from the sea that I will begin my tour of this great island-ringed lough. It is rarely visited by English yachtsmen, who are either put off by the five mile long narrows with tidal streams which run up to seven knots and sometimes more, or they are always in a hurry to be somewhere else. On the first count there is nothing to fear, and on the second they do not know what they are missing. The Irish Cruising Club Sailing Directions for going in and out are easy to follow, the entrance is now lit, and most of the pladdies (submerged or half-tide rocks) inside have been well marked. Details of navigation lights within the lough are available from the Killyleagh Sailing Centre, Killyleagh, County Down (tel: 0396 828511). However, you should not attempt to enter on an ebb or even go in anywhere near the bar during the ebb in a south-easterly when that area becomes a maelstrom. But on the flood – whatever the wind, even a south-easterly – it is like getting out of the sea and into a duck pond, albeit one that moves you along at a fast rate. The lough resembles a bottle, and when high water is coming up outside it tries to get into the neck but is stopped by the water still coming out, so high water for Strangford Lough is always two hours behind high water outside. It must, therefore, be read from Strangford village not Killard Point at the entrance.

Coming from the south there is the disadvantage of having to punch an hour or two of flood outside before it takes you into the narrows, but coming down from the north you are with the tide on the approach and going up into the lough. When leaving the lough to continue north everything is in your favour. The exit can only be made on the ebb, and if the narrows are entered at the very end of the flood as it turns into a slack you will have a good four hours of the ebb outside to take you north. Going the other way, southwards, you can leave at any state of the ebb and find a large area of slack water south of the narrows where the tide divides at the level of the Isle of Man. If you initially went into the lough for shelter and are not sure of the sea state outside you can go through the narrows on the last of the ebb, take a look outside and, if you do not like what you see, get back in the lough on the first of the flood. For the coastal cruising family I sincerely recommend scheduling at least a day, or better two, for a cruise inside Strangford Lough. It is big and open enough in the middle for regular cruiser racing, while inshore its truly emerald islands and a sylvan river provide a score of sheltered channels and back-waters for lying snug or pottering in the tender whatever the weather outside. It could be blowing a full gale in the Irish Sea,

Portaferry, with Strangford village on the opposite shore; in the narrows between the tide can run up to eight knots

but in Ringhaddy Sound on the west shore a child could safely sail an Optimist.

Immediately inside the narrows there is a choice of two stopping places – Portaferry on the Ards Peninsula on the east shore or Strangford itself, half a mile across the water on the west side. For every shoreside comfort the Portaferry Hotel is the answer. John Herlihy, the owner, is much more hotelier than publican, although his place serves both functions. He bought a run-down, tin-roofed inn and turned it into a very comfortable hotel with first class cuisine, especially sea food. He claims to have contracted to buy the whole catch of king prawns from the lough, certainly in season they are always in abundance in the restaurant or bar, and they really are enormous.

Many of the visitors are sea anglers who come for the skate fishing – catches of up to seventy kilos have been known. There is a sprinkling of very Irish type pubs notably Dumigans, no bigger than a small room so there is no chance of avoiding the locals – and who would want to? On the quayside is the Queen's University Marine Biology Station whose staff also man the local inshore lifeboat. I was given a rather hairy ride in it with, much to my surprise, a female crew. The station is not overtly open to the public, but they seem willing to entertain anyone with a serious interest in their aquarium, thirty different species of stuffed Strangford Lough ducks, geese and waders and recordings of 1,500 species of marine creatures.

Looking quite unimportant and jostled by later buildings is Portaferry Castle, a sixteenth century tower house which matches its opposite number at Strangford. A third tower house and the most interesting one is Audley's Castle, *577 505*, at the head of Castleward Bay. They were all part of the Anglo-Norman occupation of the coast of County Down. In late mediaeval Ireland, in time of danger, a landowner protected his family and retainers within his tower house, essentially a defensive structure and made up of a series of superimposed chambers. They had little furniture and their floors were 'carpeted' in summer with rushes a foot deep on which they slept, which were replaced by straw in winter.

The car ferry does the double crossing between Portaferry and Strangford every half-hour, and when the tide is in full spate it literally crabs sideways in an effort to make a diagonal passage. Anyone contemplating making the ten minute crossing in his own boat would do well to remember that 400 million tons of water pass between the two villages four times a day; no wonder the Vikings dubbed it Strang Fiord – violent inlet. There are quiet eddies inshore, but anywhere near the centre of the narrows the tidal stream may be running up to eight knots, that is over nine miles per hour, so a boat would need to be capable of maintaining ten knots to avoid being swept well off course. During the full ebb an under-powered boat could be swept five miles down to the bar, if not sucked into one of the fierce whirlpools or dashed into the rocks on the way down. Quite big fishing vessels have been carried onto rocks by the outgoing tide and foundered. There is a fine viewpoint of the narrows from the roadside by the stump of an old windmill, *599 505*, which stands on a hill above Portaferry. From there the dog leg track of the crabbing ferry boat is traced by its wake, and on clear days there is a line of sight over the archipelago of small islands along the west shore.

Strangford village clusters around a double cove which forms its twin harbour, one part for the ferry and the other for fishing boats. A sloping green leads up to the Lobster Pot, an old pub which has been developed into a sophisticated and popular house, especially with yachties. It has a spacious bar with comfortable seating, two good restaurants, one of them extending onto a patio for warm evenings, and it is open on Sundays. On the other side of the green is The Cuan Bar, better known as Sharvins, and the very opposite of the Lobster Pot. On my first visit a few years back it was small, dark and long overdue for a coat of paint which, fortunately, the landlord had not given it. Small as it is, there is room for a piano and an organ which customers make good use of so there is often a bit of a sing-song of an evening. Brandon Sharvin is a keen sailing man; mention the subject and you are 'in'. When I was last there his pub was closed for renovation, but I have since been assured that its character has not been damaged. Both pubs are good drinking holes in their way, but The Cuan Bar attracts the Catholic part of the village, while the rest share the Lobster Pot with the visitors. There is no hotel in the village, but there are several bed and breakfast houses and a secluded caravan site, *580,489*, one of the prettiest I have seen, each caravan having its own small lawn and all tucked away among the trees of Castleward estate. A note of warning: while it is only half a mile from Strangford to Portaferry across the water, it is fifty miles round the lough by road and the last ferry leaves at half past ten.

Castleward estate covers 800 acres with fourteen miles of park and woodland walks giving fine views over the lough. The gardens are among the most beautiful in the British Isles with giant oaks and beeches, rare foreign plants and exotic palms. The open glades are at their best in the spring when they are carpeted with daffodils and bluebells, or later when the paths are walled with azaleas and rhododendrons. The house was built between 1762 and 1773 and is an architectural oddity. In 1759 the property was inherited by Bernard Ward, MP for County Down and Deputy Governor of the County, who decided to build himself a larger and statelier mansion than the one existing. His taste was for the Classical style; his wife Anne was of a whimsical mind and wanted a home in the Gothic fashion. The result is a building with two contemporaneous but utterly different façades – Classical on the west side and Strawberry Hill Gothic on the east; within, the rooms also alternate front and back between the two. It is a house full of surprises, none greater than the Gothic boudoir with a fan vaulted ceiling based on that of Henry VII's Chapel at Westminster Abbey. Before the house was finished Mr Ward had become the first Viscount Bangor, and when it was completed the separation of the house into two styles was followed by the separation of the viscount and his lady. Among the outbuildings are a mid-Victorian laundry, the original tower house built in 1610 and now incorporated in the farm buildings, a Greek temple folly and two water mills. Temple Water in the park is a decorative canal made in 1724, recently restored and stocked with wildfowl representative of the various species to be found on Strangford Lough.

There are two ways of reaching Castleward; from the Downpatrick-Strangford road or by water. At the foot of Audley's Castle, on a green mound by the shore, there is an old stone quay which has floating water on its north side at all states of the tide. From there it is a half mile walk through woods to the waterside entrance to the grounds. Much nearer is the larger quay, *575 497*, and concrete slipway of the Strangford Sailing Club. Most of its members have cruising boats and one or two are always away during the season, so there is certain to be a vacant mooring. When their club house is closed you can make your number with Mr Avington who lives in the first cottage just inside the waterside gateway of Castleward. He is the Harbour Master, and also collects your entrance fee if you are not a member of the National Trust. Should you stay on your boat he will row out and charge you a nominal sum for an overnight stop. Naturally, he prefers that you row to him. You can holiday at Castleward in one of the cottages in the grounds or in one of their flats which sleep eight people. Bookings are made through the National Trust Bookings Secretary, Rowallane, Saintfield, Ballynahinch, County Down.

The Audley family was established on land around the lough in the thirteenth century, being among the earliest Anglo-Norman settlers in Ulster. Their castle was built in the fifteenth century and sold by James Audley in 1646 to his neighbour Bernard Ward, grandfather of the first Viscount Bangor who built the great house. But Audley's Castle had already been abandoned by 1724 when its romantic aspect was used as the focus for Temple Water. This tower house is nothing like the grand edifice of Castleward, in fact today it is no more than a ruin, but is great fun to wander around and climb up and down in. It is unusual in having the complete circuit of a walled courtyard or bawn although now reduced to only a few courses. It would originally have been a self-contained defensive barracks with quarters for retainers and workshops enclosed within the walls, not unlike the

Audley's Castle, one of the mediaeval tower houses built by the Anglo-Normans during their occupation

toy fort of our nursery days but without the drawbridge. The tower is built of split stone rubble with sandstone dressings. Projecting turrets protect the doorway with an arched drophole above for stoning or pouring boiling liquid on attackers. A spiral staircase in one turret reaches to a roof and gives access to chambers at various levels. From the roof you get an uninterrupted view across the lough to Portaferry. With few signs, no guides or souvenir shop, you are left to your own devices and imagination – and that is the kind of ruin I most enjoy.

Round the headland beyond Audley's Castle is the Quoile river running south-west. Once navigable to Downpatrick, it is now dammed three miles from its mouth leaving a wide estuary broken up by nine islands which can be sailed round at high water. A deep channel at all states of the tide leads to a pool off Castle Island, *509 490*, where the Quoile Yacht Club have their home in a truly rural setting surrounded by high wooded shores, totally sheltered, and with floating pontoons in deep water. The club house stands above the pool with members' caravans and children's swings and roundabouts on terraces around it; it is very much a family club. Beyond the dam the Quoile river is strictly for the birds, having been made into a sanctuary, but it is a great place for nature watchers and for children to swim in, being much

The Quoile Yacht Club is totally sheltered, surrounded by high wooded shores and with floating pontoons in deep water

warmer than the lough. The river remains wide as it meanders almost to Downpatrick with the road following close alongside. The river banks beside the curving reaches have been landscaped as roadside parks for sitting, watching and picnicing. And very pretty it is when all is green and the sky blue.

The river should be left on the outskirts of Downpatrick for a visit to the cathedral, a good compact Georgian-Gothic building with a lot of richly carved woodwork and a Celtic font. It is built on the supposed site of St Patrick's first stone church, and in the churchyard is his reputed grave covered by a simple slab of rough granite incised with a Celtic cross and the word 'Patric', both well worn as one would expect in so ancient a monument. But do not be deceived; the stone was put there only in 1900. If he is there he is not alone for the remains of St Brigid and St Columba are said to have been re-interred beside him in 1183. Several places have claimed to be the burial site of St Patrick, another leading contender being Armagh. What is more certain is that he died about 465, probably in the village of Saul, three miles to the north-east where, in 1932, a good replica of an early Christian church and round tower, *509 464*, were built by the Church of Ireland to commemorate the fifteenth centenary of his landing in 432 at Ringbane, *530 489*, where the tiny Slaney river flows into the Quoile. Anyone with a boat on Strangford Lough could include a pilgrimage (at high tide) to that landing site in a cruise up the Quoile. Or it can be reached by twisty lanes off the main Downpatrick-Strangford road.

Continuing north along the west side of the lough you come to a quiet water area of channels and lagoons among some thirty islands and islets, all low laying but slightly steep to on their north sides with shallow slopes to the south, which is how the glaciers formed them. They are beautifully green, a few are lightly wooded, while one or two have only isolated trees like the hairs on a bald man's head. They are good picnic places, and a young family could have a very economical mini adventure holiday with a day boat and a tent, camping on a different island every night; they might have a few sheep for company or, more likely, a lot of rabbits.

Ringhaddy Sound behind Islandmore, said to be the most sheltered anchorage on the whole coast of Ireland, is most attractive both for its rustic setting and for the variety of boats, big and small, which are moored there. The water is very deep, down to fourteen metres in parts, but the Ringhaddy Cruising Club have invested in floating pontoons, *535 583*, with water points which visitors are welcome to use for a stop, or to stay overnight free of charge. There is also an old stone coal quay against which one can dry out for a small fee, but which serves more often as a good platform for photographing this pretty spot. There are dozens of such quays all round the lough, many of them now very broken down and far from road or habitation, but at one time they were

Down Cathedral at Downpatrick, a Georgian-Gothic building with richly carved woodwork and a Celtic font

the only way that isolated farms and settlements could be supplied with coal and other heavy materials. After Ringhaddy any amount of time can be spent exploring the maze of islands up to White Rock which is *the* yachting centre of the lough, where the Strangford Lough Yacht Club, *525618*, has a very fine club house, big slipway and drying out posts. It was the original yacht club on the lough, and they race the oldest fleet of boats – the River class. These twenty-eight-foot keel boats were Mylne designed and built, all twelve of them, in 1921. Originally it was the Lords Londonderry and Bangor and their friends who raced them from White Rock out to sea and in to Belfast Lough with paid hands to sail them home single-handed afterwards. Today these veteran yachts are owned by a mix of professionals, businessmen and artisans, and race on Wednesday evenings and Saturday afternoons. But it is the size of the Club's cruiser fleet which is unexpected – about eighty of them. At White Rock you can hire a dinghy, a Drascombe Lugger or a cruiser, by the day or for a week's charter, from Irwin Yachts who also run a sailing school.

On Sketrick Island above White Rock Bay is Daft Eddy's, *525626*, a farmhouse converted out of all recognition into a pub with holiday flats, an off-licence and a bar busy all of most days with locals and sailing people. But it is Daft Eddy's food which draws the crowds. All year round from Tuesday to Saturday they serve buffet lunches of outstanding quality and quantity. They also do buffet suppers and restaurant dinners and, from time to time, organise special French, Italian, Greek and other Continental evenings. Daft Eddy was an eighteenth century smuggler, and the landlord is a retired twentieth century GP.

You can sail from the mainland of Britain across the Irish Sea and direct to the Down Cruising Club's landing stage within five feet of a freshly drawn pint. You do not have to get into a dinghy, you do not have to tie up in a harbour and report to anyone, and you do not have to pay harbour dues. Their club house is a magnificent bright red lightship formerly called *Petrel*, *524627*, which they bought for £2,000 off Trinity House in 1968. Attached to the land by a companionway and sheltered from every direction by a ring of islands, it is as near perfect a setting for a club as one could find. In the thirty-odd years of its existence the club has grown from a handful of founding members to 170, who between them own 100 boats. In the bilges of the lightship there is the bar, a small wooden dance floor and a stage. The members have a long history of entertaining old age pensioners, polio victims and thalidomide children on their boats. The club's main event of the year takes place during the 12 July fortnight – the time when less amusing people are busy dressing up in bowler hats and marching behind Orange Order bands. Then members make their traditional cruise up the Ulster coast to Carnlough for a slant across to Gigha en route for Tobermory. If the weather allows, they go out round Ardnamurchan, past the Small Isles and up the Sound of Sleat to Plockton at the seaward end of Loch Carron; a pretty place, once a fishing village and now gentrified but with good shoreside pubs and palms swaying on the sea front; it's a 'private' branch of the Gulf Stream that succours them.

Mahee Island a little north of White Rock is considered the limit of easy pilotage up the west coast of the lough. From there all the way to Newtownards there are extensive shallows and drying areas, and the pladdies are not marked as they are to the south. The whole area is an undisturbed haven for waders and migrants. Mahee, which has a golf course, thrusts well out into the middle of the lough and is joined to Reagh Island by a causeway, and Reagh itself is linked to the mainland by a bridge. It is a route worth taking to see the Nendrum monastic site, *525637*, on Mahee. Discovered in 1844 and still being investigated, it is a very complete example of an early monastery which was destroyed by the Vikings around 974. There are three concentric cashels, the stump of a round tower, remains of a church and monks' circular cells all on a high point overlooking the lough. A restored gable end of the church has a sun dial with Celtic ornamentation. St Mochoi (Mahee), a convert of St Patrick, is said to have worked so hard on building the church that a little bird came down from heaven and sang him to sleep for 150 years; a charming Irish version of the Rip Van Winkle story. If going by small boat from White Rock or Ballydorn, I would advise tilting the outboard and rowing the last thirty yards to the shore as the seaweed is solid and tenacious.

There is a little creek which runs from the top of the lough into Comber; it is actually the estuary of the Comber river. Below the road bridge outside the town you will find a padlocked hut. Looking through its smeared and dusty window it is just possible to make out the rudimentary tools for tea making. This is the Comber Yacht Club. In the creek there lies as good a collection of old dream boats as in any East Anglian backwater. The east side of the lough has only one sailing club, *593636*, and that is at Kircubbin, opposite Sketrick Island. Conveniently for the locals on that side of the water, their bar is open on Sundays for racing. A little further up the road towards Newtownards, the big town at the head of the lough, is Grey Abbey, *584682*, one of my favourite ruins because you can wander around them at will, and substantial and romantic they are too. It is a well preserved complex of a once great Cistercian abbey with roofs and large sections of walls removed giving aspects such as those seen in architects' cut-away models. Walls with great windows are joined by arches but open

You can wander at will in Grey Abbey, a once great Cistercian abbey now open to the sky

to the sky, giving a sense of space probably even greater than did the original complete building. You can walk where monks walked in prayer, and at the same time see where cooks prepared meals and gardeners tended vegetables. With an Historic Monuments leaflet in hand you can let your imagination put stone and men where now there is only emptiness.

The abbey was founded by Affreca, daughter of the king of the Isle of Man and wife of John de Courcy, the ill-fated Norman conqueror of Ulster, which reminds us that today the only 'foreigners' who have the good sense to sail in any numbers, and with any regularity, to the delights, natural and social, of Strangford Lough are the cruising yachtsmen of the Isle of Man. The visitor could spend hours reading the scores of inscriptions on the momuments, like that to five children who are remembered as 'all God's lovely loans'. Several to the Montgomery family remind one that Monty was an Ulsterman. The family seat, Rosemount, is across the road. One Montgomery, Sir James, was, we are told: 'by pirates shot and thereof dead of March 165½ by them i' the sea solomnly buried'. Grey Abbey is also a little village of about 600 souls which has developed into a centre for good antiques, the other one in Northern Ireland being Hillsborough.

The last site of interest round the lough shore is Mount Stewart, *553697*, a National Trust stately house where Lord

Castlereagh, Foreign Secretary during the Napoleonic Wars, was born and raised. It is largely eighteenth century with nineteenth century additions. But Mount Stewart is best known for its fantasy garden full of rare and exotic trees and plants and amusing examples of topiary, although it is the statuary which most people go to look at. Nothing Classical, Victorian or arty, just fun things – dodos, griffins, satyrs, dinosaurs, duck-billed platypi, monkeys, crocodiles, a cat playing a fiddle and a mermaid with a harp. Sculpted by local masons, they were installed early in the 1920s by Edith, Lady Londonderry to amuse her children.

To get an overall, oblique view of Strangford Lough go to the monument at the top of Scrabo Hill, *477 726*, outside Newtownards, via the ring road which circles its base just off the A20. It is only 600 feet to the top, but from there the whole length of the lough to Portaferry is laid out below you. But do go on a fine day with clear air and, if the sun is shining, early morning or evening to avoid having it in your eyes.

Rowing buffs may be surprised to learn that the shells in the Oxford and Cambridge Boat Race are derived from the old Strangford Lough longboats, one of which was introduced to Oxford by an undergraduate from Strangford in 1816, and promptly won all its races.

Lough Erne

OS 1:25,000 Sheet of Northern Ireland, Fermanagh Lakeland, Lower Lough Erne and Upper Lough Erne

Where can the discerning inland cruising enthusiast find quiet, uncongested and clear waters to explore amidst inspiring scenery but with discreetly placed facilities waiting for him when he has sufficiently 'communed with solitude' as Wordsworth put it?

There is one still-unspoilt and magnificent waterway and that is Lough Erne, the largest of the cluster that makes up the Lake District of Fermanagh in Ulster. It is, in fact and in character, two lakes; the Upper in the south and the Lower in the north – the sort of upside down nomenclature one might expect in Ireland! And the two are joined by a five mile navigable river. From one end to the other is fifty miles, and there are 300 square miles of cruising and fishing water broken up by 145 islands forming water mazes in which to play hide and seek with a boat – and seeking without finding very often for, although there are eight hire operators around the lough, their combined fleets amount to little more than one boat for every five square miles of water. High cliffs, sandy bays, thickly forested shorelines, broad reaches and secret backwaters through reed beds and water meadows, together with an abundance of archaeological and historical sites on the shore and islands are all there in almost infinite variety. It is also arguably the best coarse fishing water in Europe and there can be few places where anglers are made more welcome. There must be at least a hundred fishing stands around the shores and in the river section. Coarse fishing is open all the year round, game fishing is restricted to the period 1 March to 30 September. Bream, perch, pike and eel are plentiful in both loughs, with brown trout and a few salmon mainly in the Lower one. Salmon fishing has deteriorated over the last twenty-five years because of the construction of a hydro-electric dam at Ballyshannon on the tidal reach of the river Erne in County Donegal. Pike and brown trout are indigenous, and the Lough Erne brown trout are something rather special. Not only do they have big, red spots and a deep golden colour, but are on average very much bigger than others of the species. This is because they are late developers; they do not come to sexual maturity for at least four years and so have a phenomenal growth rate during that period. There is now a policy of restocking the lough with 'normal' brown trout which become sexually active at eighteen months to two years old. The trout and salmon fishing is in the shallow and rock-strewn waters round the edges of the lough where the motor cruisers cannot go, so there is no conflict of interest.

Fifty public landing stages are scattered around the shoreline and among the islands, and at most of them two boats would constitute a crowd. There are a few popular places where boats do congregate in large numbers and where the gregarious can get together, notably at Enniskillen, the county town of Fermanagh on the river section between the Upper and Lower Loughs. The

Derryad on the smaller Upper Lough with one of the fifty public landing stages scattered around the shoreline and among the islands

This slab of rough granite at Down Cathedral in Downpatrick on the Quoile river is supposed to mark the site of St Patrick's grave, but it was only put there in 1900

Down Cruising Club's quay and club house, a magnificent bright red lightship, on Strangford Lough

The twelve-mile broad reach of
Lower Loch Erne with the Cliffs of
Magho beyond; this wide open expanse
of water can kick up a heavy sea

From Knockninny Hill there is a wide panoramic view over almost the whole Upper Lough Erne archipelago

Lord Erne's cot on Upper Lough Erne; these boats are indigenous to the lough and have been used for centuries as transport between the islands

Lower Lough is the grander of the two with open water allowing passages of nine to ten miles to be made on quite rough water in strong winds. In the extreme western corner the lough becomes the river Erne which is navigable for a further five miles to Belleek on the border with the Republic. This is a small town with a marina, hotel and a large pottery which is open to the public. They manufacture a lustrous, creamy-coloured porcelain embellished with basketwork and flowers of extraordinary intricacy which is, by current standards of taste, rather kitsch. Fortunately for local employment it is in great demand with American collectors. The southern shore of this reach is dominated by the Cliffs of Magho, with a path from a jetty leading to the 1,000 foot high Lough Navar viewpoint overlooking some 100 square miles of the lough and the Atlantic to the west. By car the viewpoint is reached along an eleven mile scenic drive up through forests starting from Falls Bridge, *074 546*, on the Garrison road off the A46.

On the opposite side of the lough is the village of Kesh up a river and nearby the Lakeland Marina, *162 641*, a charter firm run by an ex-naval commander from Devon, with a fleet of impeccable boats that has attracted take-over bids from foreign operators. At the southern end where the lough starts to narrow and become speckled with islands Manor House Marina, *206 534*, has its own landlocked harbour in the 100 acre parkland grounds of the Manor House Hotel. This is a likely home port for sybarite sailors who might appreciate the ambience of a country house hotel in semi-Classical style with its Italianate interior and panoramic views from bar and restaurant as a change from chugging round the lough. Here it might be apposite to add that the people of Northern Ireland seem to have enormous appetites and wherever you eat prices are similar to those in England, but you get gargantuan portions for your money. Victualling is, in some respects, even cheaper than in England. I have taken on board two large T-bone steaks of excellent quality for only £3.50.

Round the corner from here in Gublusk Bay are the hangars, *207 527*, of the old Killadeas flying boat base, from where Catalinas hunted German submarines. It was one of them which first sighted the pocket battleship Bismarck making her fateful escape into the Atlantic in 1940. The first flying boats flew in 1935, and in all 3,290 were built in Canada and the USA. They had a cruising speed of 120 miles per hour with a 3,000 mile range and a maximum speed of 190 miles per hour. The wings, with a span of 104 feet were mounted on a pylon above the body to keep them and the two 1,200 horsepower engines out of the spray. These craft were amphibians having wheels which folded up by their sides when landing on, or taking off from, water. The base is now occupied by the Lough Erne Yacht Club which was formed in 1818, at the end of the Napoleonic Wars, by a number of wealthy and aristocratic gentlemen. The original membership was made up entirely of local families who owned boats and raced against each other in an informal way. But all too soon the keen edge of competition required racing rules, and each family built boats to try and outsail the others. In the early years the club was based at Crom Castle, *365 238*, the seat of Lord Erne, and they raced five tonners in the Upper Lough. When drainage schemes lowered the water level in 1880 racing had to move to the Lower Lough. The club was far better known in the last century than it is today. Its members would go to Cowes Week in August and afterwards invite their friends among the Solent yachtsmen back for house parties and sailing on the lough, such invitations being considered a singular honour. As early as 1821 the club published the first pleasure cruising chart of Lough Erne, and they raced the first centre-board dinghy in Europe, the Una, when it was brought over from America in 1852. Jack Tipping, the Honorary Secretary from 1887–91 invented the fin keel for his boat *Mischief*, which he had built by Charles McCabe of Enniskillen. In 1906 the club took delivery of eleven, 23-foot keel boats designed by

The extraordinarily intricate basketwork and flowers of Belleek porcelain is in great demand with American collectors

Devenish Island has Northern Ireland's most extensive remains of mediaeval Christian settlements, all within a few minutes' walk of the jetty

Linton Hope and dubbed the Lough Erne Fairey class. Eight of them are still racing as a class with their original Edwardian gunter lug rig.

Devenish Island, which sits like a plug at the bottom end of the Lower Lough at the entrance to the river section through to the Upper Lough, is the one island that every crew visits. The attraction is Northern Ireland's most extensive remains of mediaeval Christian settlements. The twelfth century round tower, eighty feet tall and the best preserved in Ireland, can be climbed by internal ladders for a commanding view in all directions – after all, that is what round towers were built for. The ruins of an Augustinian Abbey begun in the twelfth century, the remains of a small oratory, parts of a priory, a sixteenth century mausoleum and a large number of ancient gravestones are all within a few minutes' walk of the jetty. For the historically minded there is a wealth of detail to be studied on this site, all of which is explained in a leaflet available from the caretaker of the miniature museum there. From here the river then winds south to Enniskillen and around it, making the town an island, and after a few miles opens into the Upper Lough. There is one lock worked electrically, but you are in and out so quickly you hardly notice it. Broad Meadow Jetty in the heart of Enniskillen is served by the Lakeland Forum, a superb sports centre. The town is quite interesting with some old parts, a military museum and a variety of eating places and pubs. I must recommend a visit to Blakes of the Hollow, as Irish a pub as you could ask for with five snugs, which has remained un-tampered with for 100 years. It would be a very melancholy fellow who did not get into some earnest or amusing conversation there.

The majority of crews spend most of their time in the Lower Lough, which is perhaps one of the reasons why I prefer the Upper Lough. From the air, or on the OS map, it looks more like a mangrove swamp or a broken jig-saw puzzle than a coherent lough. But those scattered pieces of a puzzle are good solid ground. Many are complete islands, but many more are linked together and to the mainland by tenuous causeways. They are so tightly packed together that from the water one gets the sensation of exploring a never-ending skein of little rivers bordered by every shade of green that God created. From time to time the water opens up a bit and all of one side of an island or the full shape of a promontory can be discerned, but most often one is in a maze, and to motor in a straight line for more than a few minutes is rarely possible. Navigation is simplicity itself as all channels are marked by numbered red and white 'spades', the red indicating the no-go side. The Navigation Guide is also printed in red and white areas with the numbered markers shown. It is therefore always easy to know exactly where you are, and by reading numbers through binoculars courses can be decided well ahead.

It was into this enchanting labyrinth that I took a tunnel-stern Isis 700 to find the limits of navigation in the far south of Upper Lough Erne. Like a nineteenth century explorer seeking the source of the Nile, I had a dozen or more options, but only managed to look at three of them – the beauty of the place demanded a slow pace and there was so much to interest and delay. Leaving the miniscule marina of the Lisnaskea Yacht Club I first circled round Inish Rath Island with its mellow Georgian house, *337 272*, hidden in the centre of a twenty-four acre wood, every tree of which is clothed in rich lichen – proof of the pure air. I had in the past known Sam Crawford, the owner, and been envious of his island home. There is something atavistic about living on a small island, particularly if it is rather wild and overgrown and your house is screened by the dense foliage of old trees so that it is like a secret place. Sam found just such a place when he went camping as a Boy Scout on Isish Rath. After half a lifetime of

This twelfth century round tower on Devenish Island is eighty feet tall and the best preserved in Ireland; it can still be climbed

entrepreneurial travel in Africa and the Middle East he was able to buy the island and opened the house to paying guests who wanted a temporary retreat from the outside world and a jungle playground for their children. To my horror I saw that beautiful island had been cruelly scarred by a great swathe of tree felling and, on inquiry, was told that the island now belonged to the Hari Krishna cult and was overrun by people in saffron robes and shaved heads. The trees had been cut to provide an approach path to a helicopter pad. They have built four new jetties where one rickety but picturesque one had sufficed, also a road round the island. Local reaction is mixed. Some people said they do no harm, but others were of the opinion that they were undercover agents for the KGB! Perhaps the latter were indulging in a little Irish humour, but the KGB could not be more alien in that place.

Driving away from that disappointment I went north to the jetty, *279 315*, at the foot of Knockninny Hill to climb to the 630-foot summit for a view over almost the whole archipelago of the Upper Lough. That is a little expedition which anyone visiting the lough should make to get the measure of this amazing waterway. With late afternoon sun over your shoulder the islands lie like clusters of emeralds on a length of blue silk. Now and again a boat underway creates a moiré pattern. As far as the eye can see are the greenest of green fields, dark forests, distant mountains and the occasional glint of other tiny loughs. But the sun needs to be shining and the air clear. The last time I was on the hill I was privileged to become one of the first dozen or so people to be guided to a newly discovered and very rare double court cairn (ancient burial ground).

From Knockninny I sailed south to my most favourite spot in the Upper Lough, Crom Bay. It is a pool at the meeting of five channels and surrounded by two islands and five fingers of mainland. Peeping through the trees can be seen the ruins of Crom Castle built in 1611, the later Gothic Revival castle completed in 1834, Derryvore church, *354 237* across the water from it, and Gadd Island, perfectly round and just big enough to support a castellated tower which, while looking quite dramatic, is no more than a nineteenth century folly. The castle and all that can be seen around belong to the Crichton family, descendants of settlers from Brunston, Scotland, who became the Earls of Erne. On Sundays Lord Erne and his family cross the 100 yards from the castle slip to the church in a cot, a flat-bottomed, punt-shaped boat indigenous to the lough and used for centuries to carry people and cattle around the islands. A lot of the slipways are built of rounded stones so the end of the cot just rides up them and people can step ashore dryshod. Originally the cot was a dug-out cut from a single oak, and in this form was probably used to repel the Vikings who were stopped at the mouth of the river Erne in 830, but managed to reach the lough itself later when they ravaged all the monasteries. The church, rebuilt in Victorian Perpendicular style in 1885, is surrounded by bog oaks with short fat trunks and luxuriant crowns, which in mid-summer are bedecked with purple hairstreaks. These small butterflies were recorded recently on the lough for the first time in ninety years.

In the south corner of the Upper Lough the Woodford river – charted as 'unsuitable for cruisers' – winds through an incredibly beautiful pastoral landscape to Ballyconnell in the Republic, a lovely boat trip – at least it used to be. For the time being the frontier bridge, *342 195*, at Aghalane on the A509 is in ruins and the fallen stonework blocks navigation. It is a navigation seemingly plagued by misfortune throughout its history. The Woodford river is an extension of the Ballyconnell Canal which, in the mid-nineteenth century, was part of a commercial waterway linking the Shannon with Belfast via Lough Erne to carry iron ore to the city's port. Unfortunately, a railway built at the same time killed the project after only eight boats had passed through, and the canal locks have long since fallen into decay. There are many canal lovers who would like to see it reopened, but there are others who fear an invasion of the tranquil Erne by hire boats from the overcrowded Shannon. I managed to get as far as Aghalane bridge and go ashore to talk with Mrs Bullock in the garden of her seventeenth century thatched waterside farmhouse. She explained how the bridge had been built across dry land and then the course of the river diverted to flow under it. Her garden was full of butterflies – brimstones and silver washed fritillaries, small blues and dinghy skippers. In her wild garden she showed me the Irish damsel fly, a bamboo-like insect, and an otter's hole in the river bank. Over tea and cakes our conversation turned to poteen; here I will add that I have more than once been treated to a taste of the stuff round the lough shores, though not at Aghalane. To be safe to drink it must be crystal clear without a hint of a bluish tinge. There are many flavours, all as potent as each other. Several years ago I was presented with a half-bottle with a disguising vodka label on it, and there is still a drop left. Mrs Bullock told me the story of a cache of poteen which the police were holding many years ago when it was stolen, so they had to buy on the black market to replenish their evidence. Then there was the man who sold it as a cure for swollen ankles – rubbed on, not drunk – and it was so successful that he made enough money to pay his fare to America.

My next probe was up the Erne river to Belturbet, over the border, which boasts a very small but beautifully engineered marina, *362 172*. The river is wide and deep enough for motor cruisers all the way to the town, which is the limit of that navigation. There was no sensation of having crossed a border, and in fact when under way in those parts it needs close scrutiny of the map to know which side of the wiggling frontier you may be on at any one time. Locals of both north and south are likely to be talking across a narrow bit of water as you pass between them, and both sides give an equally friendly wave and 'good day' to the red ensign. Belturbet was an excuse to try some Guinness brewed and drawn as it should be – not that they are ignorant of the facts of life in the North where the Guinness is also real and in the best places takes ten minutes to draw. The difference in price between north and south did somewhat spoil the taste though.

Next I made a diversion up a tributary, the Finn river, to see if I could get under Wattle Bridge, *425 202*, below Castle Saunderson where the river is almost totally blocked by reed beds. Castle Saunderson, more great house than castle, now in the Republic, stands on a hill at a bend in the river looking down on the North. Early in the last century it was as much a part of the social scene as Crom Castle. Edward Saunderson, a former owner, built racing yachts for himself and his neighbours. Rounding the bend below the castle it was still possible to discern the cut which led to the overgrown boatyard, of which a few stone buildings still stand. There would have been no bridges to restrict sailing in those days; traffic of man and beast was by cot, scenes that would have inspired Constable had he ever gone there. At Wattle Bridge the clumps of reeds were more off-putting than the low narrow arches of the bridge itself. However, with a little hesitant bumping of soft mud and by weaving an erratic course between the reed beds I got through. The commotion among the locals occasioned by my arrival in those waters so far from the nearest charted navigation and so close to the border brought two of Her Majesty's Customs Officers onto the bridge. Having gone upstream of them I heard them call that I could not continue downstream and under the bridge – without giving thought to where on earth I could have come from! They had attempted the passage, they said, in a Dory with an outboard drawing eighteen inches and failed. The tunnel-stern Isis spun in her own length and returned the way she had come, leaving the Customs men with something to scratch their heads about. The way back to base was through another network of backwaters away from the marked channels and rarely visited by hire cruisers. They were, nonetheless, negotiable with care, and rewarding too because the wildlife, being undisturbed, was more prolific. At regular intervals stately herons gave me haughty looks, but refused to take flight for the camera. A boat on the lough makes an ideal hide from which to watch mallard, teal, wigeon, shelduck, grebe and black scoter and to sometimes hear the cry of the corncrake.

The combined efforts of the Northern Ireland Office, the Fermanagh County Council, the Northern Ireland Tourist Board and the boat hire companies have given Lough Erne amenities second to no other waters in the British Isles. Pontoons, landing stages, picnic areas with barbeques and fuelling points are well constructed and maintained, and sited wherever they might be needed. Yet nowhere has blatant development been allowed to take root, let alone grow. Local eating and drinking are good, far better than in comparable places in England, and served with wit and good grace. Most of the pubs have character, as do the locals in them. Conversation is still holding its ground against the juke box in County Fermanagh. Ashore the natives still outnumber the tourists, and of the latter the Continentals are more in evidence than the British, so although you are still in the UK it is a bit like going abroad. If you are at all sociable beware of asking someone the way early in the evening for you may find yourself bidding them 'goodbye' at midnight. And if you have a memory for jokes you will come back with enough Irish ones to last you a twelve-month. In 1609 Sir John Davies wrote of Fermanagh: 'If I should make a full description thereof, it would rather be taken for a poetical fiction than a true and serious narration'. After 379 years I believe his sentiments would be the same.

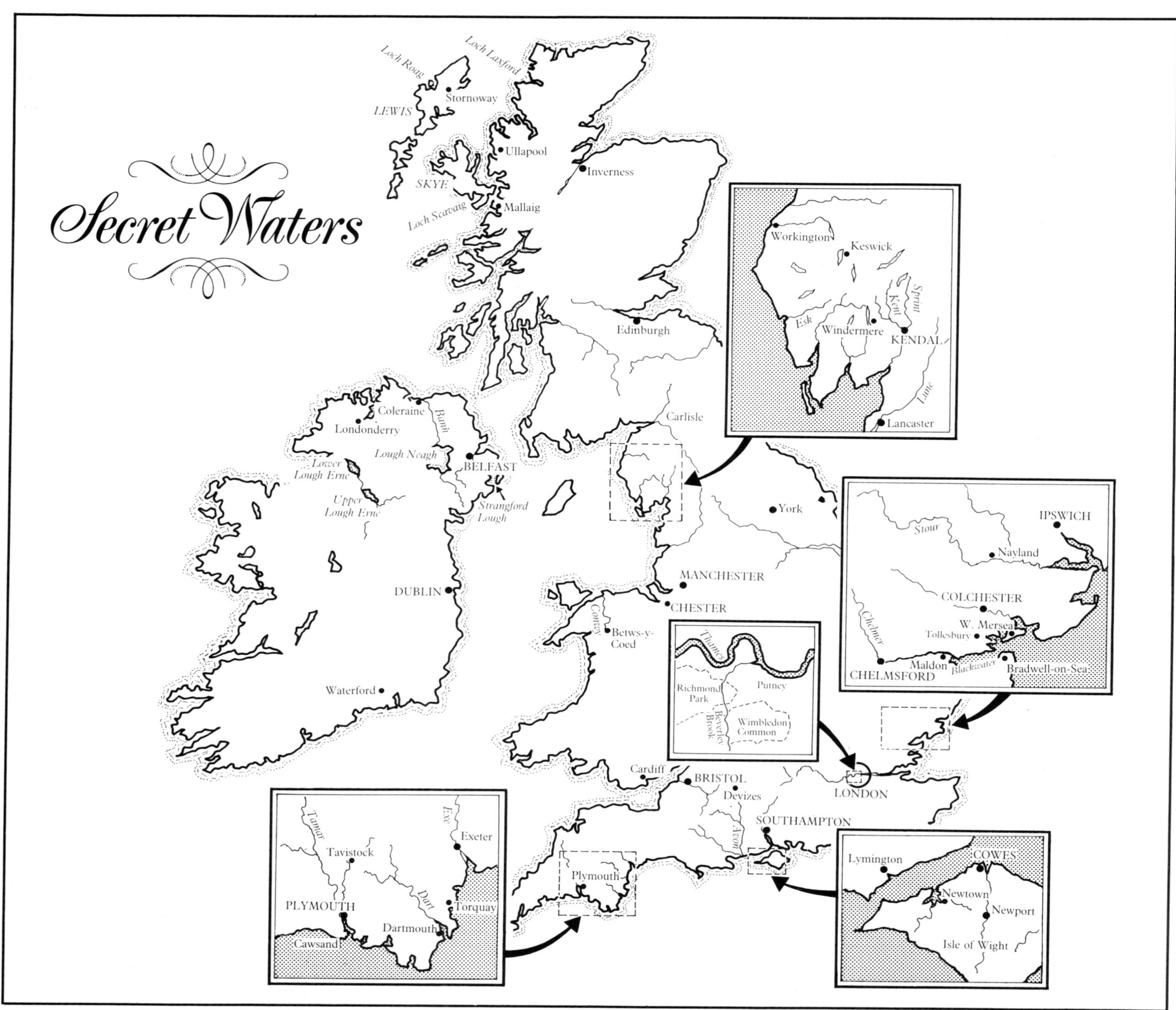

Secret Waters
Loch Roag
Loch Laxford
Stornoway
LEWIS
Ullapool
Inverness
SKYE
Mallaig
Loch Scavaig
Edinburgh
Workington
Keswick
Esk
Kent
Sprint
Windermere
KENDAL
Lune
Lancaster
Carlisle
Coleraine
Londonderry
Bann
Lough Neagh
BELFAST
Lower Lough Erne
Upper Lough Erne
Strangford Lough
York
IPSWICH
Stour
Nayland
COLCHESTER
Chelmer
W. Mersea
Tollesbury
Maldon
Blackwater
CHELMSFORD
Bradwell-on-Sea
MANCHESTER
CHESTER
DUBLIN
Conwy
Betws-y-Coed
Thames
Richmond Park
Putney
Beverley Brook
Wimbledon Common
Waterford
Cardiff
BRISTOL
Devizes
LONDON
SOUTHAMPTON
Avon
Tamar
Exe
Exeter
Tavistock
Dart
PLYMOUTH
Torquay
Dartmouth
Cawsand
Plymouth
Lymington
COWES
Newtown
Newport
Isle of Wight

INDEX